The Last Stand Of Mr America

The Last Stand Of Mr America

Jason Flores-Williams

CANONGATE

First published in the United States of America in 1998 by
Caught Inside Press

This edition published simultaneously in
the United States of America and Canada in 2002 by
Canongate Books, 14 High Street, Edinburgh, EH1 1TE

10 9 8 7 6 5 4 3 2 1

British Library Cataloguing-in-Publication Data
A catalogue record for this book is available upon request
from the British Library

ISBN 1 84195 198 6

Typeset by Palimpsest Book Production Limited,
Polmont, Stirlingshire
Printed and bound by CPD, Ebbw Vale, Wales

www.canongate.net

This morning Sheryl Barnla and I carried a heavy writing desk
into a small room.
No one else was there.
Agradecimiento y amor, chica.

Chapter One

FUCK THE DARK whatever of my soul, all the poetry in this place adds up to nil. The carpet is filthy, full of jizz and excretions. A shot of Jamesons to purify. I had to sneak in a pint. You can't buy a drink here. Sickness everywhere and I can't even get a drink. When did this whole game turn upside down?

The light shines strange. Down in Mexico you got the red light district with the whores hanging their fat tits out, spreading cunt that radiates brown stink out to the young American looking to cheat on every woman he's ever known. Those are the whores you fuck. Lay your ten bucks down and fuck them drunk. Go around the corner after the mescal starts to kick in. The lizards yelp when you squish their heads into the dirt with your boots like a Nazi on Kristalnacht. You turn that corner. That's when you get to the heart of the matter. These are the 12-year olds . . . After all the numbing self-control, after all the bullshit, after all the times you've sat around with your little girlfriends, sipping your cocktails, wearing your clothes, acting like you're a notch up on the sickness. You turn that corner, mescal bottle in hand, saying, 'My God my God, why have you forsaken me?' Eli Eli Lama Sabacthani?

I see that wide-eyed little whore staring straight at me. Nervous? Awakening morality? Kind of thing where I give her five bucks and a second-grade reader to improve her condition and then be altruistically on my way? Fuck no. I stare her down like Cortez eyeing a brick of gold. I swagger up to the porch, not taking my eyes off of her for a second. My dick swells with every step so it's nearly bigger than she is by the time I get to her. The sky is all Hades, pollution oozing down. Her eyes dart back and forth, twitching from years of abuse. Her fat Mexican brother lies on the porch, drunk on cerveza. He shoves her toward me with his boot and smiles. I wink at him. If he lived back in the States, I'd invite him over to watch the Steelers.

A permanent sexual stench floats in the air, reaching down to my balls, shriveling and pumping. I am tucked hidden in the corner of Rockets and Missiles – a sex club that is raging queer boy faggot every night except Saturday. This night.

They get the post-rave scene happening here. The little raver chicks with their funky little shoes and puffy jackets, they're like Catholic school girls in uniform. They've got the hypocrisy of style. They know what it is to walk the fine line of whore untouchability. Swig of the Jamesons, baby. If they made rape legal for a day, I'd take nine of them down.

The only light coming into the long hall is from the side rooms and the coke machine at the other end – a red and white candle that's going to save us all from thirst and darkness. I spy a little raver with her boyfriend. He clings to her nervously, not wanting anybody to touch or even look at her. He wants to act like he's crazy, down for the count. Capable of swapping, swinging, fucking around, but he's a scared American boy in hip clothes. Society's values are his values. His arm is around her waist, tight. She squirms the dance of false freedom. The last thing she wants is some fucked up, twisted son of a bitch sticking his nine-inch cock in her ass and calling her Pooh Bear. It's a competition to see who can fake being more real.

The televisions near the entrance show porn. Two transvestites are getting it up the ass from two gay guys. It's a weird mish-mash gender fuck. They switch off, the trannies now trying to fuck the fags. The standard porn music fills the air – little guitar riffs and synthesizers – sort of relaxing, really. One of the fags leans over to suck the other's dick, but it's barely hard enough to get a mouth on. I have no idea what drugs they're on. Maybe acid. Wait, one of the transvestites just blew a weak load in the fag's hair. He laughs, pets his ass. More Jamesons.

A strangely normal looking woman situates herself by the first door down the hall. Normalcy in the shape of anything, especially a single woman, is scarce here, so I walk on down. I brush against a black tranny with straight red hair, a complete dog of an individual who barely passes as human, let alone woman. This red-haired thing in size 12 pumps looks like the dude I played basketball with a couple of days ago. It could be him. It is him.

I take a stand by Miss Normal. She is non-descript white trash, possibly fat but I can't tell in the dark. A question mark of a woman, but good enough for a fuck. Nudge up to her, swig the Jamesons, nudge some more, brush the hand across her unfortunately large ass, but still no dice. She's transfixed, looking through the window in the door at what's going on in the room. Her mouth is slightly agape. I see her with the same look watching TV at home. I envision bugs flying into her mouth, millions of them. I'm too handsome to be ignored. I look in through the small window in the door.

A domination scene – complete Halloween bullshit. A woman and two men. The woman lies on her back on the bed. She's thin, junkie-style emaciated. An unhealthy, unfertile, trashy broad, twitching back and forth. Her clit is pierced in an attempt at credibility. A black scarf covers most of her face. I imagine that she's horsey-looking, big teeth and thick nostrils. Her labia is excessive. It hangs out of her vagina and scrapes along the bed, every so often getting snagged and pulled away from the rest of her shaved, brown cunt. A clean-shaven, beefy vagina is an okay thing, but there's something trailer-park about hers. It reminds me of teenage pregnancy.

Her wrists are 'held' by soft-looking ropes that come down from the ceiling. It's more of a struggle for her to keep her wrists in the ropes than to get herself free. She tilts her head up at an angle so she can spy out from under the scarf. She sees we're watching and yelps loud. Her tits aren't bad.

The men are fat, hairy, and dressed exactly the same: leather straps, studs, executioner's hoods and Levi's 501's. The same guys who used to play Dungeons and Dragons and call each other names like Dwork and Grork.

Dwork lightly whips the chick's stomach with a soft piece of leather, while Grork, probably her husband, strokes her face and offers 'consolation.' The look on his face is disgustingly earnest. It's as though, if she can somehow make it out of this thing without renouncing the secrets of the dungeon, then they will be rewarded with 30 hit points and vorpal blades. I reach in my coat for a pull of Jamesons and accidentally knock open the door. Dwork and Grork look up instantly, scared

'You're not supposed to disturb scenes,' panics Dwork in a nasally voice.

'Yeah, read the rules, man,' echoes Grork in the same voice except higher.

I swig the Jamesons, deliberately taking my time. After a good ten seconds I say, 'Hey, sorry,' and slowly close the door.

I turn to Miss Normal and hold out the Jamesons. 'Want some?'

She has jowls and is a lot older than my first impression. Any moderate interest I might of had is gone. 'I don't drink,' she says.

'Enough said.'

I brush past her. She gives a pissed off 'harummph', but I don't give a fuck. If you're not attractive then you've got to be enthusiastic; they work in indirect proportion to one another. The US Government doesn't spend it's tax dollars trying to convince Cambodia to be its friend. Either it is or it isn't. If it gets in the way, it will be brushed aside. Makes no difference in the grand scheme of things. She steps after me as women will when defeated. Victory.

People in Rockets and Missiles don't come together, they coagulate like algae or fungi or lower creatures that have no bearing or compass. It's a huddle, a non-unified hanging out in close proximity, where the only sort of communion is that of hiding. A woeful unity, like a group of old fags dying from AIDS going out for a last cup of coffee.

My fellow straights are the ones who fascinate. Two guys with muscles, sheltered most of their lives, cruise in on the scene looking for answers. They have holes that go miles wide and fathoms deep.

They wear their hats backwards in apparent rebellion. These sad wearers of Gap clothes and sensible ear rings are now on the other side of the fence, dangerous territory. They stand next to each other, expressions of lostness mixed with nervous laughter. They got a whole fucking Macbeth brewing under the surface ready to blow. Nine out of ten times it won't happen. But give me that one, the one straight-arrow frat-boy with just enough of a glitch in the family history to send him into a pair of panties and garter belts. That's the kid who's going to bring this whole American house of cards tumbling down.

The trannies are both a lesser and superior breed. They're anti-American turds, who in their fucked up sexuality, support the building in ways they can never understand. No one wants to be them, but they get to be everyone, boy and girl. Three surround the straight boys by room number two. Pull from the Jamesons, a little trickles down my black button-down shirt.

One of the three trannies, an Asian in a tight black mini-skirt, coos and twists behind the straights in a warped version of femininity that could never be perceived as feminine.

The white tranny next to him is even worse. He, like the rest of White America, is flabby and of poor posture. Nonetheless he flaunts himself in a plastic dress that shows off every disgusting ripple, fold, and chunk of cottage cheese.

Hips out toward the straights, moving to and fro, so I can see traces of penis under his red, plastic dress – it becomes clear to me that this fucking bitch of a man would suck the shit out of my asshole. He stares at the back of one of the straights' neck's, breathing heavily. Periodically, the straight reaches back and brushes his goose-pimpled, creeped out neck like he's shooing a fly. I fear for little America if left alone in a room with this vile creature of the deep. Then again, fuck him. Let him rot with a tranny cock in his mouth and the jizz of a 100 other twisted invertebrates dripping down into his eyes.

Miss Normal, who despite my scowl has followed me here to room number two, stands around trying to look cool – in her case, an absolute impossibility. Her best bet would be to go get a secretary job and shut the fuck up.

Another swig of Jamesons and I further nuzzle into the algae to get a view of what's going on behind door number two. As usual the algae leeches up some attitude: the straights in the presence of another straight try to act cool and ultra-hetero, the trannies shiver at the possibility that I might be stepping in on their gig. On further inspection, they start sending me out their twisted vibes. Miss Normal, hurt as she still is, tries to ignore me, but ends up huffing and puffing in frustrated confusion. Fuck them, I get my view.

In contrast to Dwork and Grork and their junkie wench, some real shit is going down here. Five freaks packed like sardines into a box of a room. The gig is well lit and dare I say well in hand. No bullshit accoutrements. They are utilizing the small space in a grand manner.

At the beginning of one of the greatest TV shows ever, Good Times, the one with JJ Walker and all that, they showed a funky mural of blackness that I had no interest in as a kid, but now see as a means to understand the room before me. Like the mural, the scene is pure action and can't be understood in static terms. The movement is frenetic, up and down, three-dimensional fucking and sucking, enough to make a good boy sick. Twisted bodies like a World War I documentary. Eyes rolling, showing whites and dilation in sweet denial of everything but sex. These are the people that sex clubs are about. They should all wear Rockets and Missiles jackets when they're not here wreaking havoc on each others' genitals and orifices. If Nike enters the world of underground sex, these people will be the first to sign endorsement contracts. Big condoms with swooshes. Black and white ads directed by Spike Lee. Michael Jordan sucking on a dildo dunking from the free-throw line.

The left side of the mural is domination of the highest caliber. Humiliation par excellence. The sort of action that must have devastating psychological effects on the submissive party. There are dents in the world and this is one of them. It is mesmerizing, Roman Coliseum type of shit.

Huge, ripped muscles with veins screaming out the forearms and biceps – this is one faggot who has come to play. He is naked with a shaved chest and a full shock of brown hair. He has the mustache of the queer leather scene. I've only seen a few people capable of his facial expression, and they were fucked up, mean to the core. It is the grimace of pain that at the same time is a smile. The nightmare face of pure sadism. He doesn't give a fuck about who's going down, as long as someone is going down. The need to dominate. In 1930s Germany he'd be a Nazi, in Norway a Viking, in Turkey an Ottoman. As it stands he is a ripped and ready-to-kill American faggot who will take a little hetero boy with all his dreams of upper-income tax brackets and BMWs and make him eat his own shit, then fuck him in the ass for not chewing properly. An Icon.

The fag on his knees before the Icon is Little Boy Blue, a young, strapping fucker who surely gets his own share on the fag scene. On his back is a tattoo of a joker with the earth in his hand. It's big, takes up his whole muscular shoulder-blade area. He's at least six feet tall, completely naked, white, tight ass sticking up in the air begging for someone to rip his cheeks apart and stick something – a cock, a bottle, a GI Joe doll – deep inside of it.

A blow job is not a blow job is not a blow job. It's a single malt where quality is everything. Even amongst the better blow jobs, there are delineations between good and bad. Of course the first stop is whether or not the sucker swallows. Then it's a matter of what's done with the tongue and the teeth and the approach and so forth. The issue is complex beyond description. The basic distinction that can be made concerning the truly exceptional hummer is whether or not it is performed in the spirit of degradation: Joe Buttfuck out in the burbs may have gotten lucky insofar as his wifey-poo can suck the chrome off a tailpipe. Still, when she's down there taking both balls into her mouth at once in the infamous tea bag, he's stroking her hair and saying shit like 'I love you, baby. You're my life and I can't live without you.' What's going down on their kingsize bed with the children asleep and Letterman blabbing in the background is not degradation. It's the *Joy of Sex* guide book keeping their marriage fresh and free of litigation.

The Icon and Little Boy Blue are involved in an extravaganza of degradation, a high order affair of shit-level suffering. God bless them, it's heavy.

Little Boy Blue is taking the Icon's massive, hairy, horse-cock into his throat so deep it's got to be banging against his spine. Every so often his head kind of goes off to the side and the horse-cock nearly blows a hole out the side of his cheek like he's Dizzy Gillespie. He's not just taking the behemoth into his mouth. He's doing it in a violent, rapid fashion that can only be described as supra-athletic. This kid is the shit. He deserves an award. If he put the same energy into investment banking, he'd be a fucking trillionaire.

Every ten or so sucking movements, the Icon (and this is where the degradation comes in) grabs his monster prick and slams it against Little Boy Blue's face. I can barely see the front of his face, but with every cock slam Little Boy Blue winces and his head gets knocked over to the side. This is not the light whipping of Dwork and Grork, but a downright dick slam to remind the world of who's who and to establish the order of things now and forever. The Icon doesn't seem to especially notice the amazing blow job he's getting, but when he whips his dick out of Little Boy Blue's mouth and slams it against his face, his twisted grimace deepens in a Naziesque joy. This is power and it's fucking good to see. There are still people in the world who aren't fucking around and it's an honor to be a part of it. I feel like I'm shaking hands with a serial killer, or better yet, watching him getting fried on TV – if those assholes would ever get the balls enough to show it.

To further their sick glory, the Icon reaches with his burly paw down Little Boy Blue's back to his ass. With two fingers he separates the cheeks and looks down to get a view of Little Boy Blue's red eye. The Icon is adroit. He takes his index finger like a scooper and penetrates the anal cavity. Little Boy Blue is filled with freaky love and sucks the behemoth even deeper and faster so that it's going to bust out the back of his neck like an alien any second. The Icon is so strong that he lifts Little Boy Blue off the ground a couple inches by his asshole. Little Boy Blue winces in pain, and the Icon responds by extracting his cock and slamming against his nose. Little Boy Blue goes at the cock even harder than before. The Icon grimaces leisurely. He is an enemy of the people. There is snot in his mustache.

My leg asleep, I move back and forth. The Asian tranny notices my movements and mistakes them for signs of wanting to get buttfucked by her and her gang. She moves over, releasing a horrible bad breath spray on my face and neck. I give her a look of total disgust, which she interprets as an assent and moves behind me, her little Asian face a foot behind my neck. Instinctually, I start doing the fly swat like straight boy. Nothing registers. Out of the corner of my eye, I see the Asian tranny give a quick smile over to Cottage Cheese, white tranny. It is the smile of the made man, seen around frat boy bars all across this great nation. When the target chick moves from beer to tequila and 'accidentally' rubs hand against crotch.

This is too much to take. I hit the Jamesons for courage and look back at her. Her eyes are squinchy, fucked up confidence. The sort of eyes that say, 'I got this one in the bag.' Our faces are six inches apart. Her lips are parted revealing dark, crusty teeth that are no doubt a product of Chinese dentistry and drug use. Her eye shadow is dark blue. Her lipstick, pinkish red. Despite a solid inch of pancake, I see acne. This 18- or 19-year-old little Asian boy is disgusting.

In a murderous utter, 'You mind not breathing on my neck.'

He steps off like I don't know what I'm missing.

I return to the Good Times mural. The Icon and Little Boy Blue are still rocking. The Icon having evolved from a one finger anal penetration (an exhibition sport at the Olympics) to a full-hammer fist fuck. Little Boy Blue goes at the behemoth ferociously.

Turning to the right now, away from the Icon and Little Boy

Blue, the mural only intensifies. Three queers redefining the ménage a trois.

The fag in the middle, on the bed and on his back, is at least 50. He isn't fat but his tits sag like old boobies. It makes me think that at one time he was taking estrogen, thinking about becoming a woman, but at the last minute decided that the life of the male faggot was too good to leave. He's ugly. He has greasy hair that spirals all around like the corporate man's doo on a bender. He has a wiffy little mustache that is both pre-teen and old fart. He has skinny ankles and long, dirty feet. His shoddy, red and blue, thrift store dress is piled in the corner.

He, The Sickness, is on his back because there is no other place he could be. Room number two has the same surgical table as farcical shithole room number one, but what contrast in utilization! The Sickness' skinny legs are straight up in the air, pure missionary. Standing at the end of the table, facing the door, and fucking The Sickness with cool vehemence, is a stately plump, hairy Italian who looks like he should be reading to his grandkids with a cigar in his mouth, not pounding the shit out of a pasty, middle-aged man. The Italian is probably 45 and handsome in a swarthy, Mediterranean kind of way. He is awash in the self-satisfaction of the immigrant made good.

There is the scene in *The Killing Fields* where the hero has to escape across a field of human bones and remains. The feeling is that if he can make it out of that shit, the rest of his life will be gravy – one hundred percent enjoyability no matter what the fuck he's doing. A day spent doing taxes, ecstasy. An enema bag, bring it on. The Italian's countenance is walk-in-the-park sheer contentment, no worries ever again.

Near the greasy head of The Sickness is a Character who is part of the scene, but strangely independent. He routinely inserts his small wiener into the mouth of The Sickness. The Sickness loves this and laps at it coquettishly, as if all that is going down amounts to nothing more than being really cute. The Character takes the head of his little dick and tries to stick it in the nose of The Sickness and they gaze at each other in a collective giggle. These guys have an intimacy, but it's hard to conceive of them knowing each other, as their looks are so different. The Sickness is The Sickness. The Character is a standard thirty-something, alternative guy with a couple of shitty tattoos and long, brown hair. Average faggot. Probably an artist or something.

The Character might be considered the weak link in the mural if not for the dildo that he's fucking himself in the ass with.

The complete picture of The Character: right hand on his little wiener, putting it into the mouth and all over the face of The Sickness. Numerous and average tattoos except for the one on his forearm: a house. Left hand holding a big, white dildo that he inserts into his anus with nearly the same ferocity as Little Boy Blue and the Icon's behemoth. The physiology is tough. The Character's ass is at a weird angle. Back in elementary school, the challenge of 'patting your head and rubbing your stomach' was occasionally thrown down. This guy must have been the champ. I want to try it: wagging my dick around with the occasional jack off and jabbing my asshole with a dildo. Not literally, but sort of try out the motion with my clothes on for the sake of a good challenge.

The Character requires a lot to cum. The way I see it, if all he needed to do was jack off to the Playboy Channel, then that's what he'd be doing. His motives are on the up and up. He's clean. He's in this scene because he needs to be and necessity is the mother of invention. He's not The Character, he's Eli Whitney. I wish him no harm as long as he stays away from me. A man driven by such needs can only have an unlimited downside. Plus, that tattoo of the house freaks me out. I can't see it too well but it looks white picket, suburbs, the whole thing. With that American concept hanging over his head, he can be nothing more than a time bomb.

He has now left the dildo well inside his ass with his cheeks tight around it and is focusing his energy on jamming his dick in the mouth of The Sickness. The Sickness squirms most affectionately. The Italian keeps pumping away, staring up at the white ceiling. Hail Mary full of Grace the Lord is with thee . . .

A guttural 'yowl' and I turn my attention back toward the Icon. The behemoth is fully out, Little Boy Blue on his knees shaking, cowering at the feet of the Icon. Fist clenched in the air like Black Power at the Mexico City Olympics, the Icon drops his meaty paw down on the shoulder of a frightened Little Boy Blue. His steel grip tightens, every muscle in his Lou Ferrigno guns rippling in orgasmic rage. He forces Little Boy Blue's blondey face up to the behemoth. His other hand grabs the shaft, busts out a few lightning fast strokes and in an explosion not seen since Hiroshima blows his load all over Little Boy Blue's face and neck. Little Boy Blue begins to wheeze and cough as though mustard gassed. The Icon's grimace deepens, and he opens his mouth in a belch.

'Oosh,' I hear from one of the straights, and the transvestites immediately gyrate closer to him.

The Italian, in symphonic response, pulls his shit-covered dick out of The Sickness and starts beating off like a wild monkey. The pasta eater is working hard, sweat pouring down his face. I never realized it before, but he is shitfaced. Stumbling so that his back smacks against the white, thin, cheap walls of Rockets and Missiles, he busts an admirable load straight up in the air to about eye level then collapses Indian style on the floor. A look of immigrant's delight is now permanently etched on his face.

Eli Whitney, a.k.a. The Character, is feverishly trying to match the other power brokers, but it's an obvious no go. He goes from two-handed masturbation to insertion into The Sickness to self-titty stimulation to jamming the white dildo in his ass to opening his mouth in weird dilations as though trying to catch raindrops or falling jizz. Nothing works. The Sickness, in a show of altruism, if that's possible, laps at Eli's balls while jacking himself off. He then turns his head away from The Character and blows his own wad – a weak stream of runny snot. The Sickness coos and curls up into the fetal position. The panicking Character can come up with nothing to save himself. Inevitably, the lactic acid overtakes his forearm and he retires into pure dejection. No one in the room could give a fuck.

With the show over, the straights haul ass down the hall. The trannies follow them, bumping past other trannies in their myopic pursuit. Sexual flotsam and jetsam fill the dark halls. Amongst them are Dwork, Grork, and the Miss Labia from room number one. They mill about like a band who just got off stage now waiting for adulation. No one pays any attention.

The outstanding mural has taken hold of me, catapulting my testicles in a testosterone cook-off. The door to room number one is wide open. Miss Normal is standing next to me and that's enough to proceed. The American male must understand that the American female will have sex at the drop off a hat if treated in cavemanlike fashion. It is not a complex process. It doesn't require a Ph.D. Women, in spite of themselves and their protestations, want that thing between their legs to be used properly. Blood and piss comes out there, nasty stuff all the way around, and in that capacity they're like fags. A sense of dirtiness is always dogging them. The ultimate, farcical, cover-up bullshit is this Earth Mother crap where vaginal excretions and other crotch products are made to be holy. Women have perverted themselves, confused the issue beyond reason. The bottom line is that chicks do what they do to add melodrama to their mundane lives. I imagine that truly powerful women, those in political office, rock star babes, big business broads, love to get down and fuck.

I grab Miss Normal and pull her into room number one. She tries to act like it's a problem and it could be, but I don't give a fuck. This is a sex club, I am an American White Boy, and she a sub-par chick who will never have any better. If I were to rape her with a fucking baseball bat, it would be one of the highlights of her life. I don't like her, I'm not attracted to her, I don't know her, I don't want to talk to her, I just want to fuck her. A cum depository. Nothing more.

I get her in the room without much of a fight. I kick the door closed behind me and there's a moment of silence as we face off like gunfighters in the Old West.

Stupidly, she speaks. 'What do you want to do?'

'Shut up.' And before she can act offended I whip my pants down and say, 'Suck it.'

Her method is predictably average. Doesn't take it too far deep into the mouth, hesitant at times, a little tooth action, snorting, some coughing for melodrama. She's so full of shit she makes me sick. It's two minutes into this thing and she hasn't even got a taste of my balls. I hate her. This is the rote predictability that will contribute toward the downfall of America. What's more, with this fucking method there's no way in hell I'm going to cum. I glance behind me and see two men staring at us through the window. Roles reversed, I see how fucking weak the watchers appear.

I push her off my dick and she falls back on her fat haunches. She's wearing jeans, which sicken me in their plainness. Wranglers. For one brief second I'm intrigued by the why and how of her being here, but I crush it immediately. I'd rather die than engage her.

'I'm going to fuck you now,' I say emotionlessly.

She leans back on her elbows in a way that she must perceive to be sexy, but in reality is horrific. Lisping intimately, as though we actually have something going, 'What did you say?'

I will not engage. I will not engage. 'Take your fucking pants off and let's fuck goddamnit!'

She looks hurt and something twangs deep inside me. I reach down and grab her shoe, a non-descript leather job befitting a feudal serf. 'I'll help you,' I say gently.

This invigorates her and she hurriedly pulls her pants down.

She's not wearing any panties. On an attractive woman this would be something to behold, but on her it's disgusting, bringing to mind not sexuality but a woman who has ran out of underwear because she's too lazy to go to the fucking laundromat.

This broad, in strictly scientific terms, is a fat bitch. Her pubes, if they weren't totally unshaved and looking like a briar patch, would be impossible to see due to the fat that hangs from her stomach. Pizza hut and McDonald's. Greasy fat lard and rotting babies. Bloated pig corpses and fried monkey brains. I picture her taking a dump, reading *People Magazine*. I want to die.

Her legs, to my abject surprise, aren't bad. They redeem her insofar as my ability to stick my dick in her. She has left on a little midriff and I'm fine with it. In fact, it's entertaining. One of the funniest things on the planet is a person naked from the waist down. It's like they're on constant defecation alert. Anywhere, anytime, they can drop down and blow out a turd. All the while their torso stays warm, and for that matter even stylish.

Shoes and pants off, her black socks still on, I'm laughing, I reach out to a glass jar that is full of condoms and slap one on. She makes a motion toward the table but I see no reason to mount it. Especially considering who was just on it – chic a la Dwork and Grork. Plus, getting up there would amount to officialization. This is a portrait of me blowing a load, nothing more.

I roll her over and the ass goes immediately into the air. It's big but not heinous. A heinous ass might have killed me on the spot, but a big ass with intimations of plump has an atavistic appeal. I grab her by what should be her love handles, but they're oh so much more. To grab her sides is to dig into a tub of lard, a black hole of cellulite. In times like this a man can only suck it up. Above me always in such situations is my freshmen high school football coach, who I'm sure was a closet-case sadistic faggot. He would run us boys into the ground before practice even started. Then, he'd try and run us through his version of the West Coast offense, so complex it would make Bill Walsh shudder. At full energy we wouldn't be able to comprehend the plays. In our state of exhaustion, it was the ultimate lesson in futility. When the games would come around and he would call the plays in, we had no idea of what the fuck he was talking about. The quarterback would take the snap and do what he could, which amounted to zilch. Out of eleven games we won one – the one the coach couldn't make it to because his fat wife was dying of diabetes. We called our own plays and killed them. I scored three touchdowns. After that season I never stepped on the field again.

I begin pounding. The vagina is loose, like fucking air. I consider ripping my dick out and ramming it in her ass, but the thought of the Italian's shit dick quickly squashes the notion. For her part she seems to be enjoying it, spewing out a lot a lot of 'oh yeahs' and 'fuck me's.' She could be faking, but I could care less. I just want to cum and get the fuck out of her.

I try to fantasize. I go with this chick from college: huge tits, good ass, great fuck, Kendra.

I picked her up at a party one night. We went back to my pad and got naked immediately. Drinking tequila, fucking, sucking, listening to the Doors. Heaven. I came like five times. Her pussy was tight and clean. She wore black lingerie, the kind of panties that go right up the butt crack. I titty fucked her for more than an hour. She had sexy lips and beautiful, soft brown hair. The sweetest and best thing about the night was that I spent 30 minutes trying to get it in her ass.

I do everything I can to envision her, to reincarnate her in the here and now. My mind strains, but all I can catch is glimpses. Little parting shots of her lips and tits. Goddamnit. Try. Try . . . I see her ass but then it fades, frustrating me further, especially when I look down and see what I'm actually fucking. The comparison in itself is enough to send me into depression. I have to cast Kendra aside fast before the whole ship sinks.

I keep pumping. She keeps yapping, begging me not to stop. I try going faster, then slower, then deeper, then shallower, but nothing makes a difference. It is a matter of anatomy. She has a bottomless sink hole for a vagina. Maybe if my dick was the circumference of a beer can I could get something out of it. I slap her ass a couple times out of frustration. She goes, in her annoying little voice, 'Oh yeah, daddy, spank me. Spank me.' I stop. The last thing that's going to happen here is that she cums, and that I slink off unfulfilled.

Next fantasy: I went to Cancun with a beautiful girl I dated for two years. We spent all day drinking margaritas, making out on the beach. She had the sweetest blue eyes and the longest, most fragrant brown hair. The picture that always gets me is of her in a hand-woven, Mexican dress, lying back on the sand. She pulls the dress back real slow to reveal her pussy. She says, 'You ready to fuck me, baby.'

With every pump this bitch's ass ripples fat, and the thought of Mexico love hurts me. I shouldn't have brought it to mind. That beautiful beach scene is reserved for quiet jack off's of reminiscence, late night in a mellow mood after work sort of shit. Not for this rat hole Rockets and Missiles. I stop.

She's immediately rolls over. 'What's wrong?'

I ignore her and pull out the Jamesons from my coat pocket. Take a good pull. I have a throb in my frontal lobe.

Without any instigation she starts sucking at my dick. The same sub-par blow she was giving earlier. The last vestiges of Cancun are still in my mind. I take another hit of Jamesons. My Mexico love was still a virgin when I got a hold of her. I should have sacrificed her to Baal to ensure that I should have such quality for the rest of my life. I look down at the head bobbing on my dick and it becomes clear that somewhere down the line I fucked up. I would sacrifice this one in a second but the gods would probably throw her back.

The blow job being another dead end, I pull her off me. She's so into it that I have to use both hands to wrench her mouth off my cock. She looks up at me concerned. 'What?'

I have to keep trying otherwise all of this effort is wasted. 'Roll over again and stick your ass up high,' I say.

She gives me a funny, questioning gaze. I quickly nix it with a scowl. She rolls over.

'Now spread your ass cheeks so I can see your asshole.'

I'm hoping to God it's not going to be too bad. Her white butt in the air in the stretched out position takes on an encouraging averageness. If her asshole is clean, I have a shot.

She peels her cheeks apart revealing a tight little sphincter, pink and normal in all regard. Women in general keep it cleaner then men, and this is always good news. She's performing valiantly, really digging into her ass cheeks and spreading them far and wide. I am confronted with pure asshole and effort. Her knees dig into the ground uncomfortably. Her black socks are still on. She says nothing. I whip off the rubber, toss it into a corner, situate the head of my dick about an inch away from her anus and commence jacking off in furious and focused strokes.

A sick, last ditch fantasy: In the college days I came across an Amnesty International report entitled *The Abuse of Women in Islamic Nations*. By the time I put the article down, I had a hard on so blistering that I was forced to find a hidden corner of the stacks and bust a nut that ruined a whole volume of Congressional abstracts.

A young, American Peace Corp worker was knee-deep in an Iranian clinic all day. Tired, sweating, no longer able to stand the heat, she removed her chador. Within minutes she was accosted by a Muslim priest, an Imam, and brutally escorted to backroom Islam.

The 'Holy Man' decided to invite his pals over to teach this Westerner a lesson. In strict adherence to the teachings of Allah the magnificent as dictated to his one true prophet Mohammed, they sodomized, gang raped, and forced her to perform oral sex and other such goodies for 15 hours straight. After which they dumped her on the streets more naked than she was before.

A 17-old Iranian punk is already married three years, destined to fuck no one else but his ugly wife for the rest of his life. His friend pulls him off the streets where he was on his way to mosque and leads him to the back room. There he encounters a hot, naked American babe with whom he can do whatever the fuck he wants. He pulls down his pants and props that healthy, white, American ass up into the air . . .

I keep jacking, trying to get my head into the mindset of that Iranian punk plunging into that Peace Corp pussy, my friends cheering me on so that all is right in the world. Go . . . fuck her, do it, pump, grab her hair, fuck her, do it man, do it . . . this is your dream . . . I look down and see fat white ass, cheeks spread apart and know that there ain't no fucking fantasy in the world that's going to save me. Enough. I fall back on my haunches, let go of my dick and grab the bottle. My semi-erect cock goes instantly limp. My balls squinch up into my stomach, trying to hide from the world. I take a huge pull and kill the bottle.

After a moment she lets go of her cheeks and flops around. 'What's wrong, honey?'

Her concern makes me even more dejected. 'Fuck you,' I say. 'Don't call me Honey. I'm not your fucking husband.'

Hurt, she must have thought that I was going to take her to dinner and a movie. 'What?'

'I can't cum.' I almost say it's because she's too fat, but I hold back.

Emotionally, 'Why?'

I pull my pants up and gather myself up off the floor. 'Forget it, thanks.'

'But . . .'

'Drop it, all right,' I interrupt. Then I blurt, as much to myself as to her, 'No interest in this. Don't push it.' Her pants still off, her fat still hanging, I open the door and blow through three leering creeps: two guys and a tranny. I glance back. The two guys enter the room, taking their shirts off as they go in. She's set. This is a good night for her.

The dark hallway at this time of night becomes less occupied but more full at the same time. Transvestite leeches and slumping homos take up more space as the night goes on. Weird, on the street you never notice them, but in here they reign. I fell afflicted but when don't I feel afflicted? This is standard operating procedure sanctioned by the authorities. If it weren't for Rockets and Missiles there'd be rape and bloodshed on the streets. Whether or not I'd be instrumental in it I don't know. One can never say what one would actually do until one is there, swept up in it.

I take a moment to straighten things up. Through my frontal lobe headache and physical drunkenness, I realize I have blue balls and should do something about it. Tuck in the shirt and scope the scene. Nothing but trannies and desperate straights now. It's late, maybe four in the morning. All the ravers have gone back to their apartments to get eaten out by their boyfriends. I can see them now, talking about their crazy night at Rockets and Missiles. They use guys like me to turn them on. 'Did you see that one weirdo in the corner drinking all that whiskey?' asks the boyfriend. 'Yeah,' says the girlfriend. 'He was kind of cute.' And this is where it gets sick. The boyfriend, in the safety of his apartment, says, 'You should have said something. We could have had an orgy,' and puffs his cigarette in superiority. The girlfriend looks up at him in awe, then proceeds to give him an outstanding blow job. Go fuck yourself, you piece of shit. I'll kick your fucking raver ass and sodomize your girlfriend.

Upstairs there might be some action. At least there's a porn room up there that shows some really good shit so I can jack off. Down the hall, I move past the leechy lascivious trannies. Earlier on they just breathed their bad breath. Now they reach out for dick and smack their lips. If someone were to scrape the pancake off their faces, this entire hallway could be painted three times over. All in all there must be close to ten of them hanging out. This is their own little red-light district, except no fat tits and no ten-year olds. They stand by the doors, leering and hoping for one of the few remaining heteros to grab them by the ass, pull them in and whip out his cock. They would suck it off in a New York minute. No charge. Fuck, they'll pay you.

Avoiding all the tranny grab ass is impossible. Invariably one of them gets a clean shot at cock. To react against it would be a waste of energy. For every space there is a price. The price of this space is a slight compromize of my heterosexuality. When I first started coming here it bothered me. Now I understand it's part of the game. You have to give up something to get something. Unfortunately for me, it ended up being a fat piece of white trash ass that is now being gang banged by God knows how many people and probably having the best orgasm of her life. Good for her. I pull a couple of Franco Harris moves to avoid most of the tranny cock and ass grabs. At the end of the hall are a couple more rooms, the coke machine, then the stairs.

I peer into the room on the right, two fags buttfucking. One of them blows me a kiss. I ignore. In the last room on the left the door is open. I peer in before I hit the stairs.

Reviewing herself in the mirror is a rail-thin vamp of a creature, tall, almost two dimensional in essence, like an elongated Toulouse-Lautrec. Black nylons with the line that runs up the back. White designer pumps that set off the nylons in cutting edge fashion. The skirt is not mini, but loose flowing above the knee, red. It hugs the legs and ass just enough to give an idea of the perfection that exists underneath. Up top a worn but clean black, t-shirt that hugs two perky little tits. The hair is black, well-conditioned mystery. The face is black-lipsticked aristocracy. The skin is the alluring ghost-white of the Eastern European.

This razor-sharp sexuality, so unnecessarily reviewing itself in the unworthy mirror, comes together to form the most beautiful transvestite I have ever laid eyes on.

Amidst the bad breath, the leers, the cock grabs, and the cottage cheese, she is holy.

Gracefully, so unlike the dementia that fill these halls, she straightens herself and looks over at me. Not a smile, nor a scowl. Only a recognition that I am there and admiring her. Out of nervousness, I reach for the Jamesons but remember that I killed it. I shift my balance, placing a hand on hip. I strike a pose trying to look sexy. Never before had I given one ounce of thought to how a transvestite might consider me. With her, I am again an attractive, young, successful male intent on convincing not only myself, but her.

She saunters over. In a lilting alto she says, 'Hello.'

'Hello,' I slur and do what I can to sound more articulate. 'What's your name?'

I have seen attractive transvestites before who upon closer inspection reveal foible after foible. She only gets better. 'What do you want it to be,' she says.

'I want it to be what it is,' and instinctively lean toward her. I have an erection.

She pauses, then smiles confidently. 'Then it's Lady California,' and holds out a dainty little hand. On her index finger is a silver ring. It is a snake curled around a quarter moon. Her fingernails are dark red.

I grab her hand in a shake. Women often don't know what to do with a handshake. They fear that if they grasp too strongly they'll be perceived as masculine, yet, if they do it too weakly they'll be perceived as sheepish or inferior. The end result is usually not even a handshake, but a quick touch and a slimy evasion. Lady California, who is a transvestite and therefore subject to especially complex handshake issues, shakes my hand firmly yet softly, as a woman should.

'My name is Sam,' I tell her. 'And it is a pleasure to make your acquaintance.'

She leans closer to me so that there is only a few inches between us. I am six feet tall, only slightly taller then she is. Her body and demeanor are that of a woman.

We are making direct, sensuous eye contact. Her eyes are hazel, like mine. 'Do you . . .' But drops off in the middle of the sentence. I can feel someone standing very close behind me. I turn.

An older man dressed straight out of Victorian England eyes Lady California. He has a cherubic face. He is one of those Anne Rice vampire groupies. He looks like he has a lot of cash. He speaks in a bullshit English accent, like the Great Gatsby or some shit. 'Are we ready for me, my lady?' He is oblivious to my existence.

She pulls back from me. In the grand scheme of physical attractiveness, I'm far more preferable, but she doesn't seem to mind his presence. In fact, since his arrival her face seems to have enlivened, subtly. She may even be charmed by the old guy.

Lady California nods her head and quickly gathers her purse and coat. As she steps out of the room, she places her hand softly on my arm and says, 'Nice meeting you, Sam.' She then places her arm on the Victorian's elbow and elegantly saunters off – the trannies in the hallway part for her like the Red Sea.

Sexually excluded and therefore dejected, I make my way up the stairs, clomping loudly with each step and repeating, 'That chick has a dick, that chick has a dick, that chick has a dick.' So that by the time I reach the top of the stairs I have convinced myself of the utter foolishness of my dejection . . . but why would I have any sort of feelings of dejection? The chick, does, after all, have a dick. She is not a she, she is a man. She, I mean he, pisses standing up. There are pictures of him in the third grade where he's wearing a butterfly collar and sporting a bowl hair cut. In gym class he was on the boy's team. I remember specifically a kid named Sean who hung out with all the girls, but when it came to flag football was a terror. The guy could outrun and out-quarterback the best of us. He, if still alive, is gay and probably going by the name, Shawna. Lady California is probably no more than a Calvin, Cal, Carter, or Steve.

Nonetheless, there is something in the angularity of the her being that clings to my brain, that stirs my emotions. I still have an erection.

The top floor is completely different from the long hallway and rooms below. Upstairs is like a gay men's club. The music blares. Old New Wave: Ultravox, Alphaville, New Order. The kind of synth-pop that makes every step seem like a dance movement in German avant garde theater. In the past there have been sightings of little ravers up here. They like to move around and pretend it's a club. The old fags tolerate them, but unlike the trannies, they have no hopes of fucking the ravers. Truth is, they probably don't even want to.

I wouldn't mind . . . Unfortunately, there's hardly anyone up here. It's late. A couple of queers lie around with a tranny on a king-size bed complete with canopy. They talk, pet each other, do a little kissy kissy. I move out of the main area and into a small hallway that features a long, rectangular, Plexiglas view of a domination chamber. It's like an aquarium. Nothing's going on inside. The room is equipped with everything from a noose to a rack. These are the purlieus of the Dwork and Grork set, and I could give a shit. The only time it ever gets interesting is when the 'Big Dominator Master' shows up. It's not that I give a fuck about him, the nerd. But that the son of a bitch always has a flock of good looking club girls hanging around him to do with as he pleases. He whips their beautiful tits, spanks their luscious little asses, gets them to lick his boots. But try to get in there to do a little bit of your own 'dominating' and watch your ass. The prick actually keeps the door locked while he's performing his show. One too many drunk straights have busted in uninvited.

The small hallway empties out into a loungie area with a big wheel in the center. Once in a great while some ballsy demento straps himself on to the wheel and invites the world to spin and abuse him. These guys are the hardcores, no fucking around. When you put yourself on a spinning wheel at the mercy of strangers, then you are indeed the real McCoy. People are fucked up: straights with their repression, fags with their moods, women with their issues. You give somebody complete power over you and you're asking for it. A few months ago, these two drunk straights pulled up chairs next to the wheel and spun this little queer for nearly an hour and a half. The guy was puking on himself, begging them to stop. No one, including me, would help. This guy had strapped himself on the wheel an hour before and hurled obscenities at the crowd trying to get their sadistic attentions. People were stopping to laugh at him in his agony. Finally, the manager, some fat dyke, threatened to kick out the drunks. That little queer got a first-hand taste of the wheel of Samsara.

There's no action around the wheel tonight. There are a few people milling around. I think of Lady California's beautiful legs and a sexual shiver shoots up my spine.

'That chick has a dick,' I repeat aloud to myself. 'That chick has a dick.'

There are two small rooms at the far end: the porn room and the juice bar. I can see that the thrift-store couches in the porn room are occupied by old fags, so I decide on the juice bar for a night cap. Normally I wouldn't go in, but sometimes you have to hit every angle to gain a sense of closure. It's like stopping at the neighborhood bar for one last drink after a big night. You don't expect anything, but you need to do it.

Out there somewhere is the platonic form of a juice bar with shiny happy people sitting around in sweat pants snorting wheat grass – a far cry from this little alcove. Only one kind juice is served, apple.

The rest is soft drinks and other brand name crap like Snapple and Nestea. There are three stools and an old Lazy Boy. A window offers a mesmerizing view of a naked furniture warehouse across the street. The juice bar is the darkest room in Rockets and Missiles. It is the size of a large walk-in closet. I enter and take a stool.

A conservatively dressed tranny is tending bar. She wears polyester pants and a dark sweater. There is a non-sexual energy to her, like a real bartender at a pub, and it's kind of refreshing. 'What can I get for you?' she asks in a down to earth voice. There is nothing leering about her whatsoever.

Tiredly, 'You have any coffee?'

'Just made some,' she says proudly and turns to the small coffeepot behind her.

Above the refrigerator hangs a framed picture of Divine. What a fucking hero that fat ass must be to these people! She turns around with a large cup of coffee and says, 'One dollar.'

I lay a buck and some change on the bar and take a sip. Not bad. She leans against the refrigerator, facing me. I couldn't tell before, but I think she's Latina.

'So how was it tonight?' she asks. She has a soft, but masculine voice. I respect the fact that she doesn't go to great lengths to try and hide it. Her sweater reveals no tits whatsoever.

'All right,' I say. 'Ups and downs, same old stuff.' I pause. 'What about you, how was your night?'

She sips from her own cup of coffee. How these men in women's clothes achieve such frailty is a mystery. Her arms are like twigs. 'Slow,' she says. 'Things have been quiet around here lately.'

'Making any money?'

'Oh yeah,' she says and rolls her eyes, 'a million dollars.'

I chuckle and sip my coffee. A truck rolls by on the street below.

She picks up again, 'So you had a boring night?'

I think of Lady California, but repress. 'Yep, screwed around a bit, but that's about it.'

She rolls her eyes in a 'tell me about it' look. I empathize with her. We're all trapped, but she's got it tougher than the rest of us. From what I've gathered, the fag scene is the worst when it comes to being yourself. If you lisp right, dress right, and fuck right, you can have all the friends in the world. But if you're idea of fun is going to a baseball game and chilling out with a beer, that is to say, *the straight pleasures*, then you could be in for some community acceptance problems. In a faction as cliquey and tight as the transvestites', the rules of the game have to be a hell of a lot tougher.

'What about you?' I ask in the nicest tone I can muster.

'You not having fun?'

'Fun, hon?' she says in a sarcastic way that endears her to me. 'I don't think so, unless fun is working two boring jobs so I can live in a bad apartment.'

A little surprised, 'It seems like this would be a cool job.'

She rolls her big, Latina eyes in a slightly disapproving way. 'This isn't a queers dream, babe,' she admonishes. 'There's a lot more to life than Rockets and Missiles,' and leans forward and says in a hushed tone, 'even for a pervert like me.'

We stare for a few seconds, like dogs trying to figure out what to make of each other. The visual sniff turns out okay, and in a move that would make any hetero male proud, she says boldly, 'So what the hell's your name anyway.'

I hold out my hand. 'Sam. What's yours?'

She grabs it firmly. Confidently, as though she could have no other name, she says, 'Miss Nowhere.'

We release and I decide that I like her.

'So what the fuck are you doing here?' I ask. Then I take a sip of my coffee, sort of hiding behind the cup in case I came on too strong.

In no way offended: 'The same thing you're doing here, hon. Except trying to earn a living.'

'And what is it I'm doing here?'

'That's up to you . . .' she says philosophically.

On the counter behind her I notice some books. One is an old favorite of mine, *Human, All Too Human* by Friedrich Nietzsche. I would mention the book but would no doubt be embarrassed by her knowledge, as I've forgotten nearly everything interesting that I studied in college. Instead, I bring up what's really been on my mind.

'Can you tell me about someone named Lady California?'

I expect a wry smile or some kind of know-it-all expression. To my surprise I get a straight answer. 'A beautiful woman,' she says. 'Do you want me to mention you to her?'

'No no no,' I respond quickly and immediately feel like a geek for getting freaked out. 'I mean, ummh, I just met her tonight.'

She seems disappointed by my predictably hetero reaction. 'Oh.'

An awkward silence, I can't forget who I'm talking to. 'Tell me something.'

'Yes, Sam.'

'I was talking to her tonight when this old guy showed up and escorted her out. Do you have any idea where she went?'

'There is a vampire scene here in town,' she says plainly. 'They go there together.'

'Yeah, that's what I figured. That Anne Rice shit, huh?'

'Yep,' she says with a smile. We share a chuckle that makes us trust each other a little more.

After a moment and a sip of coffee, I utter nervously, 'She's pretty attractive.'

Firmly, no doubt in her voice: 'She is beautiful, Sam,' and sips from her coffee with both hands around the cup.

Chapter Two

THESE PEOPLE HAVE no idea what it takes to operate effectively as a public relations specialist. The work requires a psychology of the spirit, an understanding of the human condition. Who knows more about what's really happening in America: a public relations specialist or some ivory-tower shithead with a Ph.D. in philosophy?

To do my job well I need a command of the language beyond that of the thinker. All they have to do is present an idea. If the world doesn't understand it, so what? Who the hell knows the true thoughts of Thomas Jefferson much less Walt Whitman – democracy's fucking poet. By the time an original idea seeps down into the head of the average asshole, it's so diluted it has no meaning.

It is my job to ensure that the average asshole has a meaningful comprehension of necessary items. Public relations is fundamental to the human condition. Without it there's only shitting, eating, and sleeping. The gap between necessity and quality of life must be bridged. Required is the heart of the psychologist, the mind of the sociologist, and the soul of a philosopher. No small order.

Investment is the hallmark of respect, and I see none of it happening here. It's not a good feeling to know that inferior colleagues are better equipped. These people think they can stick me in this shithole of an office and without any support, day in day out, and get top quality work. It's downright abusive. I don't like to make waves, but I have no recourse other than to take action.

Re: last month's convention, related matters.

Tom,

As I'm sure you know last month's convention was a success. Kudos to the staff for doing such an excellent job!

I know that you are extremely busy as of late. I can only say that your work in gaining us new accounts has been unprecedented. You are to be congratulated!

Please thank Dick for me in regard to his generosity. Without him I wouldn't have been able to stay so late on the convention floor and get the work down that I did. Thanks to Dick for going above and beyond the call!

Tom, if I may, I would like to broach a subject that I have mentioned to you on several occasions. Realize that I, probably more than anyone else on staff, know how hard you work. If I were you, I doubtless wouldn't have time for the small requests of everyone here, either. Again, thanks for all you do to make this such a great place to come to work!

Still, I do wonder if you may remember my mentioning a request for a laptop. I know the budgetary pressures you are under and would never bother you for anything that would further strain the department's finances. Take it from me that I know first hand the sort of juggling that needs to go on around here to keep everyone happy. (And let me assure you that this is the happiest department in all of Liberty Telecomm International!)

Still, as a member of the public relations community and as a representative of Liberty Telecomm International, I think it important that I (we) be on par with my colleagues in regard

to current technologies. You see, while on the convention floor
I could not help but notice . . .

A knock at my office door. Ignore. I'm flowing.

. . . nearly all of the public relations specialist in attendance, many
of whom are my friends, had the latest in hi-tech . . .

'Sam!'

'What?'

'Did you forget?'

Forget, Dina? Never. Not for one moment could I possibly forget that you are one of the juiciest pieces of meat I have ever had the pleasure of laying eyes on. Sure you could lose ten pounds or so, but I'm not going to hold it against you. Your natural sexuality could handle another 15, maybe even 20 pounds. For a woman like you, physicality is an afterthought, but what a physique you possess. Those tits, those legs! Your plucky spirit. I see you partying with all your hip, little friends. Drinking, smoking and talking until three in the morning. Oh yeah, I know you get fucked a lot. You and your 1940s, big band style. I love your dresses. You're like a walking cocktail hour. Dyed-blonde hair and fancy barrettes. Patent leather shoes and white socks. Twenty-two years old with menthol cigarettes in your purse . . .

'Sam!'

'What?'

'What is your problem?' She has a unctuous voice, the kind that gives strong clues as to how she might sound in bed.

'I'm involved in something big right now, Dina. Sorry, but it requires total focus. What's going on?'

She grins and leans up against the doorway. She's wearing a black skirt that stops right at the knee. No stockings. I turn her on, I know it. 'You totally forgot, didn't you?'

In her spell. 'Forgot what, Dina?'

She shakes her head, mocking me affectionately. 'The sales guy, remember? You're supposed to interview him and do a story or something like that?'

A chill goes down my spine. I play it off cool, though. 'Oh yeah, sure. What's that, later today?'

'Ugghh,' she says and rolls her eyes. 'He's like at my reception desk right now, Sam.'

'No shit.' I'm doomed.

Nonchalantly (it's my problem not hers): 'Like what should I tell him?'

My mind is a chess computer of permutations and possible moves: I'm sick, out to lunch, broken hand can't type, busy with the president, choking on a seed, in the bathroom, working with the handicapped. I don't even know who this man is. He is someone important, though, that much I remember.

I'm up from my desk. 'Stall him out for five minutes,' I plead. 'That's all I need. Okay, Dina?'

She shakes her head, laughing at me. 'I'll try to keep him entertained.'

'I know you can,' I wink.

'Anything for you, Sammy.' I immediately get a boner. I want to do her on the floor.

The office is a pigsty. There is a stack of *New York Times* occupying the only other chair in the office. I see the cover story on the top issue concerns a newly elected leader in Iran – probably one of the guys who raped the American Peace Corp worker. Scurry around the desk and toss the stack in the corner where he won't be able to see it. The new leader is supposed to be a moderate. Super, now they'll only allow 2 guys instead of 20 to rape a woman for showing her elbows. The memo is still on the computer. Can't let him see it. Can't let him think that there's anything but job satisfaction and love coming out of this office. Scurry back around the desk, save it for later. It won't save. The disk is full. Fuck it, no time. Erase it and write it again later. Problems like that just don't go away. Straighten out the desk. Toss a copy of *Rolling Stone* in the trash. Get the pens in the pen drawer. Paper clips in the magnetic paper clip holder. Miscellaneous papers on the floor where he won't see them. The desk wobbles as I clean it. It is so fucking cheap. How the hell can I make a good impression with a desk that looks like it's a WalMart reject? Scrape off a wad of hard gum and toss out a piece of Kleenex. Get rid of the entire box it'll make it seem like I'm always sick. Wait . . . He might be sick and need one. It's a sign of hospitality. Pick it up out of the trash can and put it back on the desk neatly on the corner. The computer is all out of wack. Get the keyboard in line with the monitor. Wipe the dust off the monitor with a Kleenex. Toss the Kleenex. Fart. Wave my hand so he doesn't smell it. Quick clothing survey: dark blue, worsted wool pants fresh from the dry cleaners, white, cotton blend shirt, dark blue tie with little red Tabasco sauces on it. Fine and dandy. The great plus of having sexual tension in the office is that it keeps everyone looking sharp. If it were all men in here we'd be doomed. Sit back in the chair and try to relax. Confidence is everything. Whatever I think, is what it is. Learned that in a motivational conference in Denver. Good city. Lot of women there. I wonder what's taking Dina so long? Is she fucking him? He's probably trying to get a date, the son of a bitch. That would be just great. I write something on the asshole making him look good, then he gets to fuck Dina. I will have no part in work that doesn't elevate me. I need payoffs. If not my own personal laptop, then sexual favors. The executives have their own massage therapist. Some Swedish chick who goes around their offices from two to five every Friday and rubs them down. Who the fuck do these people think they are? Don't they understand who I am? They should be coming down here daily and kissing my ass for sticking with the company for two years. Where the fuck is this guy?

They hired some lady six months ago to do a color scheme evaluation. The whole point was to make us more effective. This new-age bitch with an associate's degree in corporate psychology decided that the best color for the walls was a light mauve. Mauve! Now I enter this cube every morning having to deal with light brown carpet and mauve walls. There's no window. Company policy dictates that we are only allowed to adorn our walls with one company-approved poster or print. My first submission, a Gauguin

I purchased at the Metropolitan Museum while on vacation in New York, was rejected due to 'nudity that might be offensive to our clientele.' The second poster, now hanging, is a painting they supplied me of kittens. These people are involved in trying to shape culture. They are dead set on infecting the mindset of everyone who works here. The first thing a fascist leader does is appoint his best friend as minister of culture. I know, it's my dream job.

I can hear them walking up the hall. Dina talking loudly, flirting.

'Here we are George,' Dina says boisterously as she steps into my office. Like nearly all attractive women, she loves being the center of attention.

George is tall, predictably white, standardly handsome. I make him out to be 35. 'Thank you, Dina,' he says in a ultra-sincere way. 'It's been great talking to you.'

I stand and offer my hand. 'Sam.'

He grabs and pumps in the shake of the salesmen. 'George Johnkers. It's a pleasure to finally meet you, Sam.'

Dina winks at me and mouths, 'bye.' I hadn't noticed before, but her lipstick is a different shade then it usually is, a darker red.

We sit. George Johnkers is a fine example of guydom. The right sort of non-confrontational hair that is well groomed but not too well groomed – a guy would never spend too much time on hair. An athletic build, but not too athletic, because part of being a guy is achieving a little gut – an affluent sign of more work than play. At work, a guy is always dressed well, in a suit, like his father before him. At home it's all t-shirts and jeans. To be a guy is to be non-extreme, but to be too non-extreme is to be a wimp and not a guy. The main thing about being a guy is that you are yourself – within the societally accepted notion of being one's self.

George Johnkers smiles. It's going to take the most adept guyhood to figure out what the fuck I'm exactly supposed to be doing with this guy without letting him know that I don't know what's going on. The bottom line is that a laptop would eliminate this sort of confusion.

I lean back in perfect guyness. 'So, George. How are things out there? Lay it on me.'

George Johnkers leans back in his chair as well. Part of the guy thing is to mirror the other guy. 'It's like wildfire out there, Sam.' He has that salesman's voice that makes you feel like every word he says is the most relevant yet uttered in history. 'I tell you, my friend. When I first started, it was just me and a couple other bravehearts out there. Now, I have twenty quality people on my team and I'm looking to bring ten more aboard within the next six months.'

'Wow.'

He nods his head like a made man. 'Things are happening, Sam. It's all there for the taking. For go-getters like us, the potential is unlimited.'

In spite of knowing he's full of shit, I can't help but get a thrill out of being called a go-getter. I need to get more information out of him. At this point all I know for sure is that he's big in sales. 'It's really going on for you guys out there, huh?' I ask. 'People really seem to be coming around on telecommunications products.' I look for any clues in his face that might help me. Nothing. I add, 'A sea change from what it was a couple of years ago, huh?' And lean forward on my desk.

He leans forward, mirroring, resting his elbows on his knees. He has a gold Rolex. I must be careful. 'Can I tell you a story, Sam?'

'Sure,' this guy is a pompous ass.

He situates himself into storytelling mode. I see now that the modern version of the storyteller is not the writer, but the salesman. 'I was in Seattle a couple of weeks ago. You know how it is up there.'

'Of course.' I have no idea what he's talking about.

'Anyhoo (I hate when people say "anywho"), year ago, and this is just between you and me now, buddy . . .'

I give him an assuring look. He, of course, does the same.

'A year ago,' he shakes his head gloomily, 'I was on the verge of writing Seattle off. I know it sounds terrible, but things just weren't happening up there. When you have a great product and a staff that works all day every day and you're still not selling, sometimes you have to say, "Look, it might just be that these people aren't ready for the help I'm trying to give them."' He says this defensively, as though I might accuse him of not trying.

'George I know what you're saying.' He leans back and this time I mirror him. 'I know how tough it is out there.'

'Sam,' he says, beaming in wonder at the miracle that is Liberty Telecomm International. 'Would you believe me if I told you that Seattle is now one of our best cities? That it has our third largest customer base on the West Coast behind San Diego and Fresno?'

'Are you kidding me?'

'I am telling you, Sam,' he says with a deeply profound look on his face. 'The time is now.'

I shake my head in prolonged disbelief. 'Will you excuse me for just a second, George?'

'No problem, Sammy.'

'I just have this little thing to take care of,' I say. 'Don't forget what we're talking about, this is good stuff,' and get up from my desk.

In reverence: 'How could I, Sam? This is what it's all about.'

The minute I get clear of the office I haul ass to reception. The entire department consists of five mauve cubes for the public relations staff, with two large offices for the heads: Tom and Dick. Reception is up front.

Reception is reception, as opposed to any other space in the building, because it has three padded chairs and four copies of *Field and Stream*. Sexy Dina is sitting at her desk, legs crossed, smiling like she's been waiting for me the entire time.

'Dina,' I say, panting. Who is . . .' but before I can say another word she waves her hand, quieting me like a Buddhist master.

'Sam Sam Sam,' she says. 'What are we going to do with you? George Johnkers is the head sales rep for the entire western region.

He is here for you to write a 20-page biography on him that will be distributed to Liberty Telecomm's entire sales force. He's like a guru or something.'

'Dina, you're a goddess.' I bow to her, turn, and run back up the hallway, stopping before I get to the office to compose myself. Collected, I enter.

'These people,' I say to George in frustration. 'I have to be in a million places at once.'

'Hey,' he says knowingly, 'you don't have to tell me about it, buddy.'

I retake my seat. 'So explain to me how a guy as young as you – what, 27, 28 – becomes head sales rep for the entire western region?'

Flattered, he says, 'Sam, you're not going to believe this but I'm 34.'

'What?' I say, acting shocked. '34? How do you do it?'

'Good work and good living,' he says with pride. 'I never miss a day on the job and I never miss a meal.'

'Words to live by,' I say. 'George?'

'Talk to me, Sam?'

'You had me worried there for a second.'

'How so?' He asks, concerned.

'I don't know if my ego could have taken a guy younger than me running the whole show out west.' I wipe my forehead in mock relief. 'But come to think of it, 34 is not that much older than 29.' I give him a joking, worried look. 'I think I'm threatened.'

We both laugh. The one sure way of getting someone on your side is to tell them how successful they are, 'You're on the fast track,' I say to him.

'Hey,' he says with a start. 'From what I hear, you're driving right next to me, buddy.'

We laugh again in the warmth and security of the mutual admiration society.

After a moment we get serious. Too much on the job frolic isn't guylike. Work is the priority. It's why we're here. 'So let's get down to business, George.'

'Let's do it,' and adjusts himself seriously.

I reach into the main drawer of my cheap desk and pull out a microcassette recorder. I put it on the desk between us. He is impressed by this. I am coming off as well-prepared, a tribute to raw intelligence and cunning. Proudly, I hit the record button and in an official tone: 'The following is an interview with George Johnkers, 34-year old head sales rep of the entire western region.' I pause, then add, 'A real go-getter.' He winks and smiles.

I talk like I've been preparing for this interview for a month. 'George, as you know you've come here so that I can write a comprehensive, 20-page bio on you that will be distributed to the entirety of Liberty Telecomm's sales force.' Pause. 'First George, I will say that it is an honor to have you here.'

A little nervous now that he's being recorded: 'Uh, it's an honor to be here, Sam.'

'Great.' My speech is both perfunctory and profound – a true professional. 'What's important to me, George, is giving the people an idea of where you've come from, your struggles, who you really are.' He nods his head enthusiastically, really sucking up what I'm saying. 'As I'm sure you've experienced, it can be somewhat intimidating for the beginning salesman to approach a man of your caliber and ask for advice. However, if these people know that you have roots like they do, that you put one shoe on at a time, then you're going to seem that much more approachable, and that's good news for all of us.'

He leans directly over the microphone. 'I agree, Sam.'

I feel in control, handsome even. 'No need to lean over the recorder, George. Relax and enjoy.'

He overcompensates by leaning way back and folding his arms behind his head. 'I getcha loud and clear, buddy.'

'Super. Now tell me where you're from, describe it. The people out there need to know, George.' I am filled with self-importance.

He thinks for a moment, he seems slightly confused. 'I was born right outside of Chicago, but that's not really where I'm from. My dad was a sales rep for IBM, so he was transferred around a lot. Now he's retired right outside of Phoenix.'

Like army brats, the children of IBM aren't really from anywhere. I reiterate, 'What about you, George? Where would you say you were raised?'

After more thinking he says, 'Me and my brother went to a couple years of high school in Salt Lake City, so I guess you could say that that's where I'm from.'

'So you have a brother?'

'I sure do,' he says proudly. 'I come from a big family, a brother and three sisters.'

'Wow, ' I say. 'Impressive.' I'm actually not impressed, but I don't know what else to say. 'How was it in Salt Lake?'

'It was great.' For George, everything is great.

'Were you involved in any extracurricular activities, George?'

'You betcha, Sam. I was all-district honorable mention on the football team.'

'So you were an athlete?'

'You better believe it.'

George Johnkers is too much of a guy – like somebody handed him the script and he's spent his whole life memorizing it. People on the whole are average and dull, but even in their averageness they usually find a way to assert themselves as individuals in some small way. Johnkers is more archetypal than real. Like The Icon at Rockets and Missiles, except nowhere near as interesting. 'Were you involved in any activities that you think might have contributed to your success today?'

He slaps his knee. 'That's a great question, Sam. The values my father instilled in me – hard work, duty, and discipline – have made me the businessman that I am today.' Straight from of the script.

'What about your family. What do they do?'

Beaming, his face reaching apogee. 'They're all successful salesmen, Sam. The only one who's not, my oldest sister, is married to one of the top sales reps at Microsoft. Can you believe that!'

'Amazing,' I say.

This is a man living a meaningful life. He has no doubts, no questions. Every goal is within his grasp. He exists in the blissful throws of structure. He adjusts himself in the chair excitedly and I see that his red tie is from The Rush Limbaugh Collection.

'So what about college, George?'

He makes a cryptic hand movement, signifying something collegial but I'm not sure what. 'The University of Colorado, Sam. The Buffaloes!'

'What made you decide to go there?' A guy like George Johnkers has a reason for doing everything that he does. He never just ends up.

'Family tradition,' he says with pride. 'They have a hall named after my great grandfather there.' He holds his head up perfectly straight and recites, 'All Johnkers attend Colorado. All Johnkers are Buffaloes.' These are the tenets of which lives are constructed. He repeats the sign and says, 'Go Buffs!'

The world can be divided into two kinds of people – those who have structure and those who don't. George Johnkers doesn't know it yet, but he and his kind are becoming a minority. 'What did you major in, George?' I already know what the answer is.

'Marketing.'

'Top of your class, George?'

A small but nonetheless noticeable change – his head tilts downward and he slouches over slightly. This might be interesting, except now a difficult silence has hit the room. I don't want to have to overcome anything. Despite my general unpreparedness and his being an idiot, the interview itself has proceeded well.

I wait for him to say something but he doesn't. Nothing.

I consider breaking the silence, but before I can, he reverts back to his old salesman self as quickly as he receded. He is now performing the quiet sell, reaching out to me on a gut level and talking man to man. 'I was hoping we wouldn't get too much into this, buddy, but the bottom line is that I don't have anything to hide. This is my life and I'm not embarrassed of anything that I've had to go through to get to where I am today. Fire away,' he says.

The guy has me intrigued. 'Talk to me about college, George.'

He sets right in. 'When I was in college at Colorado I was in a fraternity with a great bunch of guys. We were the best house on campus, let me tell you.'

'I bet.'

He is looking more and more comfortable. I have a feeling that he's told this story a number of times. That right now I'm less involved in an interview than I am in a motivational speech. There's nothing I can do. I am back to being unintrigued. Fate has brought me to this moment so that I can suffer. 'Fraternity life at first is great, Sammy.' His expressions are perfectly choreographed. 'There are parties, women, social events, intramural athletics. It's a great time, Sam. One fun ride.'

I nod like a psychiatrist. I should have gone to grad school.

'The problem, though, Sam . . .' His eye contact is at once threatening and reassuring, sheer melodrama. 'Is that the party doesn't stop. And when the party doesn't stop, we lose sight of our priorities. And when we lose sight of our priorities, we destroy ourselves.'

I nod some more. He is now in full motivational mode, like an evangelist except he's sitting in a chair. 'My first year in college, Sam, was drunken debauchery. I would tell you all about it but I don't remember half of what went on,' he throws his hands in the air in choreographed bewilderment. 'I would go to the bars at night with my fraternity brothers, wake up the next morning and not remember how I got home.' He lets out a deep sigh dramatic enough to earn him a scholarship to the Actor's Studio, 'I would be with a woman, and when I woke up, not know who I was lying next to.' He pauses to make sure that I know he really regrets that one. I squint my eyes in false commiseration, and he continues. 'My studies went out the window. I did just enough to get by and nothing more. All I cared about was where the next party was. My life was out of control, Sam. I was on a sinking ship headed for disaster.'

Where else would a sinking ship be headed to?

He stares directly into my eyes. I realize for the first time that to be unnerved you have to care. I am not unnerved. To him, this testimonial is the kind that changes lives, causes earthquakes, cures disease and sends the stock market into overdrive. 'My parents came up all the way from Phoenix to be with me on parents weekend. They were so excited, Sam. Coming to visit their children at Colorado meant more to them than the world.' He again sighs, but this one is choreographed to indicate regret and loss. His eyes well up, 'You'll have to excuse me, Sam. This is hard for me to talk about.'

Triumphantly, I reach over and hand him the box of Kleenex. 'Not to worry, George. I got you covered.'

To my chagrin he deems the Kleenex as unnecessary. As I suspected, the welling up was for effect – part and parcel of being a good salesman. Tears would be unguylike. Even in the throes of a testimonial, guyhood must be maintained.

He exhales loudly and sits up straight in his chair. His resolve dramatically firmed, he continues. 'The first day they were in town we made plans to meet out that night for dinner. They wanted to see me earlier, but they knew I had class. They were so concerned about me not missing any school that they,' he gets a little choked up, 'spent the day shopping so they wouldn't bother me.'

If this dope hopes to ever use this story as some kind of motivational sales tool, he needs to drop the reference to his parents sacrificial shopping. Nowhere in the American psyche does shopping exist as a painful activity.

He continues. 'That day, Sam, there was a party. The fraternity used to like to go out to the reservoir with beer and some food for a barbecue. Usually it wasn't that big a deal, but for some reason the word got around about it, and a lot of people were going. It was going to be a big party, Sam,' he says slowly with a sick look in his eye. 'A big fraternity house party at the reservoir.'

'I had made up my mind that no matter how good the party sounded, that I was going to follow the righteous path and not go debase myself and my family by neglecting my priorities. Right before I went to class, though, my fraternity brothers came over and started putting pressure on me. I was weak, Sam. I had no resolve. I was like a boat without a rudder. Whichever way the sea took me, I went. Before I knew it, I was at the reservoir partying and drinking myself into oblivion.' He shakes his head in despair. 'My self-esteem was at an all-time low. My grades were just barely average and I was drinking almost every day.' He despairs again. 'I hit rock bottom, Sam. And the truly sad part was that I didn't even know it. To me, everything was fine. In fact, I once told my brother on the phone that it was the greatest time of my life.'

I haven't talked in a while. Have to throw something out to show that I'm a professional. 'So what happened with dinner and your parents?'

He ignores my question, doesn't want his flow interrupted. 'Because of the drinking, I lost track of the afternoon. In the back of my mind I knew I had to meet my parents, but I kept telling myself that it was hours away. The truth is, Sam, that deep down I was ashamed of myself and was scared to face my family. I was so lost that I was avoiding the two people in the world who loved me most.

'Like an animal, I drank beer, flirted with women, played volleyball, frisbee, and even went swimming. I tell you right now that I thank the Lord that in my drunken state I didn't drown in that reservoir.'

I tap my pencil on the desk. I wish he would cut the bullshit and get to the point. Like a good salesman he notices my slight withdrawal.

'The bottom line, Sam, is that that afternoon was the worst afternoon of my life.' His voice rises, the denouement approaches. 'I had completely broken down morally and spiritually. All of the values my parents had worked so hard to give me I was tossing aside in the name of having a good time. If it wasn't for a conscientious and faithful friend, who I to this day respect and admire, I would have skipped dinner with my parents and drowned myself in alcohol and women. As it turns out, even though my friend reminded me and was good enough to drive me to the restaurant, I was still five minutes late. It pains me to this day to think of the look on my mother's face when I arrived at the restaurant smelling of beer. My body was filthy and so was my soul. It was the worst moment of my life.'

Like an actor at the end of a monologue, he bows his head.

'So you're saying that you didn't actually miss dinner with your parents?'

He shakes his head. 'No, Sam. But I would have, if it weren't for my friend . . .'

He hangs 'friend' out there in a way that forces me to ask: 'Who is this friend, George?'

He exhales and looks deeply into my eyes like a lover at a restaurant. This is it. The point of his entire spiel. 'Who that friend was . . .' he is speaking very slowly '. . . doesn't really matter. But the friend that that friend led me to, does.'

I know exactly where the fuck this is going. Still, I have to play along. 'What friend of a friend are you talking about, George?'

'Sam,' he says, 'that friend is our savior, the Lord Jesus Christ.'

I spent the first 12 years of my life immersed in the Catholic tradition. I went to Catholic school, did penance, ate communion, and was even confirmed – the last group of 12-year olds allowed by the Vatican to be sworn into the church. After me they knocked the age up to 16.

I never liked it, was never into it, and certainly didn't know what the hell it was really about. To a kid, god is all about give and take. A kid skins his knee, he figures that sometime in the next couple of days something is going to go right for him. A kid does something shitty like punch a girl in the nose, he figures he's on God's shitlist and somewhere down the line he's going to have to take a hit. From day one, every lesson about the almighty has to do with kicking ass on the bad and uplifting the good. The issue gets confused because the people who God uplifts sometimes don't seem so good.

The minute I hit 13 and could make some sort of stand, I got out. I was already on all the priests' shitlists anyway. Once my pals and I broke into the rectory and stole three boxes of communion wafers. We spent the afternoon throwing them at each other and seeing who could fit the most into his mouth without choking. They could never convict us, but they knew we did it. When I informed them that I was no longer going to be available as an altar boy, they happily escorted me out the church door.

Catholic guilt is bullshit. Any smart kid knew that the church was just a big racket to make parents feel like they were raising their kids properly. Without exception, the biggest partyers, drinkers, and wackos are Catholics. If a survey were conducted amongst the trannies as to early religious affiliation, I expect that most of them would be Catholic. Guilt isn't what Catholicism does. What Catholicism does is make you feel like you can get away with anything. At the end of the day, all you have to do is ask for forgiveness or stop by a church and bust out a prayer. It's not a sense of guilt, it's a sense of entitlement.

Anything you do for 12 years (especially the first 12 years) is going to have an influence on you. On the existence of God question, Catholicism has definitely had an effect. Without it I would be a devout atheist, but am now more of an agnostic who could care less. It also had an impact on my approach toward religious attitudes. The quiet, traditional devotee is no enemy of mine. People should be allowed to go about their spiritual business as long as they don't bother anyone with their beliefs. The antithesis of the quiet servant of God, however, is an entirely different story.

The piece of shit sitting before me represents everything that disgusts me in regard to religion. Loud, overt testimony and proselytization. Life built around a flimsy faith. Cheap expression and lack of logic. These people are like sports fans for God. The best thing a person can do is shut up and praise the Lord – because we are as evolved and as good as we ever will be – a thought that to me is horrifying.

The last thing I want to do is engage this creep in a religious discussion, but I am unfortunately a junkie in these matters.

'What makes you think the Lord Jesus Christ is our savior?' That was a fuck up.

He raises an eyebrow. I have idiotically belched the question for which these people live. 'You don't think that Jesus Christ is our savior, Sam?'

Squash any impulse toward integrity on this issue. Georgie has the ears of the Christian executives, and even a junkie knows that you don't use in front of a cop. 'No I didn't mean that, George,' and brush it off with a laugh. 'I was just wondering what led you to believe in our Lord Jesus Christ? I have my own reasons.'

He looks at me like I'm stupid. 'The bible, Sam. What else?'

Shakily, 'Nothing else, really. I just mean that people have different reasons for coming to Lord Jesus.'

Deadpan. 'Have you embraced the Lord Jesus Christ as your personal savior, Sam?'

Integrity is a character flaw that has only gotten people in trouble. A little less of it and historical martyrdom would be cut in half. Shit, a little less of it and history would be cut in half, which might not be so much of a bad thing. We stare at each other. The way I answer this question will dictate the rest of this interview and possibly the rest of my career here at Liberty Telecomm International. Like a good ball player when he's struggling, I go back to my bread and butter.

'Well, I'm a Catholic, George. So while we're on the same team here, we might have a little bit of a different approach to the game.'

Give George a teenage rock & roller with an I Love Satan pin on his jacket, and he'll misquote verse after verse until the kid repents with tears running down his face. Give George someone with half an education and he's doomed.

'Oh.' He is disarmed.

'Yep,' I say, leaning back in my chair in victory. 'It is good to have a friend in Jesus . . .'

Enthusiastically, 'It sure is, buddy. Our Lord Jesus Christ is the one true savior and the best friend a man can have. He guides us through the dark and leads us into the light. I knew your heart was filled with our Lord Jesus the minute I saw you.'

There may be no sweeter feeling in this life than to know that you have someone bamboozled. Or, in his case, buffaloed. 'So you found Jesus in college, did ya?'

'You know it, Sam. I asked the Lord Jesus to enter my heart at the end of my freshmen year. Nothing has been the same since.'

'Expound, George.'

'What?'

'Tell me more.'

Not knowing what expound means has no effect on him – no intellectual curiosity whatsoever. 'I tell you, Sam, it was a miracle. I started working in the campus ministry, my grades went back up, I quit drinking, and I've been clean and sober in our Lord Jesus Christ for more than 15 years.'

'Hallelujah.'

'Amen, brother. The main thing was that the Lord Jesus Christ helped me to get refocused. I was on the verge of quitting my marketing major and studying Spanish instead. I had the crazy idea that I was going to live in South America after I graduated. Can you believe that?'

'No way.'

'Yes,' he says, shivering at the thought. 'I was acting like a fool. The first thing I did after giving my life over to our Lord Jesus was to go back home for the summer and in the name of our Lord Jesus ask my high school sweetheart to marry me. I am proud to say that we have just celebrated our 13th wedding anniversary.'

Our Lord Jesus is not only a college guidance counselor but a wedding planner as well. Not bad for a carpenter who liked to hang around with hookers and drunks. ' The highest congratulations to you and your wife, George.'

'Thank you, Sam.'

'Thank our Lord Jesus,' I remind him.

'I do every day,' he says.

'So you're married, George?' Time to move this interview along. All I know so far is that he's a religious freak with a degree in marketing. The same thing can be said about half the fucking population.

'Sure am, pal. The best move I ever made was to marry my sweetheart.'

'What's her name?'

'Jenny.' A choreographed look of pure love come over him. 'Jenny Johnkers, my better half.'

'And where do you folks live?'

'Liberty's got us down in Albuquerque. Great city, close to my parents, easy access to the western region. I hear of a problem and I can be in any city in the west within three hours.'

'And what about kids? A man like you has got to have some little fellers running around the house.'

'George Jr. and David,' he says with predictable pride as he reaches for his wallet. 'David is named for my father. George Jr., well, that's obvious. Here, take a look.'

Little League pictures like every American boy has taken. The uniforms are light blue with an Intel logo. Both boys are crouched down waiting for a grounder. His wife's genetics seems to seem to have gone AWOL. They are exact replicas of George.

'David is the younger one,' he points out. 'Both made the all-star team last year. George Jr. in majors and David in minors.' He leans forward on the desk and whispers, 'You know, buddy, not too many people know about this but you can set up a college fund for your kids through Liberty. You can never start too early.'

'Good thinking,' I say. 'Being prepared is half the battle.'

'And you have to pay to play,' he says.

Guys like using clichés. They are societally approved wisdom that are easy to memorize and recognizable by most all.

'So, George?'

'Yes, buddy.'

'How did you get started with Liberty Telecomm?'

He proceeds to describe in minute detail his post-college work history. I fade out and let the recorder do the work. I've done this enough to know that when he's done rambling, all I have to is say, 'and the rest is history,' and it will seem like I've been listening the entire time. I think of Lady California, but quickly crush the thought.

'. . . the bottom line is that my dad called him and set up an interview. Within a month Liberty offered me a job, and I was giving notice to the firm in Denver.'

'And the rest is history.'

'You got it. buddy. I moved Jenny and me out to Fresno and started working my tail off.'

'And now,' I say, 'you're one of the most successful men in the company.'

He gives me a pseudo-humble look that says, 'Damn right.'

'Tell us what it takes, George. I'm a young salesman asking you to share with me the keys to your success. Fill me in.'

He collects himself, then sets in with the monologue that I know he's been rehearsing for years. Before me is the new breed of American prophet – the motivational salesman.

'I started off in this company close to the bottom, and within six months I was regional sales manager of the Northwest Corridor. I didn't get that promotion because I was lucky, but because I was willing to do what it took. They told me to move to Fresno, so I moved to Fresno. They called me at three in the morning and told me to be in Portland. I was on the next plane out. Thanksgiving Day they had to have someone in Spokane, and I was there,' and nods his head in the affirmative.

'You have to be willing to give yourself up to the company. To put yourself and your own personal needs on the back burner so the team can come out on top. It's about sacrifice and commitment. There are a million salesman out there who give a hundred and ten percent on the job but who haven't increased their client base or expanded their sales region for years. Why? Because when the clock strikes five, they forget about their job and run home. They don't realize what they true key to success is.'

I play my part. 'What is the true key to success, George?'

'That you are your job,' he says categorically. 'Everything you do in your life should be geared to your profession. You want to read a book, fine. Read a book about being a being a better salesman. You want to exercise, great. Find out which gym has the most potential clients and start working out there. You want to go on vacation, super. Take a vacation to the city where your sales base is the weakest so that you can find out more about the people. Our jobs are the cornerstone of our lives. If you lose your job, your lifestyle falls apart, you might have to relocate to get another position, your kids don't eat as well, and you sure as heck, excuse my French, won't be going on any more vacations. The job we have defines who we are more than everything else in our lives, save for our way of praising the Lord. And I tell you, Sam, the Lord put us here to praise him. And the best way we have of praising him is to be successful in our work. And the one sure sign of being successful in our work is making money.'

This line of reasoning, taken to its logical conclusion, dictates that the richest man in the world is also the most pious. I always knew that stuff in the bible about the needle in the haystack was a bunch of crap. 'What are your plans for the future, George Johnkers?' Time to wrap this up. I can't take too much more.

'More of the same, buddy,' he says with a shake of his fist. 'Keep fighting the good fight. I intend to turn some of my of focus to motivational sales conferences and audio tapes.'

'I would expect no less,' I say.

'You bet!' He says.

'Thanks, George.'

He gets up from his chair. 'So do we have it, Sammy? I have

to meet some people for lunch in about 15 minutes. Potential clients . . .'

My mind scrambles. This interview has gotten away from me – I still don't have all the details of his career here at Liberty. Time for bullshit. 'Yeah, just a couple more things, George. Your secretary gave me the information on you when she made the appointment a month ago. Still, it would be good for me to get it from you so as to make sure that there no mistakes or holes in the information.' I furl my brow in a business-like manner.

He sits back down. 'Sure, buddy. What do you need?'

'Yeah, just tell me in your own words, in the most basic terms,' I scoff like the 'basic terms' are for the idiots out there and not for me, 'what it is exactly you do, who's under you, who you report to, how things are out in the field, and exactly what it is you sell.'

He is surprised but before he can say anything about it I push the microcassette recorder over to his side of the desk and urge him to proceed by vigorously nodding my head. Like a good team player, he does.

'I am the executive sales director of the western . . .'

He prattles happily about the corporate structure, his boss, his numerous assistants, and our fantastic telecommunications products. I wonder what his wife looks like and if he ever fucks her in the mouth. His kids now seem vile to me, little pieces of shit that could very well someday be my boss. Fuck Little League and screw making the all-star team. The world is a cavalcade of mediocre superstars who are constantly being shoved down our throats. If it takes total submission to your job and company to succeed, then I don't want any part of it.

'. . . so now I'm in charge of three accounts worth more than 400 hundred thousand dollars. That means jobs, Sam. That means lives.'

I click off the recorder and hold out my hand. 'It's been an absolute pleasure, George.'

We both stand and shake. 'Same goes here, buddy. I'm so glad I finally got to meet you.'

'Have a good lunch, George. And again, thanks. You've given me some great stuff to write about.'

'I look forward to reading it,' he says.

'Hey, George.'

'Yeah, buddy.'

'Can you tell Dina to come in here for a second.'

'No problem, buddy. Take care.'

'You too.'

I put the microcassette recorder back in the drawer. I will be spending the next several days listening to the tape and finding ways to make George Johnkers look like a great guy – a task that will be easier than I would like it to be.

'Sam?'

She is a vision of sex. Freud was right about everything. This is what drives us. This is what moves mountains. I will be able to write the George Johnkers piece because she is in the world. I will keep this job so I can go out and afford the likes of her.

'Hi, Dina.'

'George said you wanted to see me?'

'Do you have a second?' I say and motion toward the chair.

'Sure,' she says in her bedroom voice and sits. Her white legs are crossed, they scream out to be caressed and held. I want to cuddle naked with her on the floor.

'Dina, I just wanted to thank you for helping me out with that guy. I didn't know what the hell I was doing, and you saved me.' This is sincere. She did me a good turn.

She blushes in my recognition of her. 'Thanks, Sam.'

I have dreamed of taking her out. Of getting drunk, running around my apartment naked and fucking till dawn as I did in the days of yore. I think of Kendra. I think of youth.

Never have I dared to ask her, though. For it is not advisable in this day and age to broach any subject in the work place which might be considered sexual. For some reason, though, maybe George Johnkers and his fucked up way of looking at things – which deep down I fear might be right – I just don't give a shit about what anyone might think. This is my own private rebellion and I insist upon having it.

'You know, Dina,' I say with a surprising lack of trepidation, 'I was thinking that later we might meet out for a couple of drinks. Maybe go out and get drunk or something. It's been a tough day and I could use something fun to look forward to.'

She becomes completely nervous and uncomfortable. At the worst I thought she might say that she's busy. At the best I thought she might actually agree. Nothing but raw, awkward silence. I am compelled to fill the space, albeit sheepishly. 'What's wrong, Dina? I hope I didn't just offend you or anything.'

This softens her anxiety. She adjusts herself in the chair and says. 'No, nothing's wrong, Sam. I just wasn't expecting you to ask me that. That's all.'

'Sorry,' I say.

'You just kind of caught me off-guard, that's all,' she says. 'Like, I thought we were friends.'

'I think we're friends, Dina. And as far as I can tell, there's nothing mutually exclusive about friends going out and getting drinks together.'

A hawkishness comes into her eyes, and for the first time I realize that this woman can be a bitch. 'That's not what you meant, Sam' she says accusingly. 'You asked me out on a date.'

This sucks. I wish I could take it back, but I can't. If she wants to be uptight, fine. I've done nothing illegal. 'If you want to look at it that way . . .' I pause, thinking about what to say. A surprising rush of resolve comes to me. I've come this far, I might as well go for the gold. '. . . then you'd be right. I am asking you out in a romantic way.' I smile. She does think I'm handsome. A girl in the marketing department told me. 'What do you say, Dina. Drinks tonight?'

She doesn't want to be a bitch. Dialogue between men and women is scripted out response. Sometimes it's hard to break through the walls. 'I think you're a cute guy, Sam. But I don't think so.'

Drag, but accepted. At least this whole mistake of mine has taken a softer turn and will not be ending on a sour, job threatening note. Still, I have to ask: 'How come, Dina? I think we could have a lot of fun.' And we could, baby.

She rolls her eyes in her sexy way and bites her lip. 'I just don't think, like, we enjoy the same kinds of things, Sam,' she says thoughtfully. 'I mean, no offense or anything, but I have a lot of alternative, sub-culture friends, and we like going to underground kinds of places. Like, I just don't think you'd be comfortable with my scene.'

This is too much. The irony is too grand, too entertaining. 'Ahh, you're right, Dina,' I say with an air of defeat. 'We probably better not go out.'

Chapter Three

CHANGE THIS SHIT. Fat fuck. Where's the remote? If I have to watch this asshole sign one more piece of bullshit legislation banning uzis for three-year olds, I'll fucking barf. What's this one he's signing here? 'The President of the United States has just enacted an historic law decreeing that ice cream will continue to remain delicious.' Fuck him. Where's the remote? Ah, there we are, under the couch as usual. What do we got next?

The ignominious South. God I hate these assholes. There is nothing worse in the world than southern politics. Shit, there is nothing worse in the world than the South on the whole. Mosquitoes and cheesy smiles. Lincoln screwed the pooch. We should have let the South stay the South and the North the North. The North would be like the Netherlands: legal pot, health care, liberal policies, strong economy. The south would be a backward Balkans nation: racial cleansing, feudal system, concentration camps, Yugo economy. These retards from Alabama ensure that every four years we elect a stupid president and Christian House of Representatives. The evangelist blood courses through the Southerner's veins like shit through the New York sewer system. Festering and shunting, shunting and festering. Change it.

The Strongest Man in the Universe Contest! These guys are fucking huge. They have names like Vognus Von Basha, Friedrich Frielander, Erlic Magnusson, Monstrance Mojioaku, Doriander Crane, and, of course, Fred Jackson from Detroit.

Monstrance Mojioaku, at the battle hammer, spins, tosses. A regal attempt. Fifty-eight yards and seven inches, a new Strongest

Man in the Universe record! Next up is Vognus Von Basha, a true champion of the highest caliber. He hails from Norway and is fearless like his Viking forefathers before him. Picks up the hammer, sets himself, spins, releases . . . oh! A disappointing attempt by Vognus. You can see the look of angst across his Aryan features. Lucky for Vognus the Ukrainian boulder roll is the next event. He has absolutely dominated the event in former Strongest Man competitions. Change it.

Public access. A bunch of college kids screwing around, pretending they have something to contribute to the world. What a fucking joke! TV is a medium that affords no integrity. Fame is a sure sign of stupidity. To be accepted on a mass scale is an indictment of epic proportions. Change it.

This starving African thing is not working. The public has been inundated with these portraits of suffering for too long. These charities have to realize that people don't give a fuck about someone who's thousands of miles away. We definitely can't give a fuck about something we can get rid of with the push of a remote control button. Change it.

Baseball. Fine, whatever, great, blah blah blah. The American pasttime, whoopty doo. It's been surpassed. The only thing it has over any other sports is its history. The most compelling is the Maris thing. Sixty-one home runs is a lot of dingers. There are some guys around today who have a legitimate crack at it. I always though our very own Barry Bonds of the San Francisco Giants might give it a run, but he's too much of a head case. The problem is that he's from Northern California, and that's not a good thing when it comes to breaking records. Living in Napa is just too fab. Makes you soft. On the other hand, this Griffey Jr. kid has a legitimate shot. He possesses all the tools: bat speed, strength, quickness, a good eye. He's also up in Seattle, which is like living in Russia and being a writer. Bad weather makes for serious concentration. His only downfall is he's subject to injury. Given one full season he has a shot, but somewhere down the line he's going to sprain a wrist and miss two weeks. Besides Griffey the only other guy is Mark

McGwire. Give him one full season and it's a lock that he'll do it. What does he hit, like a home run in every seven at bats? Giants are up 5 to 2 in the eighth. Done. Change it.

More Africans. Fuck, zap it.

Oh yeah. This can be alright. A little Spanish TV soap opera. The chicks on here are fantastic, plus it's a great way to practice Spanish. 'Que lastima,' says the Latin beauty shaking her head. What a pity is right, chica. You should be a major star and not stuck on Mexican TV having to make out with that fat viejo. Zap it.

Chinese soap operas, forget it. I have no idea what they're talking about, plus the chicks are ugly. Change it. Another Chinese soap opera! Even in soap operas they're crowded ten to a house. Aren't soap operas supposed to be fantasy? Deep down they must like being crowded in together. They have all that family and loyalty shit. If the son farts on the grandfather, he has to cut his own anus out with a dagger. Super. Let the Chinese rot. They're boring anyway, and the food isn't that good. It used to be good when the people who came over to open restaurants were real cooks. But now every Cho, Lin, and Wan thinks he can take a boat over and make a fortune opening a restaurant. I bet half the cooks in Chinese restaurants nowadays never stepped foot in the kitchen back on the mainland. Change.

Documentary time. Vietnam – the old sore that's made documentary makers rich for the last 25 years. Every documentary, no matter what angle of the war it claims to cover uses the same footage: helicopters over the embassy at the fall of Saigon, the naked little girl running from a napalm attack, the two GIs, one limping using his gun as a crutch and the other holding him up, two Vietnamese being pulled out of a tunnel at gun point. The war in Vietnam is so hip it's sick. It's all about good weed and gook whores, Rock & Roll and surfing. Every Vietnam documentary is like a music video. For something that was so bad, it sure looks good. Even the soldiers, who are usually testosteroned-nerds, look cool. They smoke cigarettes, make peace signs, and drink beer. In the future, if you want to make me hate war, don't put it on TV and play *I Can't Get No Satisfaction* in the background. Time for a snackey-poo.

Loaded up on goodies a couple days ago. Out of the living room and into the kitchen. There's not much of a hall, but the place isn't too small. Have a decent-sized bedroom in the back and parking downstairs. Nice kitchen, brand names appliances, track lighting. An upscale apartment complex.

Open the shiny, white fridge. Beautiful. The reward for all the bullshit is snacks. I have my choice. Do I want humus and pita or something sweeter? The sweet tooth tends to reign in the middle of the evening, so I move on up to the freezer. Two kinds of ice cream: chocolate and chocolate chocolate chip. It's a nice night, relaxing, got the George Johnkers piece out of the way, not a walk in the park by any standard. Go with the celebratory chocolate chocolate chip. To wash it down? In vino, veritas. Have a teak wine rack featuring a nice selection of Northern California reds. Can't stand whites, they don't taste like anything. Go with a merlot to keep things flowing, a cabernet would be too heavy – though it is the recommended wine with chocolate. Set it all down, open the bottle with my stainless steel wine opener, pour a glass in a crystal wine glass, get a spoon for the ice cream, and move on out. Hardwood floors. On the wall a print of Jasper John's flag that I bought at the Metropolitan Museum of Art.

The living room is the real gem of the abode. Two matching, black, leather couches, a green and black Persian rug, an art deco lamp, and a dark, wood, handmade table. The Hope Diamond amongst these apartmental gems, however, is the 21st century cutting edge glory that takes up the entire front wall. A lot of people keep their television, VCR, and stereo in close proximity to one another, but few people have a Home Theater Entertainment Center.

I had always thought of a Home Theater Entertainment Center as a project that a middle-aged man puts together in his basement out in the suburbs, like an ultra-light or short-wave radio. This was something much grander, much more distinctive than a simple assemblage of electronic appliances meant for entertainment. This was a unified, powerful tool intended to aid the viewer in media appreciation. I had a decent stereo, I had a VCR. What I didn't have was a stereo VCR. Likewise, I had a television. But the television was a basic, autonomous agent with no feeds but a simple cable. My home was a mishmash of electronic gadgets with no unifying theme. How could this not effect my life? Where was the focus? The symmetry?

Starting from left to right as it stands majestically before me: a five-disc CD player, a CD rack with more than 200 CDs, a 30-inch Sony television with internet capabilities, a VCR with hyper-reverse so I don't have to wait an hour for my tapes to rewind, a library of my favorite videos, a protective coaster, and a glass compartment designed with the human touch in mind.

Bookending the entirety of my Home Theater Entertainment Center are what amount to the high-tech straws that stir the cutting edge drink. Two sleek, ultra-thin, speakers that integrate the sound of the entire system. The speakers are designed to filter the fuzz out of the TV audio so that I can appreciate dialogue at three times the quality of the regular, unintegrated television. The CD player hooks directly into the speakers through an internal amplifier. Normally, an internal amp means less quality, but Sony has developed an internal amp that outstrips most any external amp being produced today – save for some of the most expensive models produced by Bang and Olufsen.

The most beautiful feature of my Home Theater Entertainment Center is that it is controlled by one, intuitively designed, remote control. Never has the complex been so simple.

A little vino, merlot does just fine with chocolate chocolate chip ice cream. Set it down on the table and pick up the remote. A great invention would be a portable snack manager. A device that could keep two or three snacks right at face level, like a snack-bar facemask, so the remote could be handled properly. As it is now I have to alternate between wine and ice cream to keep managing the Home Theater Entertainment Center. Not too bad, but a little problematic when it comes to quality of relaxation.

Enough of Vietnam. Give me something that means something, like a good sit-com or TV bloopers. Switch it around, more baseball. As vs. Yankees. Between innings, catch the score, shit: Yankees 8, As 1. News, more news. Some guy in Indiana lit himself on fire because he was homeless. Big spoon of ice cream. Change.

Two college girls are walking from Florida to Washington DC in an abortion protest. Not bad looking, a little dykish to be sure. I can't tell exactly what they're pissed off about. Oh. They have flags and crosses, must be pro-lifers. The press is making a big deal of it because one of the college girls is the daughter of one of the founders of Planned Parenthood. Basic child rebellion. Change.

An old movie. What is it? Ah, who cares anyway I hate old movies. They're so fucking dated – Clark Gable and Rita Hayworth smooch and I'm supposed to get turned on. I don't know, maybe a subtle raising of a Bette Davis eyebrow should make me rock hard, but if those guys jacking off to Bette Davis in the 1940s could see the Porn Channel, that old bitch would have never made it to the silver screen. Change it to the real deal.

Ah yeah . . . Boom, baby. Sweet Ginger Jackson. I can see her little pussy dead on. Shaved bush, clean, pink, little labia. She has a nice face, too. Kind of girl next door brunette but with a sick look in her eye.

I unbutton my slacks and drop them down to my knees. I shimmy my boxer shorts past my butt. Already swollen I give it a couple good strokes and it comes to life like a champ. To be young, successful, and erect is a fine feeling. I situate myself on the couch for maximum masturbation pleasure – dick facing the TV, feet on the floor, butt on the lip of the couch. I put the remote down on the floor and get at it.

Stroke it nice. She spreads her little twat with two fingers and coos on the phone in a scared but oh so excited voice, 'Should I put my fingers in my pussy?' They don't exactly show her penetrating her little vagi, but they cut to her sticking two glistening fingers in her mouth. She has perfect little titties that jiggle when she shakes her ass in arousal. She drops her hand back down to her twat and begins fingering ferociously. They show a close up of her contorted, orgasmic face. With her other hand she massages her little titties.

I need the visual jump start that the Porn Channel so graciously supplies me with, then I'm off in my own world with my own women. A man with an agenda, though I have no control of who or what my mind will come up with. I like the element of surprise. This time it's Dina from the office. She's over here now, stretched out on the floor, naked before the Home Theater Entertainment Center. Her ass is plump, her pussy is soft and wet. She sticks her ass straight up in the air like Miss Normal and I peel apart her ass cheeks to reveal a beautiful, clean, little sphincter. Her boobs are huge, veritable udders. They scrape along the floor. She uses one hand to massage and caress them. The nipples are pink and mammoth. I never realized this before, but part of my attraction to this menthol smoker is maternal. I want to suckle at her bosom, but then I also want to fuck her in the ass. I say, 'You ready to get fucked in the ass you little slut?' She turns her head, sucking at me lustily. 'Fuck me however you like, Sam. You know I always wanted you.' I'm stroking hard now, my cock engorged with blood, reaching almost all the way up to my navel. I have one of those dicks that really only shows it's size when I have a full hard on. I sit back and lift my legs up in the air to get a little wind on the balls. I like having my asshole spread out wide, too. One time I brought home a girl from a bar. While I was doing her I told her to stick her finger in my ass. She freaked and left. It was great.

I shove it in Dina's ass. She screams in a mixture of pain and pleasure. Pumping away, her plump ass rippling and shimmying with each thrust, my universe is in complete order – like Ahab at the helm of the Pequod. Her boobs fall, loll, roll all over the place. Sweat pours down her back, a little blood creeps out of the ass.

I diddle her twat with one hand and smack her butt cheeks with the other. I feel it coming on now. I look up at the 30-inch screen. A black chick is now getting nailed doggy style by a white boy. Fine with me. She has big tits, like my Dina. She makes all kinds of fucked-up faces, like she's angry that the white boy isn't fucking her hard enough. She wants it bad, the black bitch. Gang bang her. Fuck her in the mouth. That's what they all want anyway, to be completely fucking dominated and beaten by their man. Women hate weak men. I take Dina by the hair and yank it back until she begs for me to stop. I slap her in the face and tell her to shut up. I can feel it now, stroking harder, faster, squeezing the circumcised tip, using the other hand to rub my balls. Everything's going. I can feel the lactic acid build up in my forearm.

'You're going to take what I fucking give you, Dina. You fucking hot little bitch.'

'Whatever you want, Daddy. Please put it in my mouth. I want you to cum in my mouth.'

Shit dick and all, I stick it into her beautiful mouth. Her eyes open wide at the enormity and fullness of the situation . . . except they're not so much her eyes but a dreamy amalgamation. The change is slow, but drastic. It doesn't take long for the disturbing reality to assert itself. The eyes are no longer Dina's, but those of Lady California.

The image fleshes itself out. The angularity, the sharp features, the white skin, the soft eyes. Lady California sucks my cock viciously, her beautiful black hair tossing and falling passionately. Her rail-thin body squirms under my maleness. She looks up at me, her aristocratic vampness adding so much to the suck. It's like having my dick in the mouth of the Princess of England.

I'd pull myself out of this distorted freefall, but it's too fucking good. The best ever. Taboos break like matchsticks. Her mouth gyrates on my dick. Her eyes roll into the back of her head in ecstasy as she gives body and soul over to my sexuality. She is living for my cock. Her fingers are up my butt. I lose myself to her.

I look down from my epiphany to see her ass. Perfection. Tight, round and small like a little boys . . . that does it . . . stop. No matter what. Stop . . . Stop! I am not jacking off to a little boy's ass! It's not part of my structure. It would kill me. That was weird. Bad weird. How the fuck did that get there? Crush that tranny out of my mind. She brings up things I don't want to know about. I'm still hard as a rock. I have to finish, regardless . . .

Dina. Conjure Dina. Think of her tits. They're the one thing on her that beat out Lady California – besides a vagina of course. I'm tittyfucking Dina now. That's right, I got her back. I'm not sick, only mislead by my subconscious. Dina smiles up at me. She is full of awe and harmony. My tittyfucking her gives her life meaning. Her tits are so soft and huge. In a few years, Dina, they'll be saggy and gross. I'm tittyfucking you in your prime. A true conquest. Powerful. Just a few more strokes, grab the nipple with one hand. Make her wince and beg, remind her who's boss. More strokes. Shaking. Vibrating. Pulling. About to cum now. Forearm burning. Grab the cock and stick it in her mouth. She goes crazy, almost choking on it. More strokes, pump it in her mouth, more strokes, pump it, pull up my shirt, there it is, squeeze, boom! Ahh, Christ. Jizz all the way up to my nipples. I slump over. That was fucking amazing. A huge load. The remnants of Dina disintegrate from my mind. I am glad to be alone.

Treat Lady California as a sick aberration, like a dream. In dreams I've killed people who I wouldn't hurt if paid a million dollars. I can't be responsible for the subconscious. Who can? Still, there are issues lurking that I'm scared to deal with. Issues that could bring down the whole house of cards, Home Theater Entertainment Center included. I have to put it out of my mind. Repress it way deep down, like a good boy . . .

I reach down and pull off my sock. I wipe my belly and chest clean and toss the sock over the couch. Perfectly relaxed. Incredible jack session in spite of the aberration. I grab the remote and the ice cream. Oh, it tastes so good. The chocolate chips give it that chocolate power crunch that makes the whole ensemble swing. Change it from the Porn Channel. I need to chill from psychopathia sexualis for a bit. Switch it over to one of the big stations to catch a sit com. Sit coms are a perfect nightcap to the good jack session. They are clean, safe, and sexual exhaustion makes things more funny.

What could be better than the show of shows, the Honeymooners of our time, the arbiter and progenitor of all that is funny in America today: *Seinfeld*. Seen this one before, but it doesn't matter – good sit coms are funny no matter how many times you see them. MASH is the perfect example. Most people have seen every MASH episode at least three times, but they still watch. This is the one where Jerry falls for the roommate of a girl he's dating. After deciding that to dump a girl for her roommate is the 'toughest move in the business,' George and Jerry get down to figuring out how it can be done. George comes up with a plan – Jerry should tell the girl that he wants to have a ménage à trois with her and her roommate. She'll be so disgusted that she'll dump him on the spot. The roommate, on the other hand, will know that Jerry likes her. In a couple of weeks, when he knows his old girlfriend isn't home, he can innocently call up the roommate to discuss the situation, over coffee perhaps? A good plan on the whole, but the roommates end up going for the idea. Jerry is of course too much of a neurotic Jew to ménage with the goyim, so he ends up with nothing except the million dollars per episode that he's paid to do the show. Jerry Seinfeld is the leader of the free world. The most important man in America. If we still maintained the class, demigod, he would be one. Once in New York I saw him walking with his 17-year-old girlfriend. She was so fucking hot I wanted to die. Jerry Seinfeld is living a life that on the whole is better than mine. Where I would beg for a ménage à trois, he casually decides against. Where I would work all my life to have his girlfriend, he fucks her in the mouth without giving it a second thought. Where the average man struggles for pennies, Jerry Seinfeld has a blast making millions. He is a cut above, living in a rarefied air that only a few have experienced. They're going at it again . . .

'You make me want to die, Joanne!'

'Don't say that, Vance.'

The piece of shit lawyer and his stupid wife who live next door are the enemies of my relaxation. What the hell their problem could possibly be, I have no idea. Their lives are of TV quality perfection. Their apartment is about three times the size of mine, they have two BMWs and a maid that comes over four times a week. They have a beautiful little girl named Kelly. She is usually tucked away in her room during the fighting. Waiting through the psychological damaged, slowly losing her child mind. I don't like to think about her.

This shit has been going on ever since I moved here a year and a half ago. The walls are thin and we share a ventilator, so when I want to I can hear pretty much anything they say down to a mumble. The arguments start off like most relationship arguments, but then quickly degenerate into full-on confrontations. From there they can go in several different directions depending on what mood the lawyer is in. I once heard them yelling like they were going to kill each other. Five minutes later they were fucking each other's brains out in the kitchen, which unfortunately shares the same wall as my living room.

On the other hand, I know for a fact that he's smacked her a couple of times. I don't know how hard he hits her but I've seen her wearing sunglasses on foggy days. The lawyer is not a small guy. When he hits her, he hits her. One time I heard a smack – then nothing but silence. The daughter must have been gone that night. It was eerie waiting for someone to say something. Finally, I heard him crying, begging her to get up. After a minute, she was up and comforting him. Comforting him! Saying to stop crying and that it was 'okay.' Five minutes later they were watching TV, what they always do once the storm has passed.

I don't have a lot of sympathy for a woman who puts up with constant, abusive bullshit – especially when she's allowing her daughter to be exposed to it. She has a duty to give her daughter a chance at being happy, or at least ensure that she'll not be forever fucked up and miserable.

'You're a fucking idiot!' He yells.

I try and concentrate on the television. No more *Seinfeld*, but some new sit com that I've never seen. Standard shit, three guys living together, all in love with the same girl. She doesn't know who to pick. They trip over themselves to get her, each representing a culturally accepted male stereotype: the handsome stud without a brain, the sensitive, stable, and cute nerd, the middle guy who brings it all together. She'll obviously go for the middle when the ratings dive and the show needs a gimmick. If the writers are lucky they'll be able to spin off the new relationship.

'Why do you have to talk to me like that?' she cries.

'Because you're so fucking stupid!'

I switch it over to CD mode. All through remote control, of course. I have more than 200 hundred CDs. I don't feel like getting up, so am forced to chose from the ones that are already in the player. There's Jimi Hendrix: *Axis Bold as Love*, Nirvana: *In Utero*, and Miles Davis: *Kind of Blue*. The jazz is too soft for right now, being that my quality of relaxation has already been disturbed. Nirvana could be good, but it's getting near bed time, and it might give me too much of a pump. Jimi is the perennial superstar, varied enough to fulfill all needs in all situations. Definitely one of the greatest artists this country has produced, and therefore cast aside as an acid-tripping freak.

Click on the Jimi. The righteous entry: slam, bah dah, da da da, bah dah. Then the sweetest, heaviest, most swingingest manic voice on the planet. 'If the sun, refused to shine, I don't mind, I don't mind . . .'

'Anyone,' he screams 'who would spend five minutes talking to that leech prick is a weak, stupid, piece of shit!'

'But I work with him, how can I not talk to him?'

Turn up the volume on the CD player. 'If the mountains, fell in the sea, let it be, it ain't me.' The power of the guitar. It has a saving quality. It's all right to be sick. Sickness is the way to make it. 'If all the hippies, cut off all their hair, I don't care, I don't care.' Here comes the good part. Music is blind, it doesn't know who I am and can't see the life I lead. It forgives and absolves: 'white collar conservative pointing his plastic finger at me . . .'

'Are you calling me a liar?' I can still hear him. His voice is up a notch on the anger scale. Has that physical injury quality to it that I've heard on several occasions.

She's scared. I picture her cowering in the kitchen, begging. 'No Vance, no. I would never do that!'

Silence. I wait for him to do something but it seems to have quieted down, thankfully. I pick up the glass of wine off the table and take a good slug. By my watch I see that it's two minutes past ten. With all the distractions, I forgot that one of my favorite shows is on: *American Criminal*. I immediately grab the remote and switch it from Jimi back to television. Wait one second, yes the Giants won. Good, they'll continue to remain in the hunt for another day. Bonds, believe it or not, had a game, two for four with an RBI. Sit up straight and switch it over to my show.

I hadn't thought of this before, but considering all the knives, the kitchen isn't the best place for a domestic situation. Whatever. Nothing I can do.

Commercials commercials commercials. Already missed the intro when they summarize the villains they're featuring. This is the best show on the air today. Nothing else really exposes the relationship between crime and criminal. *Cops*, the grandfather of these shows, is little more than a couple of guys with video cameras following the police around. The show says nothing concerning the sociological aspects of the institution of criminality. *American Criminal*, on the other hand, while not overtly attempting to address the psycho-social aspects of crime, does in fact accomplish much in the way of sociological analysis. You get the violator's background, his circumstances while committing the crime, his sentence, what prison he's in, and in some cases an interview with the criminal himself. The commercial is over.

Leon Pannalokis: first degree murder, life sentence. Evidently this Pannalokis snapped one night and decided that his child wasn't matching up to his expectations at the early age of 2 ½ years. He was also angry and frustrated with his wife who left him for his partner at the construction company. He took the kid to a building that the construction company was doing for the city – a huge contract – tied him to rebar and proceeded to set the building on fire. When they found the kid he was alive but with 80 percent of his body destroyed by third degree burns. The commentator makes a point to say that there was nothing left of his genitals. The child died in a Dade County burn unit two days later after intense and unimaginable suffering. Pannalokis, after initially fleeing, turned himself in out of guilt. He was devoured by the reproaches of his conscience – a favorite line of mine that I read back in college.

'You're a fucking fool!' The asshole lawyer is starting up again.

'What are you talking about! How have I acted that would make me look like a fool in front of our friends?'

There is nothing more interesting than a human in the throes of irrationality attempting to explain things, so I lower the volume and tune into the next door neighbor entertainment center. This guy is a lawyer. He should be erudite and present a strong, logically sound case. But like a doctor who gets a boner when a hot 19-year old comes into his office, he has lost control of his mental functions. He is in a twisted reality where he can't see straight.

'You sit and talk with your legs crossed, flirting like you want to fuck! That's when everyone is laughing, Joanne! And they're not laughing at you, Joanne. They're laughing at me!'

Well done, Vance. I think of the song: *Paranoia will destroy ya.* Your turn now, Joanne. Play the role of the mollifier trying to talk reason. The more sense you try to make, the more incensed you'll make him. Every word you utter humiliates him. Be the oxygen, stoke the flame.

'Steve is my associate, Vance,' she says deperately. 'I have to talk to him about new projects. Otherwise, the lines of communication will break down. I can't be effective unless we have a good working relationship . . .'

Doctor Freud has entered the building. Look at the words.

Associate. Translation: fuck partner. Lines of communication. Translation: intimacy beyond the verbal realm. Relationship. Translation: relationship. She wants a relationship with him, Vance. She wants to fuck him. What are you going to do about it?

'There is no goddamned way that I am going to believe that your relationship with that flaming shit heel is solely professional. What to you take me for, a fucking imbecile!'

'No Vance. I would never . . .'

'SHUT THE FUCK UP! YOU'RE A FUCKING WHORE! Solid thud.

Ah yes, we know this one. Not a punch but a push that sends her onto the kitchen floor. I can always tell, because with a punch she immediately wails out, but with a push the floor vibrates and silence ensues. For her, a woman dead set on tolerating such stupidity, a push is preferable. Almost always, it serves to waken him from domestic abuse free fall and into profuse apology. I can't exactly hear what he's saying, but it's fast, furious and obsequious. The weeping tones of apology can be detected through a bank vault.

Back to my show. The next door neighbors are an interesting distraction, but I need Home Theater Entertainment Center relaxation. The Pannalokis piece is over. Sad, I wish I could have seen it in order to get some idea about his childhood. It's not worth it for me if I can't get a good glimpse into their psyche. This guy now, whose name I missed, is a murderer from the Chicago area. Looks like he shot his boss then went on a month spree where he raped two women and killed another man. Snowball effect. Once they go over the edge, they figure there's no turning back, so why not go for the gold. Of course, they're right. Once you kill someone you're done. There's no way out unless you can afford a high-profile lawyer. These lower-middle-class guys who murder are right to haul ass and go on a violent crime spree. Let's say I freaked out and slit George Johnker's throat. I would get as much money as I could and go on a rape and pillage bender of epic proportions. Get a bunch of blow, acid, heroin and start doing some real partying.

I'm a handsome guy. Not as handsome as Ted Bundy, but damn good enough to get bar girls to come out with me to my serial killer van.

'I can't keep going over and over this, Vance.' She can't leave well enough alone, she needs more melodrama, more abuse. 'I'm your wife, you have to start trusting me.'

I hear some pacing, the sounds of nightmarish thought processes.

Then, in a crystal clear voice that cuts through the walls like an audio razor blade. 'Are you threatening me, Joanne?'

Return to fear. 'No, I just meant that you can't call me a whore with Kelly in the next room. That's all.'

In human relation there is the predator and the prey. The model exists for all forms of interaction. Who has credibility as an individual capable of violence? The ultimate, determining factor.

'Get this straight: if I ever see you talking to him again . . . any of them, goddamnit . . . I'm going to teach you a lesson that you'll never forget. Do you understand me?'

'Yes, Vance. I'm sorry.'

He is now daddy. She is a little girl. This is just how she wants it. This is just how her daughter will want it. I hear a soft thud, and I can pretty well assume that it's her dropping to her knees. I hear the mumbling of apology. Their melodrama has taken a 180 degree turn. She is on the floor begging forgiveness. I hear a door close and the pitter patter of little feet running across the hall. In my mind's eye I see it perfectly. The father standing tall, the mother on her knees, crying, the little daughter stretching her arms out as wide as she can, hugging them both to bring the family together. Give them a US flag and a couple more family members and it might look like something from *The Sands of Iwo Jima*, where the American soldiers are struggling to put up the stars and stripes.

I feel noble, even a little pissed off. The night has given me an edge, a new approach. Time to start using my intelligence. I will reeducate myself on my own terms and become politically active. My first enemy will be the media. I'll pick it apart, protest outside of news stations, fight on the side of truth, hand out newsletters. The problem with this country is that no one is willing to take a stand anymore. Even if people can see and identify the problem, they're too busy and involved in their own lives to do anything about it. The first lesson of change is that sacrifice must be made. Oh, man! *Cheers*.

Big mother-loving spoonful of ice cream. It's soft now, like I like it. Put the remote down, have a nice sip of wine. Lay back and relax. This is what it's all about. This is why I work hard. I earned this. Time for me to enjoy the fruits of my labor. American society is built around the man who is willing to work hard. You put your nose to the grindstone, suck it up, do your job well, and bingo: there it is, a Home Theater Entertainment Center, chocolate chocolate chip ice cream, a fine glass of Northern California merlot, and a great episode of *Cheers*.

I sing along with the last part of it, it's one of the greatest opening songs in all of television. 'You want to be where you can see, the troubles are all the same. You want to be where everybody knows your name . . .*Cheers* is filmed in front of a live studio audience.'

Norm walks in. 'NORM!' What a great fucking way to be. Love is out there, all we have to do is grab it. 'What's up Norm?' asks handsome Sam.

'The corners of my mouth, Sammy.' A great response. Norm is the kind of guy who wakes up and looks for something good to say. He's strong and free. He gets a beer and settles in next to good old Cliffy and Fraser the witty psychologist. He has his own spinoff show, which is really very funny.

Chapter Four

I WISH I could live a normal life and not come to this shithole. I wish average questions could fill the bill: should I have the soup or the salad? Is a black button-down shirt too much of a statement? Is losing 20 out of 22 players to free agency a death knell for the Pittsburgh Steelers? Should I use Rogaine? I want to be a superficial guy. I am a superficial guy. Mostly, I want to like myself.

But I can't let go. I'm drawn to this place. I tell myself that I come to Rockets and Missiles in the name of sexuality, but I'm starting to think that the real cause is to force myself to think.

Funny, when I was in class in college all I could think about was getting laid. Now that I'm in a sex club all I can think about is whether or not God exists . . .

Downstairs in the corner once more. A low turnout tonight. The trannies are restless. They need hetero blood to keep them from turning on each other like feral cats. Early still, though, and I haven't checked it out to the full extent. I got here, found my corner, started drinking Jameson's Irish whiskey. My routine is well established.

The porn on the televisions near the entrance is strong and vile, as always. A straight-up hetero session that warms my heart to see. A redhead getting the old double penetration from a black dude and a white dude. The black guy is in the ass, the white dude is pumping the snatch. Porn producers have a thing for mixing the races. The more taboos they break the more they sell. Smart. The redhead is going off. Super-orgasmic contortion. Screaming, writhing, begging them to keep fucking her. 'One dick in my ass and one in my pussy!' She screams. 'This is my fantasy. Oh God!

I'm going to cum!' The dudes pump with all their might, their balls smacking against each other. The whole bottom side of this woman is completely filled. The black dude's mammoth cock in her anus makes it look as though she's repeatedly taking a shit then sucking it back in. Fantabulous. The white dude, who is on bottom, sticks his tongue out like Michael Jordan going for a reverse jam. These people are happy. They are fucking well and getting paid for it. They are not currently questioning the existence of God.

The god question is important because morality depends on whether or not God exists. Without God, Hitler gets away with everything. On the other hand, if there is a god, then Hitler is forever being buttfucked by every Mongol to ride with Genghis Khan. Meanwhile, every Ashkenaz, Gentile and Gypsy to fall victim to the incinerators of the final solution, feast on piroshki and drink Russian vodka while they watch his torture from sky box luxury suites.

The whole god thing is keeping me from getting my dick sucked. I should have the courage to withstand any sort of sexual encounter as long as I know I'm going to enjoy it. And I fucking know that I would enjoy having my dick in the mouth of Lady California. I can't do it, though. I feel like I'm transgressing against some god-decreed, natural order. It's like once I go to the other side there's no coming back. Normalcy is key. I want to remain normal but how normal am I if I keep coming to this place, standing in the corner and philosophizing about the existence of God. I am not normal, but then I am. What is it to be normal? A basic question but a tough one nonetheless. More importantly, however, is why do I care? Why do I want to be normal. It's like 'being normal' is some kind of blanket. If you're under it, then you're okay and warm and secure. If outside, then you're exposing yourself to all the elements. I am afraid. But afraid of what exactly? The universe, the world, America, the Christian right, my mom? Shit, who the hell am I anyway? Am I a faggot? A pervert? An upstanding citizen made more interesting by my eclectic sexuality? This whole Rockets and Missiles thing is about me coming to terms with myself. Except

I don't feel like it's me that I'm trying to come to terms with, but society.

The real question is how did 285 million people enter into the picture? I thought this was supposed to be about me? How does one divorce one's self from the morals of American society without becoming completely alienated?

The trannies have taken notice. I can't stand in this corner for too long without them sniffing out my hetero blood. A black tranny stands right outside room number one. She is waving, smiling, moving her hips, dancing. From this distance she looks good: miniskirt, thin legs, fat lips. I know from experience, though, that up close she's a nightmare. She moves toward me, sauntering. She has on a black wig, long and straight like old-school Tina Turner. Black is better than blond for the negress tranny. The black trannies don't seem to realize that blond wigs highlight the masculine features in their faces. She is eyeballing me like a piece of meat. I move away from the corner to avoid contact, making just enough facial contact to see a mix of hurt and disappointment. She actually thought she had a chance.

I am one of the few heteros here tonight. I guess the m.o. for most straights, except for me, is to check it out once and never come back. If straights come here more than twice, they avoid each other out of shame. No straight wants to be thought of as a regular. Earlier, I saw two college boys who I think I've seen before. Seeing them here made me feel good, affirmed. I'm a weak man. I move over to room number two to watch.

Pure tranny love. I've seen these two around before. They are of the older breed; more trashed and worn out than the young, hip trannies who populate Rockets and Missiles. They don't bother with lipstick or any make up, but if they do it's always put on haphazardly, as if they could give a fuck. Still, they are trannies to the core. They wear old dresses and call each other names like Ronda or Margaret. Old fag bitches who have settled into their sickness. They are so removed from the blanket of normalcy that they don't even know what cold is anymore.

I'm the only one watching. The young trannies don't want to see this. Tranny love is ugly and they don't want to be exposed to anything that reminds them of how fucked up they are. Every ounce of energy a tranny musters is spent convincing himself that the world is beautiful. It's not, though. The world can not be beautiful when you have to change so much to fit into it. The truth is that they hate themselves. They want to die. They hate the fact that they were born into men's bodies. They hate their dicks. They hate their Adam's apples. They hate their hairy asses. Moreover, they hate women out of jealousy and men for finding trannies disgusting. The last thing they need is a fucking mirror. Especially one as ugly as these two freaks in room number two.

They employ no sexual paraphernalia; they use no condoms; they are on the bed. Tranny One is lying on his back. Tranny Two is on top of him, sitting, facing the wall. There is nothing unusual about the position. There are worldwide in excess of 200 million couples performing this position this very second. The tranny on the bottom is wearing a green, full length dress. He has pulled it above his groin so Tranny Two can operate effectively. Tranny One has very fleshy balls. They flop back and forth like marbles in an old, brown, paper sack. His whole ass region is droopy. It smushes and slides all over the bed. His legs are those of my grandfather, skinny yet flabby and matted with hair. His sphincter protrudes out from his cheeks. No doubt a product of years of buttfucking. He has on a green and red charm bracelet.

Tranny Two is completely naked. I can't see his face, but if back fat is any gauge, I can only be thankful that he is facing the wall. The hair on the other trannies legs is nothing in comparison to the hair that dominates the upper back of Tranny Two. It is an oily forest of sexual dementia and mystery. The hair thins as it proceeds down his back, only to gain in strength as it reaches his butt area. I envision the German forces during World War II, fighting on two fronts – compact on the western front, thin in the middle, then foolishly overloaded in Russia. As for his actual butt I can't see it. It is totally covered with thick, black hair. More hair is on his ass, in fact, than is on his head.

Tranny Two slides up and down on Tranny One's dick. The ass of Tranny Two, while never touching the bed, flabs up and down on the shaft. He buttfucks at various speeds, sometimes going super fast so that I can hear him coughing and wheezing through the door in aerobic dysfunction, then slows so that he is barely moving. At times, he simply exists with a dick in his ass.

I catch glimpses of Tranny One's face. He looks like he's dead. No excitement, no pulse. Neither happy nor sad. Sexual nirvana. Tranny Two doesn't notice. He continues to fuck at intermittent speeds. They seem to have some arrangement worked out between them. They are both at peace. On the shaft of the Tranny One's dick, all around the balls and on his thighs, is brown, liquidy, shit. His crotch looks like a softee-freeze that's been dipped in caramel. Tranny Two neither notices nor cares. Tranny Two scratches his hairy back. Pumping at a medium pace, he leans over and kisses Tranny One on the forehead. Tranny One wakes from the dead and smiles.

I accept the shit. It is the tranny version of pussy juice. A natural function of sick love. To be disgusted by it is to be unrealistic, like watching a birth and hiding from the placenta. The kiss, however, makes me feel uncomfortable. I don't want to play spectator to tranny romance. I am not a creep. Fucking is one thing, intimacy is another. While I have no respect for these specific trannies, I have respect for the institution of intimacy. Deep down, for better and for worse, I consider myself to be a romantic. Whether that consideration is correct, I have no idea.

I turn away to allow them their perverted intimacy. I am startled by a tranny who unbeknownst to me has been breathing down my neck for only God knows how long. I feel violated. I think of her ogling me from behind, dancing, winking at her friends. My instinct is to scurry away, like an ashamed mouse. After I get a good look at her, though, the instinct quickly fades.

I've always had a thing for Latinas, specifically, young Mexican chicks. Something happens to most older Mexicanas. They get fat from too much burrito and having too many babies. The young ones, those under 25 or so, have a Catholic sensuality unrivaled in this sad land. Latinas are fire. Their asses are plump, but tight. Their breasts bloom like roses. Their skin is warm, inviting brown. Their lips are full. Their eyes, death black. They are soft darkness, like the beach just after sunset. Poverty has kept them clean. Jesus has kept them tight.

This tranny is a fine little Latina. She dresses like a whore, but with a cross around her neck. She wears a miniskirt to show off her thin legs. She has no tits, but the face is sweet, uncorrupted Catholicism. It's like it's Sunday morning in Mexico and I'm staring at a 13-year-old girl who's just got out of church, except this one has on blue lipstick and wants to suck my balls off.

I feel spicy. 'Hola señorita. Como estas?'

'Aye,' she says in a high, thickly-accented voice. 'Hablas español?'

'Si,' I lie. 'De donde eres?'

She is squirming with tranny sensuality. She is a fine little piece of meat. 'Ciudad de Mexico. Y tu?'

I feel like a fat Mexican mayor. A *patron*. This is my little caca. I can do with her as I please. 'None of your business, little bitchy. You like to suck it?'

She writhes in my dirtiness. She grabs my cock, I let her hold onto it, I can't help myself. 'Nice,' she says in a heavy Mexican accent. 'I could take it all the way in.'

I have a boner. My dick aches to be in her mouth. If she had a pussy I'd pay to fuck her. Unfortunately, she has a cock. And I'm not going to blow my heterosexuality on a random tranny. I am like the worst virgin. It's got to be special, and I don't have nearly enough Jamesons in me.

I am also confident that, if I wanted, I could easily get a good piece of Mexican ass – with a vagina and everything! There's this hot little maid who cleans up the office. She can't be older than 17. I noticed that she's been showing up early and making sure to do my office first before I leave. As she cleans, I sit behind my desk and play with my dick through my pants. One day when it's safe I'm going to show it to her along with a fifty dollar bill. I'll fuck her right then and there on the floor. That'll probably be the day that the president of Liberty, a renowned Christian, comes down to introduce himself.

Still, I need to torture her a little bit to make myself feel better. 'You don't deserve to suck it, little chi chi,' and push her hand off my dick.

'Why?' she whines. 'Por que, señor?' She is frantic, like a salesman who thought he closed the deal only for the customer, at the last second, to decide against it.

I take a good swig of Jamesons. I feel powerful. 'Because you're a bad little chi chi.' I don't know why I keep calling her 'chi chi'. It just seems to fit.

'But I'm sooo goood, daddy,' she begs, and grabs my cock again.

Righteously, I knock her hand away. 'You don't deserve to touch daddy's cock. You understand me, little chi chi?' I move away from her. Time to end this little scene.

'But daddy,' she says desperately and grabs for my ass.

The ass grab makes me angry. 'Cut the bullshit you little shit! You don't get any, and that's that.'

I walk away to a torrent of Spanish vitriol. Like the soaps, it's too fast for me too understand, but it sounds like: 'tu puto maricon hoto serrotay albracarilla moro chi chi intituto leshimon cominal. Chingatay singalotay puto mareepoot.' I know I'm being brutally insulted. Still, it turns me on, intensifying my boner. Those fiery Latinas do it to me every time.

Outside of tranny love, the little Mexicana and a couple of rancid queers, there isn't much happening down here. I have no other option than to face her: I hope she's there, I hope she's not there. I hope she's there.

My prayer to Lord High Jehovah Yahweh: 'Lord allow for Lady California to be in her room. And if she is, give me the courage to stand against society and fuck her in the ass.' That's right, I'm asking God for the courage to fuck a man in the ass. In my defense, however, I accuse God of making a grievous error in allowing for Lady California to be born as a man. I therefore amend my prayer to God, and say: 'Lord, you fucked up in making Lady California a man. Allow me to put things right and fuck her like a woman. Amen.'

I come to the door, she's there. A dark angel staring in the mirror. The innocent Narcissus of Rockets and Missiles. Tonight she wears a long, flowing, black dress, adorned in a fringe that dances over her body like imps and demons around a bonfire in hell. She wears black lipstick and a red rosary around her neck. She is the Virgin Mary on heroin. A walking requiem for my heterosexuality.

She senses me almost immediately, glances over and waves me in. As though in a dream, I step into her room. Without saying a word, she points to a chair in the corner. I sit. She closes the door to our tomb, then takes a seat on the floor across from me. I feel like an eighth grader about to be laid for the first time. My cock is erect. My mind is entangled. I can't conceive of this person as anything other than beautiful woman – a dangerous state of affairs.

In lilting alto, 'I was hoping you would come by tonight.'

Nervous, but feeling very sexy myself. 'I was hoping you'd be here.' We soak each other in. There is strong chemistry between us. I think of marriage, then quickly quash the thought. I say to myself, 'This chick has a dick this chick has a dick,' but it doesn't resonate. I'm out on the perimeter. There are no rules for this. All I see is a person to whom I'm fatally attracted. I pull out the Jamesons and take a long, stabilizing pull. I hold out the bottle.

Unlike Miss Normal she immediately reaches for the bottle. She takes a good swig then hands back the bottle. 'What do you like to do, Sam?'

'I like to do a lot of things,' I say, trying to sound sexy. 'What kind of things do you like to do?'

In a killingly sober tone, 'Whatever it is you want me to do.'

The world is here. I am in the driver's seat. The only thing standing between me and real sexual pleasure are the morals and mores that have been kicking my ass for 29 years. I could fuck her a million different ways. What will it cost me, though, in terms sense of self? Will I be able to come back?

The subconscious belches up weird memories that I guess are meant to be answers, but are really no clearer than fucking Zen koans. Me and the gang, around 7 or 8 years old, hanging out in a big ditch with our bikes. Summertime. At the end of this concrete ditch is a pile of dirt, maybe three or four feet high, with a thick board up it that could easily serve as a ramp. We debated for hours. Could it be done? Was it certain death? Who had the courage to attempt such a feat?

Toward nightfall and the clock is ticking, soon everyone will have to go home for dinner. I am one of the leaders of our gang of about ten little dudes. In these dare situations it was always either me or my best pal, Dave 'The Dog' McGruder. He was a good guy, excellent athlete, but he got a girl pregnant and married her in his senior year of high school. I have no idea where he is now.

The Dog wasn't going to do it. It was me or nobody. Without saying a word, I hopped on my bike. The gang went wild, screaming and running after me as I raced furiously toward the hill. Coming closer, coming closer. Should I pull out? Never! Baboosh!

The next thing I remember is waking up in the hospital. I had a concussion, broke my jaw, and fractured my kneecap. The board gave way the minute I got to it. Cracked right in half. I ended up flying head first into a stack of cinder blocks. Looking back, I can say that it was 100 percent worth it. I was from that point on a legend. Untouchable. In the Hall of Kid Fame.

If my old pals could see me now, they wouldn't be so stoked. The legend of Villanova Street on the verge of going fag. Jesus Christ, how did I get into this situation? Aren't I supposed to be married by now? Where are my 2.4 kids? Where's my safe house in the suburbs? My life has taken a strange turn. I am pathologically attracted to a man in women's clothes, but what an amazing manwoman she is.

'You like to suck it?' I ask.

She opens her mouth and sticks out a long, skinny tongue. 'I'd love to suck you, Sam.' And moves toward me.

The time is now. Do or die. If I don't move, I'm going to be sucked off by a transvestite. It will undoubtedly be the greatest blow job of my life from what amounts to the hottest woman I have ever been with. There are no answers, only instincts. Lady California sits next to me and puts her hand on my upper thigh. Her beautiful head is on my shoulder. I am harder than I have ever been. She rubs lightly. She is treating me gently, seducing me. My heart palpitates. I ask myself who I am, but the question has no meaning. There is only the silence between Lady California and I. Her hand caresses my thigh, almost at the crotch. Her fingernails are painted black to match her lipstick. A weird subconscious koan belches up again and I am suddenly reminded of James Brown.

Not the singer James Brown, but my friend James Brown. He is the only black friend I ever had. We went to college in New York together. He was incredibly sharp, but with a lot of psychological problems stemming from race and alienation and all the other issues that a black man trying to make it in this society has to deal with. I had a couple of chips on my shoulder at the time as well, so we got along famously. We used to get drunk at his apartment in Harlem and then go off into the city looking for trouble. We pulled all sorts of capers: we'd go up to the roof and drop water balloons on crack dealers, we'd break into Rockefeller Center and piss on the ice, we'd throw stink bombs into hip bars in the West Village. It all, somehow, made moralistic sense. The world was our enemy, and it felt right.

We hatched a plan to break into a synagogue, steal the torah, then deliver it to a tenement where we knew skinhead's were squatting. We made it to the synagogue, but by the time we got there we were too drunk. We ended up breaking down a door, tripping an alarm, then passing out in the temple, only to be awakened at gunpoint by New York's finest. They arrested us, and we spent the night in jail. Being good college boys, we got off with probation and community service.

James was more shitfaced that night than I'd ever seen him. He was out of control: causing scenes, yelling at the cops, whipping his dick out, picking fights. The cops came to separate him, but James wasn't going down without a fight. It took three cops to handcuff him and move him out. It was a thing of defiant beauty. What I remember, what flashes in my mind like a red neon sign, is what James yelled to me before they took him away.

'Tell 'em!' He screamed furiously. 'Tell 'em what it is! Tell 'em!'

I wish it wasn't so clear to me, but I know exactly what he meant.

'Be a man. Be your own man. Don't let these fuckheads take you down.'

I have failed James in many ways. More important, I have failed myself. I am not proud of who I am, and I have most certainly let the fuckheads take me down. I don't know what it exactly is that Lady California represents in my life, but I know it's something important. For once, I need to know that what I'm doing is pure. I wish I would have thought the same way before I became a public relations specialist.

She's massaging my crotch. I gently grab her hand and stare into her her eyes. 'I need some time to think about this. I hope you don't mind?'

She gives me a loving look of understanding, as though my doubts make her want me all the more. Her frail features look more stunning than ever. 'I understand, Sam. I'll be here.'

With love in my heart I quickly get up, knowing that if I hesitate I will lose my resolve and remain with her. I kiss her hand and say, 'We'll talk later.' I move to help her up but she refuses, wanting to remain on the floor.

'I need to cool down,' she says with a wry smile.

'So do I,' and exit.

Upstairs there isn't much of a scene, only a few old fags talking on the bed. I feel lost but strong, like a sturdy boat caught in a storm. There is a scene in the movie *Pale Rider* where one of the men, when discussing whether or not he should make a stand with the others against the outlaws, says, 'I'm not a brave man, but I ain't no coward neither.' The same goes for me. I am not a man of integrity, but I ain't no jellyfish neither. Lady California is a chance to be decent. I wish I had someone I could discuss it with.

I don't have any friends anymore, really. Friendships made in adulthood are all conditional. They are based around jobs, playing golf, getting drunk. They don't transcend category. What can I do? Invite a pal out for drinks after work, then ask him what he thinks about me getting a blow job from a transvestite named Lady California? Absolutely out of the question. America is a rigid place. It's all about image.

I pass by the sado-masochism chamber (where there is again no action) and move into the lobby with the big wheel. A skinny queer is eyeing it hungrily but cautiously, like he wants to get on but doesn't know what will happen to him if he does. I know just where he's coming from. I enter the juice bar.

I am welcomed immediately and enthusiastically. 'Sam, it's good to see you. Have a seat.' Music to my ears. In my confusion I've managed to come to the right, friendly place.

'Miss Nowhere, the pleasure is all mine.' I sit down at my old stool. At the other end of the tiny bar is another fellow – an old-school queen dressed in a boa. He has the look of a gay elder statesman. Definitely aged, but not frail. I can already tell that he's charming.

'Sam,' says Miss Nowhere, 'meet Quentin.'

Quentin immediately holds out his hand and says, 'Always a pleasure to meet a fellow Scorpio.'

Surprised, I shake his hand. 'How did you know?'

Gallantly, 'We wear it like a coat of arms,' he says. 'Ha ha.'

I decide immediately that I like him. I turn to Miss Nowhere.

Before I can say a word, she says, 'So what's it going to be tonight, Sam?'

There's not much of a choice. 'Coffee, black,' I say.

She leans forward and whispers, 'Why don't I give you a coffee cup for your whiskey?'

Quentin holds up his dark coffee cup to show that he's already in on the secret. He pulls back his gray sport coat to reveal a bottle of vodka. A Scorpio, indeed.

She puts a red coffee cup in front of me and I pour the rest of my whiskey into it. The deed accomplished, I put the bottle back into my dark-blue sports coat and settle in.

'So how are things in the land of the living?' I ask Miss Nowhere. I feel expansive. No reason to screw around. I sip at the Jamesons.

'I'm doing well,' says Miss Nowhere with a philosophical air. 'Present company excepted, Quentin and I were discussing how there seems to be lack of real men around these days.'

'Of real *gentleman*,' Quentin corrects graciously. 'That there is a dearth of the qualities that constitute the gentleman.' Quentin is flamboyantly articulate.

They've got my interest. 'Quentin,' I say, 'what is it to be a gentleman in today's society?'

He is a distinguished old geezer. A queer to the core. He doesn't talk, he conversationalizes. And we are now on a subject. 'The latter portion of your query, Sam, and by saying this I intend no disrespect . . .'

I nod my head reverently, indicating that I am fully aware of the laws of intelligent conversation.

'. . . is arguable – for some would say that to be a gentleman, is to be a gentleman in any age. For my part, I am yet to decide on the matter.'

Miss Nowhere is in a more assertive mood than when I first met her. 'I've decided,' she says adamantly. 'It doesn't matter if it's now or a hundred years ago. A gentleman is a gentleman.'

'I disagree,' I say. I could use a good discourse. 'Each age has its own social requirements. Our time is especially complex. Therefore, it might require more to be a gentleman than it used to.'

Quentin claps his hands together in conversational happiness. 'Ha ha,' he says. 'Your point is well taken, Sam.' He turns to Miss Nowhere, 'What do you think of Sam's point? Isn't it marvelous to have with us such an astute and handsome young man.'

I can't help but blush. Quentin is like the grandmother I never had.

'He is handsome,' says Miss Nowhere. 'Only I don't think that I agree.'

'And why not?' asks Quentin, thrilled to be moderator.

Miss Nowhere looks very nice tonight. She's wearing a brown, angora sweater and a dark, full-length skirt. Sexy, but understated. She leans on the bar, a contemplative look coming over her soft face. 'Being a gentleman isn't about wearing nice clothes and opening doors for people. Being a gentleman is about believing in what's good and standing up for it when the time comes. A gentleman has beliefs and convictions. He has a sense of justice and fairness. He gives all people a chance.'

Miss Nowhere brushes her dark hair out of her face and continues, 'Justice and fairness don't change. They've been here since the beginning and will be here as long as we are. The man who stands on the side of justice now is the same as the man who stood on the side of justice a thousand years ago. The only thing that changes are the clothes.'

'And thank God for that,' says Quentin. 'Otherwise justice would be a rather smelly affair, wouldn't it?'

We all laugh and enjoy each other's company.

After a moment and a couple sips of Jamesons I speak up. 'I don't disagree with you, Miss Nowhere, but I can't help but think that things are more complex today than they were in the past. Things were more physical back then. Life was based around killing and eating, survival. If some warlord came into your hut and started raping your wife, you either stood tall and defended her or ran for the hills. Nowadays, it's not so cut and dry. Any monkey can help grandma across the street, but who can take a stand against an oil company? We're all caught up in this big net, and no matter how we act it makes us guilty. To me, being a gentleman is all about pomp and circumstance. Smile, laugh when you're supposed to laugh, treat people kindly, don't fart in public. All the while we're driving around in a car using gas from an oil company that murders decent people in Kenya. There's no way out. Our tax dollars support wars in Central America where women are raped and children executed.' I sip at my Jamesons, not knowing if I made sense or not.

Quentin, loving a politically charged conversation, says, 'Well stated, Sam. But I'm afraid that you're somewhat of a defeatist. On your account we might as well give in to our animal natures and commence in evil debauchery. Not a bad idea on the whole,' he says with a wink, 'but it could turn a bit distasteful, don't you think?'

I raise my cup to him. 'Stated like a gentleman,' I say.

He raises his cup of vodka in elegant acceptance.

Miss Nowhere pours herself a cup of coffee. 'Justice is justice, Sam,' she says. 'It takes place on a personal level. If you think driving a car is bad, then you shouldn't drive a car. The same goes with eating meat. If it bothers you, don't do it. It all comes down to a matter of personal conscience.'

'I'm not so sure about that,' I say to Miss Nowhere. 'If left to personal conscience, this world would be – and is for that matter – a worthless pit of self-interest.'

Quentin interjects, 'You're saying that there has to be something higher, Sam?'

'I guess I am.' I don't know what, though.

'Humankind,' says Miss Nowhere. 'It is humankind that has to be higher.'

The statement reminds me of Miss Nowhere's book, *Human, All Too Human*. 'That's very Nietzschean of you, Miss Nowhere.'

She bows her head. 'Thank you, Sam. Besides being a misogynist, he was a good philosopher.'

'If you can get past the mustache,' says Quentin.

We all laugh together and sip our drinks. Quentin and Miss Nowhere feel like old friends. I can be myself. After a moment I turn to Quentin. 'Back to the original question, sir. What is it to be a gentleman?'

Quentin cogitates. I wouldn't be surprised to find out that he was once a professor. He has an academic quality. 'Both of you have stated your positions so eloquently that I don't know which side to choose. At the outset, I was somewhat of the mind that, if I may brutalize Ms Stein, a gentleman is a gentleman is a gentleman. Notions of justice and fair play are constant ones. They've been at our side in the same recognizable form whenever we've outdone ourselves and fulfilled,' Quentin says, waving his fingers to make quotation marks, '"the better angels of our nature".'

Quentin sips vodka from his coffee cup. I sometimes think that meaningful conversations are the only true actions available to us. Quentin is a man who embodies this. He puts down his cup and continues. 'On the other hand, with the rise of technology, life has become an odd synthesis of the complex and superficial. One doesn't know exactly where one stands. Thus, in reference to what you said, Sam: Helping a grandmother cross the street just doesn't seem to cut the mustard anymore, does it?'

I shake my head in agreement. I sip my whiskey. I listen.

'Finally, to answer your question,' he says, 'it seems to me that the gentleman of today is close kin to the gentleman of a thousand years passed. Yet, there is a difference. The gentleman of today must be discerning in his employment of the notions of justice, goodness, and fairness. In other words, Sam, pick your battles wisely.'

Have I misrepresented myself? I feel like a liar, but I haven't lied. He is talking to the wrong guy – overrating me on a massive scale. I am the one who watches TV while a woman gets beaten. I'm no warrior battling evil in the world. I am part of the evil in the world. Humanity is a fucking farce. Life is way overrated. The only thing that keeps me around is the possibility that I might one day end up in an orgy with six supermodels.

'I don't know about that, Quentin.' I speak in couched terms, I don't want him to think me a total piece of shit. 'There aren't any clear-cut battles anymore. You stick your head out and it's more likely to get cut off than anything else. I know I must sound jaded, but in a world without meaning, it doesn't matter what you do. So you might as well make yourself as comfortable as possible and hope that the ride doesn't have too many bumps.'

Quentin throws up his arms dramatically. 'What else is there to say then, Sam?' He pauses, slyly. 'Other than, me thinks he doth protest too much.'

A witty, if incorrect, statement. I raise my cup to his erudition. He toasts as does Miss Nowhere. 'I wish it were that way, Quentin. I wish it were.' I turn to the barkeeper, 'but modern society has a strange way of making people weak, and definitely ungentlemanly. Things in this world are more confused than ever.' I pause, then add, 'And I don't care for much in it.'

'That's not what I hear,' says Miss Nowhere quickly.

These trannies have a grapevine that puts Napa to shame. I want to deny it, not only to her, but to myself. I can't do it, though. I'm caught. Tonight, when I first left Lady California, I didn't know what I was going to do. With every second away from her, though, my resolve grew stronger. I was confident in my ability to leave her tonight without saying another word. Now, I'm like a dry sponge next to a spill. One little push and I'm soaking.

'What have you heard?' I ask.

Miss Nowhere, in her inimitable down to earthness says, 'All I've heard, Sam, is that she thinks you're an attractive and interesting guy.'

'That's all?'

'Not entirely. Girlfriend would kill me for saying . . .' She pauses intentionally to make sure that I really want it.

'What?' I beg.

'She skipped a big party tonight, just in case you were going to be here.'

'Really?' I feel like a school boy getting the low-down on a girl I like (except this girl has a dick). 'What should I do?'

Quentin speaks. 'Do what your heart tells you, Sam. And if not your heart, then your libido. Ha ha.'

'Easier said then done,' I say to Quentin. 'I have issues here.'

'And you should be thankful, Sam,' he says. 'A life without issues isn't worth living.'

I turn to Miss Nowhere. 'What do you think I should do?'

Miss Nowhere is a transvestite. Moreover, a transvestite with a soul. This is a serious question for her. She's thinking not only of me, but of Lady California as well. I'm sure that Miss Nowhere has fallen victim to the overactive sex drives of straights such as myself. I am also sure that she could give a damn about my 'heterosexual issues.' For her, there are no such things as issues, there is simply society.

'You should go talk to her, Sam,' she says caringly. 'She's a human being, just like you. She's waiting for you because there is something in you that touches her.'

I sip Jamesons and taste my own hypocrisy. I protest to how meaningless this society is, then bow down before its morals. If I truly believed in the emptiness of this world, then I wouldn't give a fuck and be out at a downtown bar drinking scotch with Lady California.

'You're right,' I say to Miss Nowhere. 'I'm going to go talk to her now.' I dramatically push my stool back and finish the Jamesons. 'Thanks.'

'Don't thank me, Sam,' says Miss Nowhere. 'It's the gentleman in you.'

'Yeah, right.' I say it to myself as much as to her. I say this to the world and to God and to history and to all humanity: don't look to me to stick my neck out. I am not above average in any way.

I hold my hand out to Quentin. 'Quentin, it's been a real pleasure.'

'The pleasure is mutual,' he says gracefully.

'Will I be seeing you in these parts again?' I ask.

A wistful smile comes over Quentin's face. 'I'm afraid not, good sir. I rarely venture out into the world anymore. I'm much too infirm for this kind of excitement on a regular basis, no matter how enjoyable.'

I notice for the first time that Quentin has on a hospital bracelet. He must have AIDS or cancer or one of those diseases that eventually gets to most of us these days. There's something beautiful about the fact that he comes here instead of going to a church or an old movie. This is a man who sincerely, devoutly, loves humanity.

I squeeze his hand. 'Take care of yourself, Quentin.'

'Ha ha,' he shakes back. 'Too easy. Take care of the world.'

These people are tough. I tip my head to Miss Nowhere and leave the juice bar for the lobby, where the fag has managed to get himself on the wheel. No one is paying any attention to him. In fact, no one seems to be on the top floor at all. I stare at him for a moment, he stares back. Neither one of us says a word. It is one of the strangest, most awkward silences of my life. He is not upside down, but sideways. I am standing straight up, a position I hadn't noticed until now. In gentlemanly homage to Quentin and Miss Nowhere, I step up to the wheel.

Like on the *Price is Right* where they go for the ten grand, I spin. The fag lets out a little yelp and to make sure that he's getting his money's worth, I say, 'Spin till you die, you fucking piece of shit. Daddy hates your guts,' and give it another good twirl.

A smile comes over his whirling face.

I quickly make my way to the bathroom, a mini-disco in itself with a small strobe light and glow-in-the-dark stickers on the wall. I piss and splash some water on my face for that oh so fresh feeling. If there were a mirror I would check myself. I head down the stairs in the direction of Lady California. I am anxious. I don't know if what I'm doing is right. I feel morally adrift. I have an erection.

I stop before I get to her room and nervously adjust myself. I step in front. She is there, reading *The Essential Lenny Bruce*. She looks serious, beautifully intense. After a moment she raises her head. Upon seeing me she immediately puts the book down. I step in.

'Hello,' I say.

Softly, 'I was hoping you hadn't left.'

I take my original seat on the floor, we face each other. 'I wasn't sure what I was going to do, but I thought it might be nice to come down here and talk for a while.'

Her movements and expressions are subdued, almost ghost-like. She exists more than she expresses, but her existence says everything that needs to be said.

'What do you want to talk about, Sam?'

'If you don't mind me asking, I was wondering how it is you're always in this room while everyone else is out there scurrying around?' I feel crude for saying it. I feel crude around her in general.

'I know the owner,' she says. 'He keeps this space for me. Otherwise, I don't think I would be down here.' She has a blunt but nonetheless gentle way of talking.

'I see . . . You like Lenny Bruce?'

'Yes,' she says. 'He wasn't afraid of anything. He wasn't afraid to be himself.'

'Do you think I'm afraid to be myself?' The question from nowhere. I don't like it.

Calmly, she says, 'That depends on who you are, Sam.'

I've had my fill of this game. Too much thinking, too many questions. This is all hitting way too close to home. 'Do you want to know who I am?'

My display of emotion seems to turn her on. 'Yes.'

'I am . . .' I feel a hot rush up my spine. The room slants. It pours me out. '. . . I am not anything that you are, okay? I don't mean to sound like an asshole, but it's the truth and I don't want to speak any untruths. You know why I don't want to speak any untruths, because that's what I do for a living. I express untruths. I am a public relations specialist. That's right, a PR man.' I rant to myself as much as to her – as though there are people inside me passing judgment. I am my own tribunal. 'And so the next question is why am I not downtown enjoying the yuppie lifestyle, but here at world headquarters for the sexually demented? Answer: because I am them but I'm not them. And it's harder to be part and not part, then it is to be fully part. Last week this guy comes into my office and tells me all about how he's found Our Lord Jesus Christ, and that he's happily married with children and has the greatest job in the world, ad infinitum ad nauseam. By the time he leaves I want to kill myself. Why? I am jealous of the guy. That's right, I am looking at him and wondering why I can't be like him. "Why don't I have what he has?" I ask myself. The answer: because I'm fucked up. I embrace society, but then condemn it. When I was a kid things were so much easier. I had it all worked out about how I was someday going to be a world leader. My plan was to get elected president, then move into the ghetto. I actually wrote the goddamn speech. My vow was to remain in the ghetto until there were no more poor children left in America. Now when I see a black kid get shot on TV, I couldn't give a shit. So now that I have no conscience, I should focus in on making all the money I can, then move into a gated community in the burbs with all the other rich white people, right? Wrong. The minute I start looking at getting myself into a position to make more money, an alarm goes off in my head, and all I can think about is setting up a free summer camp for children who have suffered massive burns to more than 75 percent of their bodies. I played football, you know? I was good. I was into it. It was maybe the last time in my life that I was pure. My dad was coach. That was before he took off. Down from where we lived there were some projects, a black man who worked with my dad lived around there. He said there might be some kids there who wanted to play ball, but couldn't afford it. Me and my dad drove down there before the season to see who wanted to play. Fifteen kids were waiting in the project's parking lot all day because the man who worked for my dad spread the word that we might show up. We weren't rich, but my dad took every kid to the sporting goods store and bought them football pads, helmets, and everything. The deal was that none them had to pay him back if they got all A's and B's on their next report card. The day the report cards came out, there was a line outside my house. Half of them did it and the other half did chores to pay my dad back. I used to think that was what life was all about – truth, fairness, helping people, all that shit. I used to believe in things. I used to believe that I was good, that people were good . . . and now I'm a public relations specialist. We won the championship that year, you know?'

She comes and sits next to me. She's so light. Ethereal. I know now what people mean when they refer to someone as not born for this world. It is a sacred condition.

'I didn't mean to go off on you . . .'

'Shhh,' she quiets me and puts her head on my shoulder. Her lips are against my neck. She doesn't try to kiss me. She stays still. This person who barely knows me is taking pity on me. She wants to help. I need no comfort, though. Every emotion I have passes as quickly as it comes. I regret only that I haven't acted upon my lower instincts. My little speech is gone from me now, as though it never left my lips. Words have no meaning, actions are illusions. There is nothing to grab onto. I am not whole.

'I understand you,' she whispers.

Understand what? I think to myself. That I am confused? That I am a contradicted ball of crap? 'I don't think there is really too much to understand,' I say to her. 'I don't go that deep.'

I hear her sigh – the natural sound of a dying world. Her hand goes back onto my thigh. Something inside of me turns and I find it all pathetic: her, me, Rockets and Missiles, human sexual activity, America, Miss Nowhere, football, God. This world is a joke that played itself out long ago. Good and evil are human inventions that give us a reason to keep going. The greatest thing that can happen to anyone is massive, assaulting injustice.

I say filthily as though I were speaking to a whore, 'What do you want me to do to you?'

There is resignation in her voice. She has been treated this way on so many different occasions, but she didn't expect it this time from me. 'You can do what you want.'

I grab her head and look her straight in the face – nothing but woman. This poor creature never should have been born. 'What is it like to be you?' I say cruelly.

She doesn't answer. It is taking every ounce of her energy not to cry in front of me. So different from George Johnkers and his contrived displays. She has had to fight for her self-esteem and is determined not to lose it to the likes of me. Finally, she says, 'Fuck me, if you want to fuck me.'

I stick my tongue out and lightly flick her nose. Her eyes are closed. She is dead, like a rag doll. Sodomy awaits. Conscience is nowhere to be found. I could kill her and not feel one pang of regret. My inner-Nazi goose steps around inside of me, begging to be let out. I become aware of being severely, grotesquely unhappy.

I kiss her for no other reason than to see how it feels. It is the same as kissing a woman. No difference, the softness, the warmth, everything is there. Her hand goes to my crotch and massages my hard cock. There is something robotic about her movements. She is adept, but I sense a distinct absence. What was once the most sensual creature I had ever laid eyes on is now the high school chick fucking me because her friends pressured her into it. I don't care. I do care. I have to ask.

'What's wrong?'

She looks at me hopefully. This is how she expects me to be. A sensitive good guy. Little does she know that all I'm concerned with is getting a premiere blow job. 'I just like being with you,' she says.

Being with me? Why the fuck would she want to be with me? I push her away.

She looks at me with intense concern. 'What is it?'

'I don't fucking belong here with you. I'm gone.' I get up off the floor.

She remains sitting. She is below me, her head coming up to knee level. 'Why are you doing this?'

'Doing what?' I am suddenly angry, having a hard time keeping control. 'Doing what?'

She lowers her head. She doesn't say a word. This is a scene that she's played out too many times. She doesn't want this anymore.

I am a ball of conflicting emotions. I feel betrayed, injured, angry, violent, horny. I lash out, 'I am a man, you are a freak.'

She raises her head, slowly. Her angular face is expressionless. She is beyond emotion. 'Sam.'

I stop before I get to the door and turn around. 'What?'

Coldly, not accusingly, like a doctor pronouncing a patient dead, 'If you are an example of what it is to be man, I'd rather be a freak.'

Shaking, 'What do you mean by that?'

'At least I have the courage to be what I am,' she says unemotionally. 'You're so weak and confused, you can't even make love to someone you care about.'

Her words shove me out of the room. Outside, the trannies stare. They mock me. I am a little boy to them, a scared little boy . . .

Fuck these people, I am not afraid. I do what I want to do. If I want a tranny to suck me off, then I'll get a tranny to suck me off. Easy. There's no philosophy here. There aren't any serious issues. This is about sex, a portrait of me cumming in someone's mouth. I have no fear. These people are the ones who are scared. They stay down in these holes, this shithole, hiding out from society. They live on the fringes. I'm the only one strong enough to live in both worlds. I don't need anything or anyone. I dictate the course of my life. I live by choice, not by fear.

Still standing in front of room number two is the hot little Mexicana tranny. She is leering at me, staring, sticking out her tongue, salivating for my dick to be in her mouth. I swagger openly over to the little Chilanga. She is taken aback, made small in my confidence.

'Get in that fucking room you little puta!' I open the door and push her in. Immediately the other trannies take notice. One of their kind is scoring with a certified Rockets and Missiles stud.

And let me tell you, girlfriend, he looks like he's ready to fuck the lining out of her!

She is on the floor, obediently waiting for my next command like a little dog. I shut the door behind us. The window in the door fills instantly with tranny faces. They are clowns come to watch the circus. I pull my shirt off to reveal my well-defined stomach. Despite alcohol abuse I retain a powerful and lean build. I like posing for this audience of freaks.

'What do you want me to do, daddy?' She coos. She thinks that she's the star here, too.

'Shut the fuck up. You don't ask any questions here. I'm the fucking man. You understand that you little bitch?'

'Yes, daddy.'

'Let me see your tits.'

The command has the desired effect. She has no tits. I intend to humiliate her for it. 'But I don't have any tits, daddy.'

'I thought you were supposed to be a girl, little puta,' I laugh. 'How come you don't have any tits?'

This is getting her good. Her eyes flit back and forth. Her head is tilted down to the ground in shame. 'I'm going to get tits soon, daddy,' she says. 'I'm starting my pills soon.'

'Shut the fuck up.' I tell her. 'I want to see your fucking titties, little puta. You show them to me now, or I'm going to get my dick sucked by one of your fucked up friends. Tu entiendes?'

There isn't a man in the world who doesn't get hard when a woman goes down by sheer force. Better yet, is a humiliating mind fuck. I am rock hard. She has on a tank top. She slowly lifts it to reveal the chest of a little boy – nearly identical to mine in the pre-pubescent years.

'You're not a girl, you're a little boy,' I say in slow vehemence. 'Pull it down now, little boy. I don't want to see that bullshit any more.'

He quickly pulls his shirt down.

'You ready to suck it, little boy.'

He's crying, I don't care. I say again, like a marine, 'You ready to suck it, little boy?'

Through his tears, he says, 'Yes, daddy.'

I put the little-boy chest out of my mind and concentrate on the face and ass. 'Little Mexican girl,' I say to myself. 'Little Mexican girl I just met on the bus. She's going to suck me off in front of all her family.' I turn around, the trannies are enraptured, fighting each other for space like Jews for bread in Auschwitz. The sickness of the world is now with us.

I drop my pants down to my knees, leaving my boxer shorts on. I slowly, intentionally, pull them down. I can hear the trannies outside yelping. I feel like a rock star. The little Mexicana before me has gotten over her tears and is itching to suck it. I give myself a couple of strokes to make it super-hard. She moves closer to me so that her face is about a foot away from my dick.

'You like this, little puta?'

'Yes, daddy,' she says, shaking in anticipation. 'I want to suck you till I die.'

'That's good, little chi chi. Open your mouth.'

She opens her mouth wide, but closes her eyes. 'I didn't tell you to close your eyes, did I?' I say. 'Open your fucking eyes so you can see my dick! So you can praise it!'

She opens her eyes wide. She looks like an innocent little girl. I give my dick a couple more strokes and begin slapping her face with my cock. I hit her in the cheeks, in the nose, in the neck, in the eyes. She laps at it like a fucking dog, quivering with excitement. She has on at least an inch of pancake. She is a classic, fucked up, little faggot. A piece of shit.

I slap her in the face, hard. The trannies outside the door squeal in delight. I am Satan. These are my little demons. The world is supporting my evil. I have no regrets. I am pure. I want to fuck God in the mouth. I want to rape the Virgin Mary. I want to see the niggers lynched. I want to ship Jews to concentration camps. I want the genitals of little children to line my walls. There is nothing in the universe that can quench my self-hatred. It is the only way I can love the world.

I thrust my cock deep into her little mouth, choking her, making her gag. I grab her thin shoulder with one hand and the back of her head with my other. She is so small, so frail. I could crush her chest in with one punch. In spite of the gagging, I push my cock in deeper so I hit the back of her throat with the head of my dick. She struggles. She can't breathe. With my cock, I pump her mouth strong enough to break a plate glass window. I shove her off me and onto the floor. She collapses into a pathetic ball, coughing and choking. I feel like a god.

'What the fuck's your problem, you little fucking whore?' I scream. 'I thought you wanted to suck daddy's dick. Get up.'

She is afraid of me, she gets up off the floor.

'Open your fucking mouth.'

She barely opens it. 'Wide! Wider! Open your fucking mouth wide you little bitch! Like your momma's pussy!'

She opens her mouth as wide as she can. I grab her by the back of the head with both hands and slam my dick into her mouth. She chokes and fights to pull her head away. This is me, the real me. No more bullshit. Time to kick some fucking ass. With both hands I keep her squirming head in place, and with all my strength thrust my cock down her throat. One thrust, two thrusts, three thrusts, five, six , seven. Pounding, pounding away. Giving her everything so I'm pouring with sweat. True violence. She can't breath. She hasn't breathed anything but my cock for 30 seconds. She is trying to peel my hands off her head, but she has no hope. I give her one more thrust and push her down onto the floor. Gagging, tears streaming down her face, streaking her makeup, she curls up into the fetal position.

Triumphantly, I turn to my fans outside the door.

Standing in the middle of the cheering, satanically sexualized audience, is Lady California. Her face reveals a pristine disgust, as though I were smearing my face with dog shit. I am everything in the world that makes her sick. The energy drains out of me like blood through a severed wrist. I look back down at the person who I have injured and feel nothing but revulsion – not for her, but for myself.

Nothing left, sub-anemic. 'I'm sorry,' I say to her. 'Lo siento.' She looks up at me and reaches out, like a wounded child asking for help from a stranger. I can't be here any more. I am tainted, lost in the sickness, and have to get out. I feel nauseous, like I'm going to puke. I look out for Lady California, but she's gone. I touch the Latina on the hand and gently brush her hair back. I repeat, 'Lo siento.'

I burst out the door with my head down. The transvestites call out to me, laughing, mocking, catcalling:

'Come on, baby. Stick it in me. I'm better than that whore.'

'You can push me down as hard as you want, sweet thing.'

'Don't leave us, baby. We need some more of that ass of yours.'

'You can fuck my mouth as hard as you want. I want to lick your tummy.'

I have brought them here. I deserve no less. Nothing is mystery. I am horribly clear on who I am.

Chapter Five

ERGONOMICS, PSYCHOLOGICAL ANALYSES of employee behavior, motivational studies, color schemes for productivity enhancement, the secrets of the ten most effective people on earth, management skills seminars . . .

In college I rented a room with this guy who turned out to be an Alcoholics Anonymous freak. He went to meetings every night, recited the AA prayer five times a day like a Muslim, had an altar in his room, a picture of Christ displaying a three-year sobriety pin, and a framed black and white photo of his sponsor – a withered, old guy with acne. He kept a drawer full of mementos from every meeting. If a girl he liked from AA dropped a cigarette butt, he would wait for her to leave, then pick it up and add it to his collection.

In spite of his devout lifestyle, he was a slacker creep. Upon going sober, AA hooked him up with a cashier's job at a cafeteria. He never left it. On his days off he would watch Star Trek all day. He had all the episodes on tape. Not once in the eight months that I lived with him did he have a date or even go out. He was fat, didn't read, and drank buttermilk. He talked to his mom on the phone five times a week, long distance.

If I were clean, sober, and dedicating my life to a higher power, I would be president of the fucking United States. I would be my own higher power. A prophet. A demigod of boundless energy. Unstoppable. A sacrifice as grave and horrible as joining AA mandates massive, vengeful, worldly achievement. People would fear me. I would take over Guatemala.

Same goes for this fucking company. If I were Liberty Telecomm

International, an ergonomically enhanced, psychologically ana-
lyzed, motivationally skilled, seminared-to-death, Christian freak
show of an organization, then I would be conducting a hostile take-
over of Microsoft this very minute. Bill Gates would be my secretary.
Alan Greenspan would consult with me before he even considered
touching the interest rate. The Dow would drop 25 points every
time I went to take a shit. The pope would hit me up for loans.

At the very least I would make sure that employees had the
proper tools and subsidies to do their jobs. I don't like having to
do this, but Liberty Telecomm International leaves me no choice. If
I don't move to defend myself, no one is going to do it for me.

*Re: A Car Allowance to Keep Personal Costs, and therefore
Company Costs, at a Minimum.*

Tom,

*First, allow me to congratulate you on the fine work you do
as head of our department. Dare I say that we are recognized
as one of the finest departments in all of Liberty Telecomm
International. Congratulations to you!*

*Moreover, if you would be so kind as to pass on my sincerest
sympathies to Dick in regard to the loss of his second cousin. I
understand and commend him for attending the funeral Friday.
Nonetheless, his one-day absence was felt most keenly throughout
our department. He is an integral part of our success. Kudos
to Dick!*

*I know how hectic your schedule is, Tom. Still, I wonder
if you might recall that I have on several occasions broached
the subject of a car allowance. As I am sure you are aware, I
commute more than 115 miles daily – a drive that includes four
dollars in toll fees. All told, my transportation costs exceed more
than 250 dollars per month. (I have retained a representative
group of receipts, which you are welcome to review.)*

A car allowance might seem like an extravagance, Tom.

However, when you consider that most professionals with any degree of responsibility in the public relations field receive a generous car allowance, and that by not receiving a subsidy I am doomed to drive an American made piece of shit, then by all means you can go fuck yourself and stick your head up the president's ass.

Sincerely,

Sam

Super. That'll get me a car allowance. Probably my own limo, too. This place is getting to me. The mauve walls, the lack of respect, this cheap, WalMart desk. I'm turning into a hamster. Run on the wheel and get a food pellet. Make pink babies. Poop in the cedar chips.

Manhood has gone out the window. The biggest scam in all of history is equating manhood with coming to work every day. Whoever thought it up is a genius. I picture a bunch of government eggheads cogitating on how to force people into tiny offices 50 hours a week without starting a revolution. 'How can we make going to a mauve office and telling lies seem important? I've got it! Hook it onto the concept of manhood!'

Eveything happens incrementally. Public relations specialist will have to live on reservations. It'll be a shithole, but the world will think it's the greatest place on the planet. We'll send out press releases promoting kivas as luxury suites. Fried bread will be called 'millennial wonder stuff.' Three-legged dogs will be billed as 'ergonomic canines.' Dirt will be 'organic concrete.'

Life is a series of knocks at the door that don't mean anything. It's Dina.

'Enter,' I say. It'll never be as relaxed as it was before, but I like to think that we've put my asking her out behind us. 'What's up?'

She looks sexy as always. A black, 1940s dress and blue pumps.

She is the stylish star of the company. Men come down from other departments just to look at her. It makes me sick how much she plays up to it. Never once have I seen her show up to work looking anything less than impeccably hip. In spite of being 'alternative,' she loves this job.

'Like, you tell me,' she says and sits down. Her legs give me a semi-boner.

'What do you mean?' I ask.

'I got a message from Tom,' she says. 'He said for everyone to meet in here at three.'

'What time is it?' I ask.

'Three.'

'So then where is everybody?' A strange question, considering I don't know why anybody would be here anyway.

'They must be late,' she says flatly.

'Oh,' I say. An oddly satisfied pause. There is something nice about keeping the flow of information to a minimum. After a few moments, though, I plod forth. 'Late for what?'

'I don't know,' she says. 'Like I said, I got this message from Tom saying to be here at three.'

'Today?'

'Yes,' she says in a condescending way, like I'm an idiot for not knowing. 'Three o'clock today.'

'Okay,' I say. Calmly, I erase my memo from the computer. Wouldn't want to accidentally kick that bad boy out into the e-mail system.

We sit in silence. In spite of what I like to think, the truth is that my asking her out has put a damper on our working relationship. Before, there was an easy-going banter between us. Now, for us to communicate for more than 30 seconds takes an effort. Little does she know that, with the amount of times I've jacked off to her, she might as well of said yes, got drunk and fucked me all night. In the future, when they have the thought police, men will be busted for masturbatory rape.

'Nice poster,' she says in reference to the company-issued kittens.

'Thanks.' A *significant* damper.

A knock at the door saves us from further smalltalk doom. Tom and Dick stand outside, waiting. Strange, usually when they want to see me they barge in without knocking.

'Come on in,' I say with the mandatory, employee-to-boss, happy face.

In comes the dynamic duo. Tom the chieftain is in his trademark blue suit. They pay him in excess of six figures, but it's the only suit he wears. I don't know how he keeps it clean and wrinkle free, but he manages to look sharp every day. Tom is a strange guy. I have heard rumors that back in the sixties he was some sort of radical. At times I can see it. He's excitable, and when he gets into something he can be downright passionate. He has a funky habit of banging his fists on the table or clapping his hands together loudly when he gets enthused. The thought of him smoking pot and protesting the war in Vietnam, though, is inconceivable. He can be an uptight square. His rise to department head has made him a company man. He is an American, middle-aged male.

'Sam, how are you?' he says boisterously. He is in one of his better moods.

'Good, Tom.'

He mills about awkwardly for a moment, then says enthusiastically, 'We need some chairs in here.'

This is Dick's cue. His status is an enigma as is his keeping the name Dick. He is not a nerd, but a rah-rah man. Word is he and Tom have known each other all their lives and have maintained a weird sort of partnership for most of that time. They're not gay. They might even be cousins. Dick seems to have no problem with being Tom's number two. Actually, he may not even be that much of a number two. I think behind closed doors things are pretty equal, but in front of the employees they stratify their relationship to keep up appearances. Pecking order is very important at Liberty Telecomm.

Why he has maintained the name Dick when every English-speaking human being on the planet considers a dick to be either a shithead or a penis, that's a mystery. People, I guess, get attached to things. They get lazy and don't want to deal with change. All I know is that, if my name were Dick, I would take out a full-page ad in the *New York Times* insisting everyone thenceforth call me Richard or be sued for libel.

After not more than ten seconds, Dick returns with chairs for him and Tom. Dina scoots over so Tom is in the middle. They face me. No one says a word.

'So what's up?' I ask, a little nervously.

Tom speaks up. 'I tell you, Sam. We are the bearers of good tidings.'

Dick chimes in, 'I think you're going to be pretty darn happy with what we have to tell you here, Sammy.'

I look over at Dina. She looks back at me, dumbfounded. 'Well, what's going on?' I ask. At least they haven't come to fire me – always a concern.

Dick takes the lead. 'Does the name George Johnkers ring a bell, Sammy?'

'Sure it does.'

Tom turns to Dina. 'Dina, my girl,' he is the boss, he gets to talk like that. 'Do you remember George Johnkers?'

'Yes,' she says, glad to be brought into the conversation. 'I met him when Sam interviewed him for that biography piece.'

Tom slaps his thigh with his hand. 'That's right!' He is in one of his better moods. Nix that, he is in a great mood. 'And do you know what's happened since then?'

Both Dina and I shake our heads.

Tom looks at Dick knowingly. 'Do you want to tell them, Dick?'

'It'd be a pleasure, Tom.'

Dick eyes us intensely for a long time, like a guru preparing to make known ancient wisdom. Dina looks a little tripped out by it. I think it's funny. 'First, Dina and Sam, let me begin by passing on to you a report made by Mr Johnkers himself to the President's Council.' I've seen Dick do this before. He has read too many biographies on American generals, so whenever it comes time for him to talk, he takes on the persona of a man addressing his troops. He makes sweeping gestures and his head tilts back, so that you get more chin than anything else.

I imagine that Dick is the kind of guy that, after a couple of drinks, starts ranting about how we fucked up in Vietnam. He continues, like Patton. 'I think you both know me well enough to know that I'm not the kind of man who compliments people just because I don't have anything else better to do. The way I see it, we pay you to do your job and by god you better do it well. Truth is, I'm a traditionalist. I think I can speak for Tom in saying that we expect a lot from the people we hire without having to pat them on the back every five minutes.'

We all look over at Tom. Tom nods.

'So,' he continues. 'Tom and I being here right now should tell you how important this all is. And what this is, is a boon to the department.'

'An absolute boon,' echoes Tom.

'It's so big,' says Dick, 'that I don't feel it right that I be the one to tell it.' He turns to Tom. 'Tom, I leave the honor to you.'

Tom is touched by Dick's magnanimity. They share a moment together while Dina and I sit by, still not knowing what they fuck they're talking about.

Tom, our distinguished leader, picks up the torch and addresses us as though things will never be the same again. Everyone in the room is riveted on him, even the kittens. 'As I'm sure you both know, George Johnkers is the rising star of Liberty Telecomm. The man is responsible for more than 15 million dollars worth of sales over his stellar career. The bottom line, Dina and Sam, is that his word is like gold with the top brass.' He pauses to make sure that all of this is soaking in. Tom loves saying *top brass*. 'The night after you interviewed him, Sam, he had dinner with the Vice-President of Sales, the Vice-President of the Finance Department, the Senior Vice-President of Product Development, and the Senior Vice-President of all of Liberty Telecomm International.' I flash to the Monty Python skit in Life of Brian where the Jews are in the Coliseum defining their groups along semantic lines: The Revolutionary Front of Judea, The Peoples' Front of the Judean Revolution, The People for the Revolutionary Front of Judea, etc. 'The word that I've received from the top brass is that, over dinner, George Johnkers could not stop talking about how impressed he was with the level of professionalism exhibited by our very own Dina and Sam.' He slaps his hands together and says, 'The man was gushing! Can you believe that? He was gushing over how professional our department is! And who do we have to thank? The two of you! Dina and Sam! The pride of the public relations department!'

He again claps his hands together and bellows, 'Thank you Dina and Sam!'

Dick throws his hands up in praise and says, 'You've made us look like the best department at Liberty!' In turn he stares us down with Pattonesque intensity and says, 'By God, we are the best department at Liberty!' And we clap our hands and shake with glee.

'I'm just thrilled to be a part of it,' I say.

'Me too, me too,' says an overexcited Dina. The men in the room take a moment to admire her juiciness. Every time she moves, her jugs quiver and loll. Fantastic.

After a moment the dust settles. This time it's Dick, in full Black Jack Pershing mode. 'That's all well and good,' he says like a tough ass. 'But that's not why we've come down here to your office.'

'No it's not,' says Tom.

'I think you know me well enough to know that if it were just a matter of . . .' he does the quote thing with his finger ' "job well done," then I wouldn't be down here in a full-fledged meeting. I think the same can be said for Tom.'

Tom nods his head. 'Absolutely right,' he says. 'This is a whole heck of a lot bigger than just a pat on the back.'

'What this is,' picks up Dick, 'is a seminal event in the history of our department.' He emphasizes the word seminal and repeats it. 'Seminal.'

I think back to my closet-case fag of a freshman football coach. Besides running us into the ground, his favorite thing was to use big words. 'The offense must drive INEXORABLY to the end zone. The defense must be a PUISSANT force against the enemy.' One time when he didn't think anyone was around I caught him in the men's locker room reading the thesaurus. I picture General Dick doing the same.

He continues, 'Three days ago an advanced copy of Sam's 20-page biography on George Johnkers was distributed to the executives and the department heads.' He pauses and turns to Tom. 'I'll let Tom take it from here.'

Tom takes a moment to gather himself, dramatically. He does have a certain charisma. Maybe he picked it up giving speeches back in the sixties. He clears his throat and begins. 'First, let me say that I am proud of all my staff. I feel that we do a great job with the resources that we have.' He stops, makes deep eye contact with each of us, then continues. 'There are a lot of good teams out there. A manager can have a good career if he keeps his ball club above five hundred and gets them into the playoffs once in a while. Last month's convention was our playoffs. We showed up and made it known that we could play with the big boys. People all across the country now know that Liberty Telecomm has a top-flight public relations department, and that we are here to stay!' He slaps my cheap desk with pride. I hope he notices how much it shakes. 'To win a championship, though, it takes something special. We don't have the resources that other departments do. We don't even have the resources that public relations departments at other companies do. Still, we have managed to assemble a fine playoff contender every year since I've been leading this department.'

'You got that right!' affirms Dick.

Dina, not wanting to be left out, says, 'You guys do a great job.'

I'm compelled to chime in. 'You sure do.' Now give me my laptop.

He moves forward quickly so as not to lose any momentum. 'I'll be honest with all of you. I've wondered if we were ever going to have a championship team down here in public relations. We've been good, mind you. But like I said, to win a championship, it takes something special.' Dramatic pause, he exhales. 'I've struggled for years with how to improve this department. I've hired and fired, brought in consultants, instituted training programs, and even organized social outings to make sure that my people were rested and mentally healthy. Besides some small improvements in morale,' he says with a tinge of sadness, 'I haven't had much to show to the top brass for my efforts.'

A moment of silence. Tom sighs aloud, then authoritatively continues, 'It's taken me a long time to understand what makes a champion. And now I know. What it takes to be a champion is having star players on your team.' He looks at me admiringly. It gives me the creeps. 'The kind of player who steps up when the pressure is on. The kind of man who hits the home run with two outs. Who catches the touchdown pass with three defenders on him. Who hits the shot at the buzzer. The sort of soldier that the rest of the troops can look to as an example. The sort of soldier who inspires the infantrymen around him to shoot better and fight harder. A team can be of playoff caliber, but until they have that star, that Michael Jordan, that Audie Murphy, they'll never win a championship.' He runs his fingers through his brown, thinning hair and takes on a more conciliatory tone. 'Up to this point, I have been guilty of one of the cardinal sins of management – not knowing the potential of my soldiers.' He now looks at me with a look that can only described as love. 'Not all soldiers come into the army as all-stars. Like fine wine, some need time to age into perfection. I've always thought you were talented, Sam. A real solid member of our team, a fine lieutenant. But I'll be honest with you, pal. I didn't know you were a Purple-Heart Superstar.'

'A Purple-Heart Superstar,' Dick echoes reverently.

Dina looks at them like they're crazy.

'As I was saying,' Tom continues, 'advanced copies of your 20-page work . . .' *A work?* Did he actually call it *a work?* '. . . on George Johnkers were distributed to the top brass and department heads. I can honestly say, Sam,' pointing his finger at me, 'that your work has spread throughout the upper echelon of Liberty Telecomm International like wildfire! You are the talk of the top brass. The job you did with the Johnkers biography has taken Liberty by storm. You have catapulted this department and yourself into the limelight. The executives themselves have taken the time to make copies of the biography so they can distribute it to their associates throughout the company. Everyone is begging for the full printing. Your biography of Johnkers is the hottest item to hit Liberty Telecomm since the NBA phone cards!'

'The NBA phone cards,' echoes Dick.

'Wow,' says Dina. The NBA phone cards were introduced two years ago at a time when Liberty was in some financial trouble. They have since made Liberty millions of dollars and opened new markets worldwide. The Dennis Rodman phone card by itself has made Liberty more than eight million dollars (two million in Greece alone). Even Dina, a non-sports fan, knows how important they are. 'Wow,' she repeats. 'The NBA phone cards . . .'

Tom looks over at Dick. Dick grabs a brown briefcase out from under his chair and pulls out what I assume to be a copy of the bio. He handles it reverently, so much so that it's embarrassing. He slides the briefcase back under his chair. 'If I may, I am now going to read you an excerpt from this phenomenal piece of work that Sam has produced on behalf of this department.' He looks at me for approval.

'Sure, go ahead,' I say.

Dick clears his throat. 'This is the first paragraph of the Johnker's biography. I would read the entire piece if we had time.' He looks at me intensely. 'Believe me, I would.'

A nauseous shiver shoots up my spine.

He again clears his throat and begins reading:

'There are people in the world who would have us believe that the American worker is dead. That the American man has crawled into a hole and given up on this chaotic world. These are the same people who question traditional values, who laugh when we talk about right and wrong, good and bad, or the work ethic. These ne'er-do-wells look out at the world and say, "Why fight? Why work hard? Why go to work at all? Collect welfare, you'll be fine!" These naysayers clammer and clang their pots of discontent so loudly that even the good man is forced into questioning. In a time when the dark shadow of dubiousness is longer than ever, in a time when dirty doubt has sullied clean certainty, in an era when malaise and malcontents have replaced integrity and innovators, George Johnkers, Sales Manager of the Western Region, stands before us like a sentinel waiting for the dawn.'

The three sit in awe, as though in front of Picasso's *Guernica*. Their appreciation is rancid. I see now that I am not, and never will be, an important human being with anything valid to contribute to society. This is my milieu. This is my theater of operations. Socrates questioned society. Nietzsche made cultures shake. Kennedy invigorated the spirit of the American youth. I captivate Tom, Dick, and Dina.

'Absolutely phenomenal,' says Tom

'Utterly significant,' says Dick.

'Really great,' says Dina.

The piece is a hodgepodge of goofiness. I started it off intending to be serious, but got too frustrated. The idea that I was writing a biography, no matter how short, of stupid George Johnkers was too much for me to take. I had to find a way to make it enjoyable. I went for the hidden commentary thing. Too many philosophy seminars and not enough marketing classes – like my advisor warned me.

The first line about the 'American worker being dead' is my own. I've said it a hundred times and I believe it. The American worker couldn't give a shit about anything but vacation and retirement. People hate their jobs. Work is lame.

'The American male has crawled into a hole' is pure Freud. I wanted to throw something in there for the one guy in this company (who I've never met) who might pick up on it. I see clearly now that it was an overestimation of the Liberty workforce.

All the crap about not working, collecting welfare, blah blah blah, is pure Republican rhetoric. It's been repeated so many times it's imprinted on my brain. I understand perfectly that the reason I can't go to Barbados for vacation is because the welfare mothers are sucking up our tax dollars. If it weren't for the niggers and the Mexicans, this country wouldn't have no deficit neither! Christ, show me one average American monkey who even knows what the deficit is, and I'll fucking pay it off myself.

I always wanted to use the term 'ne'er-do-wells' but never had the chance. The 'pots of discontent' is obviously Shakespeare, King Lear. The only line I know from the play is, 'Now is the winter of our discontent.' I saw it on a commercial for hot chocolate.

There is one legitimate jewel in the piece. It is of course heisted, but from a source that is so misquoted and misrepresented throughout history that a minor pillaging means absolutely nothing: The Bible. There is some pretty heavy writing in the old book, but none finer than that of David and his collection of Psalms.

'Like a sentinel waiting for the dawn' struck me like a knife in the heart when I first heard it in Sunday school. The teacher was Brother Edward. We called him 'Machine Gun Eddy' because he spit when he talked. Machine Gun was a decent brother. He used to be a boxer, and once in a while he'd throw a couple of jabs in the air to get our attention. I remember like it was yesterday. He put his hands in the air and said, 'To be a good man is to be a fighter,' and threw a couple of jabs. 'You gotta be prepared for the battle, "like a sentinel waiting for the dawn."' Jab jab. 'That's out of Psalms, boys. King David. The brave youngster who took down Goliath with a slingshot.' Jab jab.

Ha! I use the one phrase in the Bible that actually means something to me for public relations purposes. I am a cheap slut, an American through and through. I look up at Admiring Tom and see my future.

Dick, who looks like he wants to make out with me, says, 'You have managed to do what I thought could never be done. You have SYNTHESIZED literature and public relations. You are an artist, Sam.'

'An artist,' echoes Tom.

'Really great,' says Dina.

Although I don't want to, I figure I should say something grateful. 'Dina, Tom, Dick, I want to thank all of you for being so kind. It was . . .'

Dick interjects, furiously. 'We should be thanking you, Sam! You have brought the light of acclaim down on the department. You have led the troops through the firestorm! You have won us a battle single-handed!'

I almost say thanks, but hold my tongue. I don't want to encourage him.

Tom clears his throat. He is once again ready for our attentions. The jig, unfortunately, is not up. 'I was going to bring in a stack of e-mails from all over Liberty Telecomm ranting and raving about your work . . .'

'Ranting and raving,' affirms Dick.

'. . . but,' says Tom, 'I couldn't figure out how to print them out.'

'It can be tough,' says Dick.

'Have to have a Ph.D.,' says I.

Dina shakes her head. 'Like, I haven't even been able to figure out how to get on the Internet,' she says.

Technological misery loves company. We share a moment of ineptitude, for which I'm thankful. I need something to temper the accolades.

Tom quickly picks up. He's not about to let us dwell on foibles during such a grand occasion. 'Right now, I have three messages on my answering machine. They aren't from the top brass, or anyone else here at Liberty for that matter. Do you know who they're from?'

Dina and I shake our heads. Dick shakes his head, too, which is ridiculous. He knows who the messages are from. He knows everything that Tom knows. Dick is Ed McMann.

'The messages,' continues Tom, 'are from our competitors. Our competitors! Through their colleagues here at Liberty, they have gotten wind of the George Johnkers biography. They want to know if they can buy copies from us so that they can distribute it to their own sales force! What is going on here, Sam? Are you some kind of genius or something?'

'Darn right he is!' yells Dick. 'A great genius! Our own Purple-Heart Superstar!'

They all break out in a big round of applause.

I never realized how ugly people are when they clap and gush. They look like smiling seals. I expect Dick to start balancing a little red ball on the tip of his nose. For Dina to let out a few Arf Arf's! No wonder rock stars hate everybody. An audience is a disgusting thing.

Tom looks over at Dick, signaling his cue. Dick, letting the drama breathe, takes his time putting the bio back in the briefcase. 'Congratulations are fine,' he says like Douglas MacArthur giving the 'Old Soldiers Never Die' speech in front of the US Senate. 'But you all know me well enough to know that I don't live and die with congratulations. We should be very proud of Sammy, but being proud in this business doesn't cut it. We need more if we intend to build a championship dynasty. We have to expect more from ourselves and from each other. Life doesn't take too kindly to those of us who think they can sit on their laurels. A job well done only gives us the right to face more challenges. To pass one obstacle is only to be greeted by another – and the man of quality wouldn't have it any other way.' His speech complete, his rolls his head back and stares at the ceiling in epiphany. This was his finest hour.

'Beautifully spoken,' says Tom and grabs Dick by the shoulder. Dick lowers his head and juts out his jaw with the dignity of a two-star general. Heck, maybe even a three-star . . .

Tom's mien is changed. He's more serious. I notice, too, that

Dick has dropped the MacArthur act and moved on to a more mature Eisenhower. Dina, not wanting to be left out, tightens her jaw, fixes her hair, and sits up straight.

The front line in place, Tom commences. 'This morning I received a call from the secretary to the President of Liberty Telecomm International.' He pauses to let it sink in. 'It turns out that one of the vice-presidents was so impressed with your George Johnker's biography that he turned it over to the President's chief assistant. His intention was to pass it on as motivational reading material, nothing more. The President's chief assistant was so impressed, however, that he handed it over to the President. The President! As luck would have it, the next day the President was flying in his Lear jet to Germany, so he had plenty of time to catch up on his reading.' Tom throws up his arms in amazement at the chain of events. He has a look of wonderment on his face that says, this sort of thing happens maybe once in a million years! He continues. 'The secretary notified me this morning that the President had called her from his Lear jet in reference to the Johnker's biography. The President of Liberty Telecomm International was so moved by the biography, that he, and these are his words not mine – couldn't sleep and had to read it twice.'

'Couldn't sleep and had to read it twice,' echoes Dick.

'Read it twice,' says Dina. She repeats, 'Read it twice.'

'The secretary,' continues Tom, 'conveyed to me the President's deepest thanks and congratulations on a job well done.'

I see a laptop computer and a $700 a month car allowance. 'Tell him I said thanks,' I say confidently.

Tom shakes his head like I don't know what the hell I'm talking about. 'That's not all,' he says. 'There's more. Much more.'

The room is filled with tension. It's like we've been at a poker table where all night we've been betting quarters and nickels, and then out of nowhere someone throws down a hundred bucks. We prepare for the call.

'The President will be returning from Germany in a week. After which he is going to headquarters in New York to wrap up a telecommunications deal worth more than 22 million dollars. Once he's done there, he's coming out here. Do you know why?'

Dina and I remain silent. Dick, ever the Ed McMann, says, 'Why, Tom? What's happening?'

'What's happening, Dick, is that the President of Liberty Telecomm International, the founder of this company, a man whose total worth is estimated to exceed more than 400 million dollars, is coming here to meet with our very own Sam. And do you know why?'

Same thing: Dina and I remain silent, Dick says, 'Why, Tom. Why is he meeting with our Sammy here?'

'He's meeting with our Sam here,' Tom says, shaking with excitement, 'so Sam can write his biography.'

Shock, oohs and ahhs all around. I feel putrid.

'Not just a 20-page job like you did for Johnkers, but a full-length 100-page biography, of which the company will print and distribute more than 50,000 copies! It's going to be in book stores dammit! 50,000 copies all across the country! You'll be famous, Sam! At the top of your field! You do this right, and you can write your own ticket!' He jumps out of his chair, 'Congratulations, buddy! You're going to be a very successful man!'

Dina and Dick leap out of their chairs as well. They yell out in a mishmash of praise:

'Congratulations, Sammy!'

'You did it, Sam!'

'You're going to be famous!'

'I knew you were something special!'

'You're the best, Sam!'

'You're making us all look good!'

'Really great! Really great!'

Eventually, they join each other in a sustained applause – 20 seconds, maybe more. I am embedded in my chair. The room twists and turns, smiles and flared nostrils float in the air. I realize for the first time that nausea is a symptom of the surreal. I can't tell if I'm happy or sad. My vision is doing this weird thing where everything close seems far and everything far seems close – like the first stages of dropping acid.

I utter something to the effect of, 'Thank you all,' but their clapping drowns me out. I fixate on Dina's bouncing jugs and do my best to ride it out.

Their clapping subsides, and they retake their seats. Dick and Tom have broken a sweat. Dina's jugs have settled into a disappointing stillness.

'You've taken the public relations department to a whole new level,' says General Dick. 'Because of your efforts, we are on the verge of becoming the feature department in all of Liberty Telecomm International.'

'Thanks, Dick. I appreciate you saying that.'

'I just want to say, Sam,' says Dina emotionally. 'That I'm really proud of you. I know we joke around a lot, but I have always admired the work you do and always known that you were cut out for something special.' She gushes, leans over the desk and gives me a peck on the check. Tom claps his hands together at the joy of it all. I, of course, have a boner.

'Thanks, Dina,' I say. 'Coming from you it means a lot.' Does this mean you'll go out with me now?

The thought of being a hyper-successful young stud does of course have a certain appeal: my own secretary with big jugs, a Porsche, new suits, hand-made Italian shoes, a Rolex. With the right accessories I could run the yuppie scene, fuck my way through it. I see me in a black Porsche wearing an Armani suit with one of those super-model advertising chicks in the passenger's seat. I could be like Jerry Seinfeld, except on a smaller scale.

'This is all good news,' I say to Tom, Dick, and Dina with strategic modesty. 'I'm just happy to be a part of a winning team.'

Tom gazes at me like I'm his long lost son. Thankfully, the uncomfortable love moment passes without him reaching over the desk and hugging me. He turns to Dina and Dick and says, 'Dina, Dick? I hope you don't mind but there are some things that I need to discuss with Sam, and there's really no reason for me to keep you here. All I can say is that it's an honor working with the both of you.'

Dina happily gets up out of her chair. 'Sam,' she says. 'If there's anything I can do to help you out with anything, let me know, okay?'

I stand for what seems like the first time in days. My legs, which both fell asleep, have the pricklies. 'Will do, Dina. Thanks for your support.' We shake, and I give her a wink. She smiles back flirtatiously, then leaves. In light of my recent success, maybe I should ask her out again.

Dick, for his part, seems to be a little hurt. He thinks of this as his show and he doesn't want to miss a beat. He hems and haws and mills about, hoping that, since Dina is gone, someone will ask him to stay. No dice. He reminds me of the guy who hangs around where everyone is doing coke hoping to snort a freebie. Forget it. Finally, he accepts his expulsion and says, 'You're the man now, Sam. You've put yourself in a position to make things happen, and for this you should be proud. You know where my office is if you need me.' And like a good soldier he clicks his heel and exits.

For the first time I feel like one of the big boys. I feel like I can kick my feet up and spew shallow wisdom without anyone saying a goddamned word. Tom needs me. The bottom line is that I could take a crap on the floor and not catch any guff. I like it. It's goddamned liberating. Let it be known from this moment forward that the driver's seat is the best seat on the bus!

'Tom,' I say and kick my feet up on the desk, 'what can I do ya' for?' Only an hour ago, the mere thought of my addressing him in such a manner was enough to get me fired. Now, judging by the look of satisfaction on his face, it's how I'm supposed to act.

'I wanted to talk to you alone, Sam, because we need to go over a few things before you actually meet with the President, and I didn't want to have to deal with any distractions. Okay?'

I love it. Dina and Dick are now reduced to distractions in the light of my success. 'Let's do it, Tom.'

I hadn't noticed, but he's brought with him an old, leather valise.

He opens it and produces a large, thickly stuffed manila envelope. 'I've been saving this for a long time, Sam,' he says reverently. 'At times I wondered if I would ever have cause to use it. Now, I thank God that I made the effort.'

I'm intrigued. What could be in this magic envelope of his? Money? A laptop? Condoms for my future black Porsche conquests? 'What's it all about?' I ask.

He puts the valise down on the floor and rests the envelope gingerly on his lap. 'When I first joined this company ten years ago, Sam, I was impressed with a lot of different things. The aura of professionalism, the drive to succeed, the "people first" mentality. Liberty Telecomm International is an amazing corporation. And do you know why?'

I don't say anything. I wait for him to answer his own question.

'Because of our President, that's why. He is a fine, fine man, Sam. Our President came from nowhere and built an empire. Our President cares about his people. Look around you, Sam. All that is, is because he built it. The man is a born leader. Where others look out into the world and see closed doors, he sees possibilities. He doesn't know the meaning of the word "can't." His life is about doing. Give him a shovel and he'll dig. Give him an ax and he'll cut. Give him a telephone and he'll build a telecommunications giant! This isn't about you doing a little biography, Sam. This is about the documentation of history!'

He stops and replenishes his oxygen supply. 'I am not a great man, Sam. I know what it is to be effective and how to manage people, but I don't know the first thing about greatness. Soon, you will come face to face with a man who embodies the ideal of greatness. You must be more prepared than you have ever been in your entire life, because great men don't play games. Great men structure their lives so that every second is spent building, erecting, enhancing! The concept of hanging out is anathema to the great man. And let me tell you, Sam, if he senses you're wasting his time, even for a moment, he will pounce on you with a vehemence you can't fathom!'

He stares me down like a drill sergeant. I avoid making eye contact. 'You have to look them in the eye, Sam! Don't let them think they have you, not even for a minute. If a great man senses weakness, he can't help but attack like a shark. He smells blood and he kills. That's what makes him a great man. Kindness, in his eyes, is weakness. He understands only efficiency and ingenuity. I don't want you being ingenious with our President, though. It's enough that you survive the interview without making any major mistakes. Understand me?'

'Yes I do.'

'Good,' he softens his approach. 'I want you to know that I have complete faith in you, Sam. It is only that I feel that I would be doing you an injustice if I didn't prepare you to meet our President.'

'. . .'

He opens the manila envelope and pulls out a collection of newspaper clips, brochures, and photographs. 'Like I was saying, Sam, when I first joined this company ten years ago, I was pretty darn impressed with our President. So impressed, in fact, that I began collecting everything written and published about him. You see, even then, Sam, I knew that our President was destined to build up this empire and carve out his name in the tree of great men.'

The tree of great men? Why don't you start a fucking cult, Tom? If this is what it takes to get that black Porsche, you can count me out. Tom, in the absence of God, has nominated the President of Liberty Telecomm.

'Nice job, Tom. You showed a lot of foresight in getting that together.'

'Well, it didn't take a rocket scientist to see that the President of Liberty Telecomm was destined for great things. Great men have a way of forcing themselves upon the world.'

I detest the fact that the President of Liberty Telecomm could be thought of as a great man. I am not sure what it is to be a great man, but I am certain that the sole requirement for greatness is not owning a telecommunications company. There has to be something more to it. There must be.

'So what to do with all the clips?' I ask.

Tom carefully places them on my desk. 'I hand them over to you, Sam. I admonish you to familiarize yourself with every piece of information in a collection that has been ten years in the making,' he says proudly.

I pick up the pile. The top story is a recent one. It concerns the President's plans to take over a small telecommunications company in California. I begin reading it, but before I can get past the first line Tom brusquely reaches over the desk and retakes the pile.

Like a kid who won't share his toys, but still wants you to know he has them, he says, 'One of my favorites is this one here.' He pulls a magazine story from the bottom of the pile (he has maintained them chronologically). He holds it up like it's show and tell and says, 'This was one of the first stories done about the President. I remember the day the reporter from the business journal came down here. We were all so excited. The President himself came down to ask me how he looked. He was a lot more . . .'

I fade away to the land of the championship season. I see my dad buying the black kids from the projects shoulder pads at the sporting goods store. It's one of the few memories I have that makes my chest swell with pride. To think of it is to remember being good.

We won the first two games of the season by a total of three points. It was luck: a fumble at the end of the game or their quarterback stepping on the out of bounds line in the back of the end zone for a safety. We weren't the biggest or the fastest. We won because we played as a team. We were the Bulldogs, AKA, The Dogs.

The playoffs worked so that only one team from each of the four YMCAs in the city would make it. It so happened that we played the other best team in our YMCA division in the last game of the regular season. The winner would go the city playoffs. The loser, as they say, stayed home.

Deep into the fourth quarter the game was tied. The weather was cold, the field hard as asphalt. Perfect football conditions. I played safety and had a reputation for picking off passes. I would get one a game without fail. I had already intercepted a pass in the first quarter, so they weren't throwing to my side anymore. In the huddle, I said to the other safety, Tyus – a tall, lanky, soft-spoken black kid with an Afro like Buckwheat – to cheat up to the line, because they were going to throw a short screen to the tailback. He did like I said, picked off the pass, and returned it for a touchdown. I felt better than if I had done it myself.

We won the first playoff game easily. The other team got behind early on in the game and that was pretty much it. They didn't know what it was like to be losing. We had been losing in parts of games all year. The black kids had been losing all their lives.

'. . . but if you really want to see my favorite article, you should look at this one. This is when I sensed that the President was really coming into his own . . .'

The same team had won the Championship five years in a row, and the word was that this was their best team ever. My dad got ahold of their regular season record. They never had a close game all year. Most of their games were sick blowouts: 55 to 7, 61 to 0, 49 to 14. The closest game they played all season was 20 to 7. The coach of the team had been an assistant in the NFL for 12 years. Every dad in the city who thought his son might have some talent would get a fake address so his kid could play for him. Where other teams had problems filling out their roster, they had tryouts with more than 60 kids. Half the guys on their team had already been offered scholarships to play at private junior highs. St Vincent's, whose football team hadn't lost a game in six years, was their heaviest recruiter. Their nickname, in fact, was the Vinnies.

We were doing a pretty good job of not getting scared until my old man sat us down after practice and confirmed every rumor we had ever heard about the Vinnies. After he was done with his speech, he brought in a priest who gave us all a blessing and reminded us of how David took down Goliath. By the time they were done with us, we were scared shitless. Guys were talking about how, if they were going to die, it was okay, because at least they got to die in the championship game. I went home that night and wrote out a will.

'. . . you see this picture. This is the picture I think of when I think of our President . . .'

After a long week of no sleep punctuated by nightmares of being crushed by 60-foot barbarians, it was time to face the Vinnies. They were big. They looked like a high school team. Their quarterback had facial hair. They were cocky, too. Warming up before the game, I ran over to pick up a ball. One of their linemen kicked it out from under my hand. 'I thought the Pee Wee League Championship was last weekend,' he said. 'What are you punks doing here?' I ran back to our side with my tail between my legs.

They got the ball first and rode over us like a monster truck. It took them all of five plays to score. Their sideline was laughing at us. Their parents were already talking about where to take them for championship pizza. After the touchdown they went for a two-point conversion. They ran a trick reverse and faked out our entire defense. We were demoralized. We wanted to pack it in right there.

I hadn't understood why my dad psyched us out like he did with the priest and everything. But then after they made the two-point conversion, he brought us all over to the sidelines for a talk. My dad wasn't a poetic guy, but in this one instance he outdid himself. The old man showed a side that I had never seen, and have since never forgotten.

He told us straight out that we were the best kids that he ever knew, but that even for the best kids, life can get too big. He said that he was proud of us no matter what happened in the game, but that deep down, he believed we could win. He said that every so often in life the little guy has a duty to stand up and fight the odds. He said that if we fought for each other and not for ourselves, then the score would take care of itself.

For the first time in our lives my old man treated us – a group of black kids from the projects and a couple of white middle-class punks – like men. Men.

The offense took the field, but was shut down after a valiant effort that resulted in three first downs. We marched onto the field to face the offense that only three minutes ago had trounced us. We were scared, nervous, and unsure, but dead set on giving it all we had. On the first play from scrimmage, the quarterback rolled out looking to pass. Usually I dropped off to cover the receiver. This time I gambled and went at him.

The sound of the tackle reverberated across the field like a shotgun blast. Their sidelines, with all their adoring fans, was stunned silent. Even the referee looked shocked.

After a few choice words to the quarterback, I got up and made my way back to the huddle. Tyus, who never said more than two words all year, looked at me, then the team, and said, 'Let's kill these motherfuckers.'

Final score: Dogs 40, Vinnies 8.

'. . . anything short of complete memorization of this feature story would be unpreparedness. And you know what I said about being prepared when you come face to face with a great man like our President. You cannot waste his time. You are living in his world . . .'

Chapter Six

OH GOD, I'VE been waiting for this all summer. The Pittsburgh Steelers vs. the Oakland Raiders. Monday Night Football, the third week of the season. They never show the Steelers here. All they show is the pansy-ass 49ers. If I have to watch one more four-yard slant to Jerry Rice, I'll kill myself. How the 49ers ever won four Super Bowls with their finesse style of play I have no idea. They are the epitome of high-tech, impersonal Silicon Valley. I would not be surprised, if, when performing Joe Montana's autopsy 50 years from now, they discover a computer chip in his brain. Same goes for that fucking Mormon Steve Young and goody-two-shoes Rice. Ronnie Lott was actually pretty cool.

The Oakland Raiders are one of the few teams that I have any feelings for besides the Steelers. Nowadays they're a bunch of wannabe badasses, but back in the day they were something to behold. Criminals! Criminals and degenerates all! I think of the Stork, that son of a bitch! Gawky death. Six foot six or some shit. Nut ass motherfucker swomping down on Fran Tarkenton. I hope you rot in hell, Ted Hendricks, because that's where you'll be happy. And you! The TOOZ!! Captain Evil. John Matuszak, may your soul rest in peace. You are the most evil man to walk the earth since Ivan the Terrible! Crusher! Satan worshipper! Monster Man from the Deep! You were a beast, a vile sledgehammer of the gods. To you, men fell down in angst-filled worship. The apocalypse was upon them when you stepped onto the field. Right now you're in hell, lining up against Napoleon. You versus thirty-five thousand French troops – God help them!

More whiskey. Ahh. How fine it is to be good and drunk in my own home. I sit on my leather couch in nothing but my blue boxer shorts. Besides a headless blow job I could ask for nothing more.

Game time in two minutes. Last chance to take a pisser. Nothing better than a whiskey piss. It comes out faster than beer, cleaner, too. Soon, cars will be run on whiskey piss, and I'll be a very rich man. I like this bathroom. Nice white tiles. Five or six months ago, I was dating this chick who liked to fuck in the bath tub. Smallish tits, a perfect little ass. We'd sit in the tub for hours: fucking, sucking, drinking vino, wrinkling up like prunes. The fucking was so good that I was compelled to improve the bathroom. Put in a new light fixture and painted the ceiling a cool blue. She was arty, so to impress her I hung up a poster from the Museum of Modern Art: *Retrospectives on the Russian Avant Garde at the Beginning of the 20th Century*. I didn't take into consideration, though, that the steam from the shower would cause it to sag. Had to throw it away after only one week. The girl lasted two.

Steelers win the toss, Raiders kick off. I like this Hastings kid. He's got speed. Rod Woodson, the god of all men, used to handled the kick off returns until his defection to the pussy 49ers. Now they got this Hastings kid. No wait . . . it's not Hastings, it's Jahine Arnold. The young speedster out of Clemson or South Carolina or some shit. Damn. That's how it is. Not even the devout can keep up with it anymore. Makes me want to cry. I have to take a big swig of whiskey to save my self-esteem. Thank God there are some things you can always count on.

Steelers have the ball at their own 30. We have a new quarter-back. Excuse me, a new black quarterback. That's right, the Steelers got a brother running the show: 'Kordell!' I love him.

Handoff to Bettis, he goes for a crushing eight. He's a tank, better than Earl Campbell. Another handoff to Bettis, a bruising seven. When Bettis gets the ball, he's not only picking up yards but wearing down the defense. He goes for 30 carries and the defense is sweating it. If we could nail down not a great, but a solid passing game, we could go all the way. The key is to keep the defense off balance. To have them thinking run and then hit them with a pass, to have them thinking pass then cram it up their ass with a run. We have the receivers. Kordell drops back, looks to pass . . . Boom! He nails Thigpen 30 yards down field right at the sideline. 'Beautiful.' I swig the whiskey in celebration of Steeler's execution.

Kordell drops back to pass. He nails our fine tight end Mark Bruener for a quick and easy ten yards. They weren't expecting that, the sons of bitches. This is what I'm talking about – commitment to a balanced attack. Having faith in Kordell, sticking with the passing game. Kordell takes the quick snap, rolls out and nails Pegram on a short screen. Pegram cuts inside and breaks it for a pickup of eight. This is beautiful football.

Kordell pitches to Bettis, a crushing four yards up the gut. A monster truck. Whew. 'Fucking beautiful.' Bettis is a bona fide superstar. A champion of the highest caliber. 'I love you, Jerome.' Bettis is tired, he comes off the field. Pegram, a fine player in his own right, takes his place. It's a beautiful one-two punch. Bettis the basher and Pegram the slasher. Hand off to Pegram for a short pickup. On second thought, Pegram might not be the best option down by the end zone. I think he's best utilized in third down situations where he can swing out of the backfield and make something happen in the open field. Down in the red zone is where the big boys come to play. It's bumper cars. Little men stay home. Bettis comes back in.

Everyone knows who the ball is going to. The Raiders pack the line. Thigpen goes in motion, Kordell takes the snap, and BOOM! . . . Touchdown! It's not even fair. Bettis runs over people. The Raiders could have packed the line with a hundred guys and it wouldn't have mattered. Strelzcyk blew a hole through the line like a shotgun blast through plywood. Bettis just waltzed in. Give him some love, boys. Fine fucking drive. An abject thing of beauty. Who needs art when you have drives like this? Pure sweetness. Nice mix of plays. Kordell looked sharp. Pegram made a nice contribution. Bettis digested Raiders. Steelers up six. The field goal team trots out. Automatic . . .

These commercials are for morons. It's a crime the way they represent the business world: a handsome guy sitting with a chick on the beach answering e-mail. A super-model driving a luxury sedan in Big Sur while making deals on her cellular. What they should be showing is an out of shape, pasty white guy, caught in traffic, gnawing on his steering wheel because he's losing his fucking mind. They paint pictures so far removed from reality they make the *National Enquirer* look the *New York Times*. I mean what the hell? An accountant with an amazing body and a hot girlfriend? A lawyer with the free time to play volleyball? A CEO sailing around the world? These people are delusional. The business world is a cesspool.

A fine pull of whiskey in a toast to reality. If work is freedom, then drunkenness is sobriety.

Steelers kick off, touchback. The Oakland offense comes onto the field. First play the QB hands it to Kaufman – a rocket of a tailback – who goes for 12. They huddle up, Steelers pack the line, Raiders hit for another 12 yards on a post pattern. 'They're killing us! Where the fuck is the goddamned defense!'

The Raiders QB drops back and nails his receiver dead on for a 30-yard gain. 'Christ Almighty! Fuck!' I need a shot of whiskey after that one. If we're going to give them something then let's at least make them chew up some clock. Give Bettis a rest, for Christ's sake. Handoff to Kauffman, he busts it for nine down to the 17. 'Jesus Christ! Fuck it all!' The crowd is starting to get into it. They come to the line, QB drops back, is chased out of the pocket and nailed for a ten-yard sack. 'Fuck yeah!' Now that's what I'm talking about! My Steelers, coming up big when they have to. The QB is shaky, comes out of the huddle. The snap, he drops back, holds it, looks around, not too much pressure, lets it fly, 'OH SHIT!' Fucking circus catch all the way down to the Steelers eight-yard line! That receiver, who is it? The great Tim Brown, of course. That son of a bitch reeled that one in with one hand between two defenders. I thought they were going to pick it off! Unfuckingbelievable.

They line up at the eight. Pitch to Kauffman, cuts up inside, breaks a tackle, busts to the outside and trots in for the score. 'Christ Almighty that was horrific . . . Goddamned fucking pathetic . . .'

Time for a cigarette. Yeah, screw it, I like to have a smoke every now and then. If my heart can put up with a drive like that then my lungs can sure as hell deal with a couple of smokes. I like these non-filters. If I'm going to smoke, I want to taste it. Kudos to all you boys in North Carolina. Thanks for caring, thanks for sharing. Ahhh . . .

'Why do you insist on making a fool out of me, Joanne!'

You have got to be kidding me. Not tonight. Of all nights, not tonight. I need to relax, I don't want to hear these assholes freak out. I'm trying to watch the game here.

'I work with him, Vance. I have to talk to him,' she pleads her case like an idiot. 'They respect you, they don't think of you as a fool. They talk about how they respect the work you do and how admired you are in the legal profession.'

'How in the hell do they even know that I'm a lawyer! What do you do, Joanne, tell them every little secret about us!'

The same bullshit every time. He's a jealous freak and she's a sap. There is nothing that can be done. They are sick human beings in a pathetic world.

Raiders kick off. Arnold makes a few moves and brings it back to the 23. The offense comes onto the field.

'Don't you know how much I love you, Vance?' says the shrill voice of martyrdom. These walls could be ten feet thick and I would still be able to hear her.

'If you love me so fucking much,' he says in low-tone hatred, 'then why do you humiliate me in front of our friends?! Answer me that, Joanne!

I don't care I don't care I don't care I don't care! I am not going to let them distract me from the game no matter fucking what! Leave me alone.

Handoff to Bettis, straight up the gut for a nice five. That's right, let's slow it down and start imposing our game plan on them. The key is to put some points on the board and give the defense a good rest. Handoff to Bettis, he goes for . . .

'I am your wife, Vance,' she pleads. 'You have to trust me, or our marriage doesn't mean anything!'

. . . three yards. Not bad, three yards and a cloud of dust is fine as long as they have some five- and six-yarders in there. Drag of the cigarette, slug of the whiskey. Come on boys, let's do this. They come to the line.

'Don't you dare tell me what the fuck marriage is about, Joanne! Don't even goddamn insinuate it! I give more to this marriage in one day than you do in an entire year!'

Kordell drops back, looks for a receiver, gets chased out of the pocket, and runs five for the first down. That's fine, but he needs to look to pass. Otherwise, he's not going to last the season.

'I'm not going to stand here, Vance, and let you minimize the effort that I put into making this marriage work!'

'You are going to fucking listen to whatever it is I have to say!'

Well-executed draw play to Bettis, he breaks through the line and goes for a bruising seven. The Raiders weren't expecting that at all.

'You don't control my life!' she says in rare defiance. 'You don't tell me what I can and can not do. You are not my father.'

'You fucking got that right!' he yells, the venom building. 'I am not an old alcoholic who hasn't gotten up off the couch in 20 years except to fix a drink!'

Kordell drops back, scampers away from the pressure, and hits Blackwell for an eight-yard gain. Beautiful. Kordell can scramble around all he wants as long as he throws it.

'Why are you so cruel?' she cries. 'What have I done to make you so cruel?'

'I'm not cruel, Joanne,' he seethes. 'What's cruel is the way you flirt and flaunt in front of me. You treat me like fucking dirt!'

'How do I treat you like dirt, Vance?' she screams in confusion. 'I've given my life to you. Everyone knows that I'm untouchable because I'm with you.'

Bettis goes down for a yard loss. Kordell drops back, gets chased, dumps it to Bruener, who is taken down immediately – right at the first down marker. Shit, this is going to be a close one. They're coming out to measure it.

'Untouchable because of me! Untouchable because of me! What am I, your fucking Kaffir Boy? Little tag along piece of shit! Is that what you tell those pricks at your work?'

He got it!

'How much longer are you going to keep bringing up the men I work with?' she wails. 'When are you going to start trusting me?'

'I'll start trusting you, Joanne,' the seething hatred now fully alive, like a monster finally emerged from the depths, 'when you stop acting like an unabashed whore in front of our friends and our daughter!'

Hand off to Bettis . . .

'I AM NOT A WHORE!'

'Oh yeah?' The flood gates open. He is raging. 'Then what the fuck do you call a woman who can't leave the house for work without first making sure that her nipples are sticking out in her blouse! I don't know any other woman who dresses like you do to work! If that's even where you're going, you lying bitch! For all I know you're spreading your legs for your boss at the downtown Hilton every day! Sucking his dick for a paycheck! Tell me the truth, Joanne! That raise wasn't about a job well done, but about letting him shove it in your ass for the first time! Tell me, Joanne. What's it like being a whore? What's it like having the boys at work talk behind your back about how they fucked you? Does it make you feel special? I would really like to know, because I think it would be hard to be a whore and a good mother at the same . . .'

Enough! Fuck these shithead motherfucking assholes! All I

want to do is watch the goddamned game, but they're forcing their twisted lives on me! They can kill each other as far as I'm concerned. They're nothing but a part of it, and there's no part of it that need be saved.

I switch it to CD mode, but leave the game on. Fuck it, I hate these announcers anyway.

'What have you done for our daughter, Joanne,' he screams, 'besides teach her to be a whore!'

I hit play. I got the Nirvana in there and it's time to blast. *In Utero*, song number four. The irony is sweet music enough. The guitar comes, the strum, Kurt at his best before he so honorably quit this shitty game.

'You can't talk to me like that anymore!'

Louder! Slam it all the way up, fuck 'em all. More guitar. More Steelers! More everything! Go Bettis GO! Whiskey in the gullet! Sing it brother sing it!

'Rape me. Rape me, my friend. Rape me. Rape me, again. I'M NOT THE ONLY ONE! AHHHH I'M NOT THE ONLY ONE! AHHHH I'M NOT THE ONLY ONE! AHHHH I'M NOT THE ONLY ONE!'

'Go Kordell, you son a bitch!' Fuck it, run. Shove it up their ass. Do what you have to do. 'Win Baby! Win!' Do it for me! Line it up, hand it off to Bettis, slam it up the gut, slice into shit. Destroy! Blast it for 12. Kill those motherfuckers! No one deserves to be alive!

'I'M NOT THE ONLY ONE! AHHHH I'M NOT THE ONLY ONE! AHHHH I'M NOT THE ONLY ONE! AHHHH I'M NOT THE ONLY ONE!

Go! Roll it back, you got him, hit him. Beautiful! Twenty fucking yard gain. Life! 'I'm not dead! I'm not dead!' I'm alive. I'm living. You can't kill me. There's nothing to kill, you motherfuckers! Give it to Bettis! Give it to Bettis! Yeah! Go Jerome. Go! At the 30, the 25, cutting back inside. You can't take us down, you motherfuckers! 'GO!' Fuck it all! Knocked out of bounds at the ten. We'll crush you all. There's no stopping us anymore!

God is with us. Come on Lady California, I'll give it to you up the ass!

'I'M NOT THE ONLY ONE! AHHH I'M NOT THE ONLY ONE! AHHH I'M NOT THE ONLY ONE! AHHH I'M NOT THE ONLY ONE! AHHH I'M NOT THE ONLY ONE!'

You got him, Kordell, throw it, throw it . . . no, don't run! Fuck it, run! 'Run you motherfucker!' Cut to the inside, you got blockers there . . . ohh shit, slammed like a motherfucker. What the fuck? Fumble! 'Oh no, not a fucking fumble.' Not here, not now! Death! Who the fuck has it? Who the fuck has it? 'NOOO!!!' Not the Raiders! How the fuck could this have happened? I told you! 'I told you not to fucking pass goddammit.' You son of a bitch, you had him wide open. It was automatic. Now it's Raiders ball at the fucking two yard line. Son of a fucking bitch. 'Goddammit.' More whiskey, I can't take this shit . . .

'ARE YOU TALKING TO ME! YOU FUCKING CUNT! ARE YOU TALKING TO ME! BECAUSE YOU BETTER NOT BE TALKING TO ME LIKE THAT, YOU FUCKING WHORE!'

Goddammit! I can still hear that piece of shit. Fuck it. Fuck the neighbors, fuck them all! Give me song number nine.

The Raiders offense comes on to the field, sing it Kurt:

'Give me a Leonard Cohen Afterworld. So I can sigh eternally . . .'

'If you call me a whore one more time, Vance, I'm going to leave you!'

'LEAVE ME! WHAT THE FUCK DID YOU SAY! IF YOU EVEN THINK OF STEPPING ONE FOOT OUT THE DOOR I'LL KILL YOU!'

'No!' He drops back and nails Tim Brown over the middle for a 25-yard pickup. That's not the way to fucking do it. When you have them pinned you got to keep them pinned. What the fuck is going on with this team!

'I'm so tired I can't sleeeep. I'm a liar and thieeef.'

'I'm tired of your threats, Vance! What are you going to do to me?'

'SIT AND DRINK PENNY ROYAL TEA! I'M ANEMIC ROYALTY!'

Another goddamned pass, this time for 20 yards. They are chewing us up. Run a fucking blitz or something. Do anything to break up the rhythm of these assholes. You're making them look like goddamned Air Coryell! Send the goddamned kitchen sink if you have to. Anything to stop them before this game gets out of control. The crowd is going apeshit. Look at them. They're a bunch of bloodthirsty maniacs!

'WHAT THE FUCK AM I GOING TO DO TO YOU? COME HERE YOU FUCKING WHORE! I'M GOING TO TEACH YOU A FUCKING LESSON!'

'I'm on warm milk and laxatives. Cherry flavored antacids.'

'No!' Another goddamned 20-yard pickup. They threw twice in a row. You knew they were going to draw to that fucking Kauffman! Where's the fucking defensive coordinator's head? What are you fucking thinking, Cowher? Anyone could have predicted that. You don't have to have a Ph.D. in Football Theory to figure it out. The defense doesn't even look like it belongs on the field. They're confused. They have no idea what's coming. Call a goddamned time out before something really bad happens.

'GET OVER HERE YOU FUCKING WHORE! DON'T RUN AWAY FROM ME!'

'STOP, VANCE! YOU'RE OUT OF CONTROL!'

'SHUT THE FUCK UP!'

'I SIT AND DRINK PENNY ROYAL TEA! I'M ANEMIC ROYALTY. I SIT AND DRINK PENNY ROYAL TEA! I'M ANEMIC ROYALTY!'

Fucking son of a bitch! Down to the three yard line with a fadeout to the corner. 'What the fuck is that shit?' 93 yards or some shit in four or five goddamned plays. What's fucking going on in this goddamned world? When did everything start fucking falling apart? Answer me that! How do you go from a great start to pure shit in the span of 20 minutes? WHAT THE FUCK IS GOING ON?

'RUN AWAY FROM ME! PUSH ME! QUESTION ME! YOU'RE GOING TO GET IT WORSE THAN YOU EVER HAVE! YOU WANT TO BE A WHORE, YOU'RE GOING TO BE TREATED LIKE ONE!'

'STOP HITTING ME!'

Lower it. Turn it all the way down.

'Stop, please stop . . .'

Thuds, like small earthquakes. One after the other and I know he's on top of her. I can hear him panting, spewing, beating her:

'You fucking bitch, thud. Fucking whore, thud. Think you're going to leave me, thud. Think you can talk to me that way, thud thud thud. Who the fuck do you think you're talking to thud thud. If you ever even fucking dare, thud, to threaten to leave me, thud thud, I'm going to fucking kill you, thud thud thud.'

No more screams. He's fucking her up.

'Fucking whore, thud, thud thud. You aren't anything but a fucking whore, thud thud thud . . .' She's hardly making any noise, only a low gurgling that I can barely hear through the wall. I picture them in their kitchen. He on top of her, totally pinning her down and wailing on her face. Where's the kid? She usually comes in and stops it before it gets to this level. This is the worst I've ever heard it.

'Thud thud thud, you're my fucking wife, thud thud thud, you don't talk to me like that, thud thud. You want to go fuck those assholes, thud thud. Stick your pussy out and make a fool of me, thud. You want to suck their dicks, thud thud. I know you fucking do, thud thud. Every goddamned time you leave this house you spread your pussy to those cocksuckers, and they laugh when they fuck you, thud thud. They give each other high fives, thud thud. They stand in the room when they fuck and give each other high fives and laugh at me.'

Quiet, save for some mumbling that I can't really make out.

The daughter must be gone. She would have been there by now.

Please stay quiet. Don't hit her anymore. I can't deal with this. There's no saving you. There's nothing I can do. Nothing will change. All I want to do is watch the game and relax. Please don't hit her anymore. I'm not a coward, but I can't help anyone. I want to be left alone. I don't need this. There's nothing to save. No one can save anyone else. This is natural for a lost world, like a bad storm. I have to ride it out. Please don't hit her anymore. Please go to bed. All I want to do is relax. I have so much happening right now. I can't be brought into your hell. I have my own problems. Please don't hit her anymore. Don't make me feel like I'm evil, when all I want to do is watch a football game . . .

Little foot steps . . . she is there, *goddammit*. The daughter is there, but was too scared to come out! God, when is it ever going to end? Why is it like this? She's only a little girl. Why does she have to see this? No child should ever see her mother with her face beat in. She won't make it back from this. She won't repair. It gets way deep into the system. She hasn't done anything to anyone. She's unlucky, that's all. She didn't asked to be brought into this. This will kill her. This will kill her. Leave her alone. You are not allowed to expose her to this. She's a child. It's not your fault, baby. I'm sorry it's this way, but there's nothing I can do.

'Daddy,' she sobs loudly, 'is everything okay?'

Shuffling, fast movements. 'Uh, everything's okay, honey. Go back to bed. I'll be in there in a second to tuck you in.'

'But why are you on top of mommy?' she cries.

'Just go back to bed, Kelly.' His voice becomes more stern. The motherfucker has the twisted nerve to order her around, like he's a good parent. 'Go back to bed, Kelly. Now!' he yells.

Don't you fucking yell at her again you son of a bitch! Don't you fucking stand on the side of the righteous after what you've done. Don't you act like you know what it is to be good. Don't you goddamned dare to pretend to be a good man, you sick motherfucker, because I won't stand for it. I'm not a good man, but I have my limits.

The pitter-patter of little innocent feet and the sound of a door closing. Stay there, honey. Don't come out anymore. Stay where you are and don't let them hurt you, because they will. They will crush you. Go to sleep, little baby.

I think of the song that my mother used to sing to me before bed. She had the softest, most melodic voice. It cast me into the land of dreams on angels wings. I hum it: 'He's my dear, my darling one, his eyes are sparkling full of fun. No other, no other can match the likes of him.'

Go to sleep little baby. You're a special little girl. None of this is your fault. I'm sorry.

Stirring in the kitchen. That motherfucker is getting up. I can hear him begging for forgiveness.

Crying. 'Oh my god, Joanne . . . I'm so sorry, honey. I didn't mean it. I just lost my temper. You know how I get. Oh my God. Wash your face off, I can't believe I did this to you.'

Sound of running water. She isn't saying anything. The piece of shit is crying while she stands there in silence washing the blood from her pummeled face. Everything is a mess. A bloody, swollen, disgusting nightmare.

'Oh God, Joanne,' he says in his disgusting wail. 'I'm so sorry. I'm so sorry.'

The water shuts off. I hear mumbling. Don't do it, Joanne. Don't give into him this time. Get your daughter and get out of there. If you don't give a fuck about yourself, at least save your daughter. She still has a chance. She's not dead yet. She might grow up and do something special. She might make people feel again. Don't do it. Fight. Even if no one else in the world could give a shit, fight! Rage against him. Get out of there.

I can hear him crying, sobbing like a child. Movement. She is with him now.

'It's okay, honey,' she says. 'Don't cry. It's okay.'

My stomach wrenches. Nothing will ever change. I was right –

there was nothing I could have done. It was none of my business. Suck his dick, Joanne. I know that after a good workout I always like to have my dick sucked.

'I'm so sorry, Joanne. I'm so sorry.'

Good for you, pal. You are a man who knows how to handle the ladies. Next time you see her talking on the phone with one of the guys she works with, cave her head in with a baseball bat. Or better yet, decapitate.

Slow movement out of the kitchen and into the living room. As usual, after a good, constructive fight, the wonderful couple sit down to enjoy some television.

The sounds are familiar. Oh, great, they've settled themselves into a nice evening of Monday Night Football. God, it's good to be an American. Things are okay. They really are. Everybody is doing great. Boy, I can hear the game almost perfectly by listening to their set. Must be real top of the line. Probably 30, maybe even 40 inches. I wonder if they have a Home Theater Entertainment Center, too? Maybe sometime we can all get together and see whose is better. Wouldn't that be wonderful? Gee whiz, sounds like the Steelers have tied it up. This is a great game.

Chapter Seven

MORE JAMESONS. MORE semen down my gullet. More to drink. Drink more. The corner pull. The pull in the corner. Standing in the corner, pulling Jamesons. Dribble dribble toil and snibble. Penis and vagina, nothing ever finer. Vagina and penis, Bill Cosby's son was Enis. Asshole and some jizz, whiskey makes you whiz. Some nice jizz and some ass, the name of the Russian news service is TASS. Blow job, hand grenade, rim suck and Le Poop – Nickelodeon, Don King, Post-it notes and soup. Asklabanza inkadinka : murigasha harizinga.

Charlie Chaplain was a klutz, black folks have big butts.

Detergent companies pollute the streams, Mexican people like their beans.

'T'is best to follow your own path, Chinese folks are good at math.

Conspirators hid behind the grassy knoll, the Caucasian male has lost his soul.

People revere me. The supercilious functionary of the reactionary component. A dogmatic distillator of the happy-go-lucky. The Jamesonian whiskey champ taken hostage by the Palestinians at the '72 Olympics. 'Mr Eat the Beans and Cut the Farts.' Captain Mendacity. The Tovarish of Truthhood. The 'Earnest and Julio Gallo of Contemporary Thought.' The abridged, 172-page, paperback version of *Moby Dick*. A bestseller. A tampon. Cartoons.

Heroic drinking. I began this morning around nine. Woke up, read the *Jew York Times*, and poured myself a glass of merlot. Oh, at first it was nothing more than a joyful lark. Saturday morning, the sun is out, the birds are singing. The air had that certain crispness that speaks vim and vigor to the American white boy. A happy, skin bracer of a morning. A sporty, menthol-smelling deodorant of a life. The Three Ss of manliness: shit, shower, and shave.

Time for breakfast? Heck no. On a fine day such as this, a man shouldn't concern himself with such triflings as eating a breakfast. The edict is clear: another drink is in order. Happily, I pour. Ecstatically, I imbibe. The softer hues stroll forward, the lights dim to a comfortable setting. Never before had ten o'clock in the a.m. seemed so grand. Freedom was the rule. Anything was possible. My wallet was full, the world awaited. None of it mattered.

The noon cometh and my bottle recedeth. To the stores! To the bodegas and the winesellers! To the whiskey coffers! To the cigarette machines! To the booze emporiums! The outlets, the retail merchandisers, the malls, the shops, the repositories, the bazaars, the flea markets, the gourmet limiteds, and the wholesale distributors. All is mine. I claim it for Sam! Samville. Samburgh. Samtown. Sam York City. Sam Francisco. Samcago. Samlanta. Sam Angeles. Samiami. Sam Luis Obispo. Sam and the Family Stone. Son of Sam. Uncle Sam. Samboree. Saint Sam. Samurai. Dr Jonas Sam. Country Sam and the Fish. The Grateful Sam. The Sam also Rises. Samovar. Sam and Dave. It's all the Sam to me. Samothracia. Now is the Sam of all good men to come to the Sam of their country.

The entire town of Sam Francisco completely sold out of Jamesams, I was left with no recourse other than the bars of this fine city.

Plop down in the chair, Mr Big. Jameson's Irish whiskey, sir. No ice. Make it neat, and make it a double. Give me something special. Make it a whipper snapper. That's right, I'm a public relations specialist. You? Oh, a coward hiding from the world in a back alley bar. Fanfrickentastic. Damn glad to make your acquaintance. Knew you were a maverick from the get-go. Win the Super Bowl this year? You don't, say? Brave man you are. Yessiree bob, a brave man you are.

I want to piss on you . . .

This old German guy on the block used to show us kids his wiener. I touched it and he gave me five dollars. I took all my friends for candy. I was the hero of the block.

Three country kids in Michigan hopped a train. The train stopped in inner-city Detroit. The girl and two boys got off. The 12-year-old girl was gang raped and shot in the face. The two boys were decapitated.

The President is playing golf in Mallorca.

No one say a word, but I'm taking another pull of Jamesons. This is sooo great, dude! So right on. So bitchin', man. I can't even fuckin' believe it, guy. This is so fuckin' right on. Way cool, brah. Oh man, can you dig this or what? Drinking whiskey in a sex club, man. Fuckin' A. This is the top notch killer shit. Really fucking sub-culture, man. Cutting edge all the way, dude. Totally alternative. Deep house. This is like the most killer rave ever, bro. You are so cool. God, I can't believe how right on you are. More Jamesons, dude. Bring the heat. Right on, brah. No doubt.

The misconception exists that heavy drinking leads to a decrease in lucidity. Perhaps at first, when the booze contributes to giddiness and not cerebrality. After a period of time, however, when the amount of drinks reaches into the twenties, the physicality of the high wears off, and a cogitative condition ensues. The condition is complex, to lesser and greater degrees inclusive of: melancholia, erudition, permanent handsomeness, sports trivia, reminiscence, hostility, pacificity, eagerness, joie de vivre, nihilism, libido intensificado, delusions of grandeur, low self-esteem, arrogance, and disdain. Ultimately, this all falls away in a particularly spiritualized self-consciousness that is most amenable to the articulate palate. La de da, la de da. The layers are pulled away, revealing a raw, manic, nearly suicidal man with no real meaning in his life other than whiskey, sex clubs, and presidential interviews. The serpent tongue rolls to and fro, like the Jersey Shore, rife with sewage and toxins. More whiskey, sir? Yes please, thank you. The service here is phenomenal. I must have you as my waiter again. Yes, my self-referential demon. I will always wait on you.

Thar she blows. Hush little raver, don't you cry, Uncle Sammy's gonna give you a penis pie. Nice face, brown hair, good jugs, no boyfriend in sight – yessirree, a real Rockets and Missiles score. Swing on in, see if I can chop down the cherry tree. Tonight might be my night. I like a woman in sweat pants. Easy access.

'You want a little whiskey, biskey?'

'What does that mean?' She's sullen. What sweet, youthful music to these jaded ears!

'That means,' I take a big pull of the fifth right in front of her face. 'That you share in the libation.'

'I don't think so.' She's young, real young. My guess is 20.

'To bad for you, little guy.' Take another swig and wipe the whiskey from my face. 'You don't know what you're missing.'

A cute little smile on her 20-year-old face. She is loosening up. 'What do you mean?'

'I mean,' I say with a wink, 'that if you want some of this,' I make a fuck motion with my hips, 'then you need to chill out with some of this,' and swig away.

She laughs. The sullen are always the first to go down – all they want is a little attention. The bender mind is a confident mind. I am urbane. A caballero. Don Juan. This eve I don the full regalia: a sport coat, a mock black turtle neck, gabardine pants, and black loafers. I am a yuppie beat poet. An unthreatening dangerous guy.

'You think I'm handsome, don't you?' I inch my face closer to hers. She doesn't move away.

'You're crazy,' she says.

'I am indeed, that's why I'm here.' She's coming around. 'Why are you here? Aren't you crazy, too?'

'I guess,' she says shyly.

'What do you mean,' I say angrily. 'What do you mean you guess?'

'I am,' she says defiantly. 'I am crazy.'

There's only one way to handle these youngsters, and that's to get to the point. 'Let's do it, then,' I say hungrily. 'Let's go in this room together. I'll make you cum like you never have before.'

Her little nose twitches, she shifts her weight back and forth – all for naught. I move in closer, corner her further. There's only six inches between our lips. I flick out my tongue and get a little lip.

'Get your ass in there,' and pull back to take a swig. All day drinking lends little toleration of bullshit. 'You're here to get seriously fucked and you know it. Don't go home empty handed. Let's get down and dirty and do some serious fucking. I'll eat your pussy for an hour!'

She is now faced with the real deal, the guy who will pull the trigger and make her call him daddy. The trannies fuck me up, but with these hetero chicks, I'm as confident as Deion Sanders. This is prime time, baby. Let's get those sweat pants off and get something going. I want to see your panties. I want to fuck you in the ass. I want to make you suck my dick until your lips fall off.

'I don't know if I'm ready for this,' she whispers.

This tall bitch with her little nose and cutey lipstick thought she had it made. All she needed was 30 more minutes, then she could have gone home to her Pearl Jam poster and stuffed animals, called her friends on her pink phone and bragged to them how she went to Rockets and Missiles.

It ain't going to happen, baby. You are now an official part of the sickness. Oh yeah, that's right, you're in over your head. It's finally happened. You've met someone who doesn't give a shit about you or anything that you stand for. I know you have boyfriends who say they don't care about anything, who sit in cafes and talk about how nothing matters. Those guys are faking it, doll. Otherwise, they'd rape your ass and throw you in a gutter.

I am empty. I proved it a couple nights ago when I sat in front of the Home Theater Entertainment Center and didn't do a goddamned thing while a woman got the shit kicked out of her. And let me tell you, Miss Tall Raver, kicking your fucking head in and shoving my dick up your ass would be no different. I understand the moral code. I am as guilty as her fucking husband. It would have been no different than if I had walked in there myself and gotten a couple of licks in. Shit, I should have. It would have been better than going to bed, then sweating and squirming all night because I was so fucked up over it. But since then I've learned. I have gained from the forced realization of my emptiness. I've made the proverbial lemonade. Now I'm a full-fledged, immoral coward. Now that it is incontrovertible and immutable that I am a piece of shit – I am heretofore relieved of all moral duty. I can do whatever the fuck I want. And what I want right now is stick my dick in your twitching, nervous, trying-to-be-sexy mouth.

'Fuck that. Have some whiskey and get in that room!' I lean on her, pinning her against the wall like a sandwich.

The body contact is warming her to the task. She's not going to get a guy like me again. If we were at a bar, I could pick her up, take her home, and fuck her. The whole point of being here is to avoid the bullshit of the one night stand. I put my lips up against her cheek and flick my tongue out onto her face. She responds by kissing my neck.

'What do you want to do to me?' she asks in a seductive whisper.

Ridiculous. I want to fuck you, that's what I want to do to you. I want to cum. I want to see stars. I want to forget who I am. I want to be dead for a while.

I pull back and force her to make eye contact by grabbing her little, white chin with my hand. She doesn't resist. 'You're going to get some cock, is what you're going to get.' I speak in the most frank, sober tone available to me. I get a thrill out of de-romanticizing this for her. I don't want to her to be happy. I want to hurt her, like I hurt. I want her to be ashamed. I want her to go home and squirm in her bed and cry because she feels like a worthless piece of shit.

'I'm going to give it to you up the ass.'

Not at all phased, this little whippersnapper is more of a nympho than I first thought. 'You're crazy' she says as she traces my chest with her finger. 'So crazy,' she repeats.

'Fine,' I say and take another pull. 'Then let's get the fuck in there.'

'I want to,' and grabs my dick, which is only semi-hard. 'Talk to me some more. You're so handsome. You turn me on. I never met a man like you.'

Through the sick haze of transvestites and creeps, I see out of the corner of my eye, Lady California. She stands at the end of the dark hall next to the coke machine. She is a vision like I have never beheld. For tonight she is a whore.

The dress is black plastic, the high-heels are black stilettos, the lipstick is that of night as are the fingernails. Her legs scream out of her tight dress in black, fishnet stockings. Standing next to the red coke machine, she appears a demoness unaffected by the flames of hell. She is the darkest purity. A goddess beyond good and evil. A princess of the netherworld.

For every effect, there must be a cause. She is the cause. Of what, I don't know exactly. Lady California is the walking breathing question mark of my condition. She is the embodiment of my confusion. How ironic, how inappropriate, that she be so beautiful . . .

Unfinished business abounds. My energies no longer lie with the girl before me. What is she but averageness? I need my confusion on a plate, or better yet, in a trough. I need terminally unusable society. Garbage. The dregs and the dogs. Give me Christ on the cross, not on the mount. Suffering, that's the ticket.

'I'm done talking to you,' I say to Miss Tall Raver, angrily. 'I've given you your chance, and you've fucked it up.'

'What?'

Ha Ha! Now that I have her, I can make her suffer. She's second fiddle now, and needs to be made sorry for it.

Lean in real close, vicious whispering through clenched teeth. 'You think you can stand here and play games with people? Hmm? Don't you know where the fuck you are? This is a sex club. A club for fucking and sucking. You don't come here unless you're serious about getting it up the ass. This isn't one of your fucking raves where you can stand around flirting all night. This isn't a bar where you can get a guy hard then take off at the last second because you decided you want to go home and watch the new Brad Pitt movie.'

'But . . .' She's on the verge of tears.

'But nothing! I'm tired of fakes. Either you're a fucking whore or you're not. Either you want it in the ass or you don't. Either you love the world or you hate it. There is no middle path. You either get down on your knees and suck cock or go home and watch cable! Don't come here acting like you're something special when all you are is run of the mill.'

'I am not run of the mill!' she cries.

'Let me tell you something,' I say coldly. 'If I'm run of the mill, then you sure as hell are too.'

She doesn't respond, but only sobs to herself. I think of Kelly, the lawyer's daughter. This is how she's going to be, and some day she'll run into a good for nothing hypocrite like me who will do the same thing. I can't help but feel some remorse.

'Listen,' I say, stroking her shoulder gently with my hand. 'You've got to be crazy to let an asshole like me have any effect on you. I am not anyone that anybody should be listening to,' I add, 'especially a woman as pretty as you.'

Predictably, the 'pretty' thing gets her – people are suckers when it comes to flattering their appearance. Tell them they're kind and goodhearted, big fucking deal. Say that they have a nice body, win a prize. She dabs at her eyes and says, 'Then why did you say all those horrible things to me?'

'I'm not really sure,' I say blankly. 'It might just be that I have problems.'

'What?'

'Nothing,' I wink and take a good slug. 'Have a good night.'

'What?' She asks in a panic. 'Where are you going.'

'To meet my destiny, honey,' I say like a cowboy.

'But . . .'

'But nothing,' I say. 'I am a sick and sad man. Be thankful our paths crossed only as much as they did. Otherwise, I would have had torn your cunt out and shoved it in your mouth.'

Her mouth hits the floor.

For the first time I understand the power and the glory that go along with being a serial killer. Looking her dead in the eye, I seethe, 'A good evening to you,' and drink a secret toast to Ted Bundy.

Know thy self . . . Ha Ha. I think of Salieri at the end of *Amadeus*, when he finally gave into his mediocrity. He sanctified the mad as he was wheeled through the halls of the asylum. A priest of mediocrity. A composer for the inept. His whole life was divinely engineered to bring him to his realization of averageness. In the end he came clean, and gave up any further pretenses of greatness. What a relief. What a triumph! Turning the tables on God, he achieved greatness in his mediocrity.

There is no greatness in my mediocrity. It is too small to be of any significance. I am on the sad inskirts. More part of society than not part, but still not part enough to be considered a part. Cowardice defines me. If I were a braver man, I would live happily on the outskirts. I wouldn't work in public relations, but maybe as a writer. I wouldn't hide in the corners of a sex club, but live an openly bisexual lifestyle. For the cost of the Home Theater Entertainment Center, I could have trekked through Nepal for six months.

I move amongst the confused, manic, and perverse. Lady California, witnessing my withdrawal from the sweat-panted raver, has receded into her room – proper etiquette for a woman in waiting. I stroll, as though taking my evening's constitutional. I am the emperor relieved to find that I have no clothes. The trannies smile, grab, and leer. I drink from my whiskey bottle and accept their antics as droll.

A weak man stands no ground. There is no striving, no sacrificing. He skips along from commercial to commercial, criticizing everything that he is not. To have a luxury sedan is indulgent. But wait 'til I buy one! Boy oh boy, I'll justify it with all my might. Whatever I am in the moment, is what's right. Whatever I once was, or consider unlikely that I ever will be again, is wrong. Success is merely jumping on the right bandwagon at the right time. And once on, convincing the world that you were on it from the beginning of time. Or, of course, until a better bandwagon comes along. One moment a rapist, the next a saint.

I am bound by nothing but my own success. Buttfucking Lady California will not hinder my success, therefore I am free to do as I please. If there were any chance that someone out in the real world might find out about Lady California, then I couldn't do it. I am completely dependent upon what the world thinks of me. As for my own set of standards . . . they don't exist.

To the door, the room with no view. There stands my baby. 'Honey,' I say with a smile, 'I'm home.'

She reaches out for the whiskey bottle and I happily oblige. If to be with me she needs to dull a few of her own issues, then God bless her. I like to think of her as suffering in having to be with Yours Truly. It makes me feel irresistible.

'Saw your face through the window a few nights ago,' I say and reach for the bottle. 'You couldn't have been too happy with what you saw.' I say this not to make amends, but to challenge. I want to make Miss Beautiful face the pig.

She doesn't say anything. She stares at me, expressionlessly.

'You must think I'm a real piece of shit?' and swig from the fifth. 'You must think I'm pretty fucked up.'

Again, no reply. She sits down on the floor in the corner. I have a raging boner.

'Why don't you say anything? I'm talking to you, aren't I?'

She reaches out for the bottle, I move over and hand it to her. After a good swig, she looks up at me and says softly, 'I'm here. What else is there to say?'

Her silence is pure condemnation, and I refuse to let her take the moral high road. 'What the fuck is that supposed to mean?'

Grab the bottle out of her hand and take another swig. 'You were there, you saw it. You came down the hall to see what I was doing, and you got an eyeful. You saw me brutalize another human being, okay? You know what I did, and you must have something to say about it.'

Softly, 'I'm not going to judge you.'

'Judge me!' Fuck her, these people are masters of the reproach. 'I saw the look on your face. You were disgusted. You hated me. You wanted me to be dead.' Hard pull of the whiskey. 'And now you have the gall to tell me that you're not going to judge me. You already judged me. You are judging me! I make you sick, don't I? DON'T I?'

She gets up off the floor, puts her arms around me and gently guides me back down. She is so caring. I am in love with this person. I have been from the minute I laid eyes on her. I dig my head into her long neck. I feel weak, tired of life, tired of myself. I feel the tears well up in my eyes. My chest is heavy, there is a lump in my throat. Without any thought I begin talking. My lungs, liver, kidneys, and organs force the issue. I feel like layers of silt are being carried away from the base of my spine. Toxins are fleeing my body.

'. . . you can find some happiness, but then there's nothing. So if there can't be that, there has to be some sort of backbone or conviction, some sort of reason for not being happy and for suffering. But there's nothing. There's not emptiness, there's nothing. I can't find a reason to be here. When I was a kid I had the best ideas, but I've lost them all. I don't mean it's some bullshit like a loss of innocence, but then in a way it is . . . I don't feel innocent anymore. There's nothing I believe in, but I'm not even a non-believer. It's like I'm floating without purpose or direction. I see the people around me, and they're the same way. Everyone is floating, but it's more me than anyone. I remember when they used to ask me what I was going to be when I grew up and I'd run off a list of all these good, honorable things. Everybody would. We were all going to be archaeologists or find a way to feed poor people or be statesmen. We never became anything. *I* never became anything. I never grew up. All I did was get older and make more money. I thought this was supposed to be about something. If anyone would have told me that I was going to grow up to be a fucking PR guy, I would have laughed in his face. Now, being a public relations specialist is more about who I am than anything else about me. I feel like I've been waiting all these years for a vocation, that something would shake me from this nightmare and I'd wake up with a purpose, that I would be clean, fresh, and innocent again. But nothing has come to me. I've tried to convince myself that there aren't any more battles, but I know there are. Right next door to me is an asshole lawyer who beats up his wife in front of his innocent little daughter. I can hear him smashing her face in. He's planting the seeds that will grow into a living hell for that little girl. All I do is sit in my apartment and hide behind my fucking CD player! I play it as loud as I can and I can still hear them! I've become everything that I once despised. I am the little company man who scurries away at the first sign of danger. I've sold my soul for a little piece of security. All my life I told myself that if the shit ever really came down, then I would be there on the right side of things, that I would come through with shining colors, that no matter what I might be up to, I was a stand up guy. Now I know it's all bullshit. I've been deluding myself all these years in thinking I was a good man. I'm as lost and as sold out as everyone else. I'm dead. There isn't any passion left in me . . .' I stop, look into her dark, mystical eyes, '. . . except when it comes to you. You are the only thing that has made me feel anything other than contempt. You are everything that I am not: brave, strong, and beautiful.' Our faces are three inches apart. I can feel her breath on my face – the only air I want to breath. From the bottom of my heart, from the last remnants of my soul, I speak the words, 'I love you.'

I kiss her. A passionate, loving beautiful kiss that awakens my core. Her lips are tender, her tongue is sweet. Somewhere in the back of my brain I know that I am sharing myself intimately with a man, but my heart, to whom at this moment I place my faith, celebrates the poetry of the feminine. This man is more woman than woman. For the first time in my life, I feel what it is to make love without sex. I stick my tongue deep inside of her mouth and lick at every crevasse. I trace the lines of her teeth. I taste her and in so doing am brought into the light that is her brave fire.

Gently, our lips part. She delicately places her lips on my cheek, then separates from me to close the door. I feel safe. She retakes her place next to me on the floor, and we kiss again – more heatedly, more sexual. We are making out like high schoolers in the back of the car. I grab her by her hair, pull her head back and lick her neck. She purrs and groans like a feline. She is my black cat. My sensual demon. My equal. My vamp.

'You're so fucking hot, baby,' I pant.

She responds by licking my eyelids with her tongue. She nips at the tip of my nose. She bites my neck, hard. She wants it. My little blackcat whore is ready. My cock is swollen with desire. I want her to feel me deep inside of her. I want to feel what it's like deep inside of her.

I rub my hand over her dress, find a nipple and pinch. She purrs with delight and puts her long, thin, black-stockinged leg over my crotch. I put my hand on her lean thigh. She grinds her thigh into my cock and slips her hand under my shirt. I flex for her, she digs in with her long, black nails. I want her to cut me. I want her to share in my blood.

'Harder, baby,' I say. 'Make me bleed.'

She claws and scratches at my chest. I feel my skin tear under her nails. She is stronger than a woman, and I am thankful. I want to be ravaged. I want to feel another human being dominate me. I want to be made small and I want to feel the danger. She paws at me hungrily, never giving an inch. Ripping at my soul, she's an angel come down to liberate me. I can feel the blood trickle down my chest, like holy water down a child's forehead. A baptism.

Out of my mind with sexual delight, I pull down her dress to reveal two, perfect, little breasts.

She pulls back and strums her nipples with her fingers. 'Do you like them?'

Without saying a word I plunge my face into her chest and feverishly lap at her titties like a thirsty dog. She holds my head against her chest and swells with rapture. Her tits are firm, her nipples bitesize morsels that I nibble and chew. I am finally getting my 12-year-old, Catholic school girl.

I squeeze her thigh. She grabs my ass. The sexual frenzy is in full swinging order. She pinches my nipple then slides her hand down inside my pants. She plays with the tip of my dick – squeezing, rolling, tracing – so I feel like I have an erection at the end of my erection. Smoothly, she undoes my pants and my cock busts out like a jailbreak. Her hand reaches down to my balls, then to my ass. Gently, so I barely notice the penetration, she sticks a finger in my asshole. In and out she goes and before I know it it's two fingers. For the first time in my life, I'm getting fucked.

I spread my legs wide so she can really dig in. I feel my asshole being stretched in all directions. To sit back and get pounded is a wonderful thing. A woman knows what she's doing when she lies on her back and spreads her legs. The hole is being filled.

In soft contrast to the hard fingering, she licks lovingly at my neck. Lady California is a sexual master. She knows both ends of the spectrum – that sex is bittersweet music made of both pleasure and pain. There is nothing melodramatic about her. This is her natural state. Fingering me and licking my neck is all the purpose she needs in this world. I feel her push up into my anus toward my balls. A jolt flashes down my spine, my cock stands on end.

'You like that?' She asks.

I wipe the sweat and hair from her forehead. 'I love it, baby. I love whatever you do to me.'

With this she fingers harder and licks more furiously. I am hot and cold. Empty but full. I bite her nipple. I pull her dress down all the way to the belly button and lick her all the way down. I insert my tongue into her beautiful, little innie and swirl it all around, giving her a good cleaning. She coos with delight, and I am happy to please. I want to impress her, to make her feel good.

She catches my rim with a fingernail and I flinch. 'I'm so sorry,' she says and begins kissing me all over my face and gently padding around my anus.

'It's okay, baby. Even that felt good,' and I kiss her on the lips.

We lean back onto the floor, me on top of her. I slide my hand up along her thigh, squeezing and rubbing at the taut flesh. She strokes my dick masterfully. I kiss her lips and descend to her nipples. With one hand she pulls my shirt up to my head, and I pull it off. She claws at my back like an animal. I love that she is leaving her mark on me. I'll go shirtless for days so all can see what it is to make love to a real woman.

Our nipples rub up against each other. We grind, lick, pinch, and bite. I slide one hand under the small of her back and she arches up, letting her head tilt back in gorgeous relief. She's so light, so ethereal, that I'm afraid I might damage her. Yet the minute I slow my pace or soften my touch, she rakes my back with her fingernails and squeezes my cock so hard that I'm afraid it's going to burst out the head. She wants me to fuck the hell out of her. I am honored and lucky.

Kissing her lips, I slide my hand up into her crotch. Her groin is muscular with none of the usual flab. I slide my hand up further and into her stockings. I come to what feel like silk panties. I have no reservations, everything is action. What is, is . . . To hope for anything other than reality is to betray her. I must accept her in her maleness.

I reach down to her ass and pull the panties aside. With my index finger, I penetrate her asshole. She moans and shakes. Her asshole is her vagina, and to my surprise it is even wet. I've fucked women before in the ass. After a few minutes of good buttfucking, the colon secretes a clear liquid that's as good as any pussy juice. Her ass is one with her mind. I can't wait to have my dick inside of it.

I can't fuck her without acknowledging her, though, and Lord knows she'd let me. She would suck my dick without any thought of reciprocation, but I don't want that. I want to make love to her. I want her to know that I care about her. Nothing else will quench my thirst. Nothing else will be right.

I slowly slide my hand up to her genitals. There, where a sweet, tasty, pink vagina should be, are two little balls and a small cock. I hold the balls in my hand and can't help but think of when we were kids and would joke about kicking each other in the nuts – because that's what they are, little nuts. I move my hand up onto the shaft. It's a limp and lifeless cock, probably good only for pissing. With her tits as perfect and ripe as they are, it's obvious she's been on estrogen for a good long while. I play around with it, but really have no idea what to do – if I'm supposed to do anything. There are some issues here that I hadn't fully considered. I think deep down I was hoping she'd be like some kind of Barbie Doll with nothing but a smooth surface. I move back down to the balls and jiggle them around. I sense that to her the whole assemblage is not even part of her body, and that there's nothing for me to do with it that would please her sexually. I move back to her asshole. I can tell immediately that she's grateful. I insert three fingers and start pumping. She has both hands on my cock – one working the shaft and the other the balls. I'm hard as a rock, but somewhat detached.

To have part, that is not part. To be in a chronic state of self-denial. To be lost inside yourself . . .

If in addition to the daily specials of the American meat grinder, I had also to deal with issues of gender identity and transsexualism . . . Well, I doubt I'd make it. I need, for the both of us, to do this right.

I pull off her, grab the fifth of Jameson's and take a big pull.

Nervously, 'What's wrong?' I'm sure her past is full of last minute rejection. Not this time, though.

I hand her the bottle. 'Nothing, baby. I just want to slow down a little bit.' And as she swigs, I run my hand through her beautiful black hair to quell her fears.

'You're a fairytale princess,' I say.

She smiles and hands me back the bottle. I swig hard. 'You going to be here for a while?' I ask.

She looks hurt, worried. I immediately kiss her and give the nipple a little pinch. 'I just want to go to the bathroom and get a drink of water.'

She grabs for the bottle and I hand it to her. She takes a huge swig, and with whiskey on her sexy black lips says, 'I'll wait for you forever.'

I take back the bottle, take a good swig then pass it back. 'Hold onto this, baby. I'll be back in five minutes.' I give her a good passionate kiss, get up and walk out the door.

I notice, thankfully, that it's the only door in Rockets and Missiles without a window. When together, we are alone.

I run up the stairs, my mind reeling a hundred miles an hour like I'm on acid. There are a lot of people in the place tonight. Funny, on the one night where I'm totally occupied, the raver chicks show up en masse looking for action. The Yin and the Yang. The checks and balances that keep the whole karmic show on the road. I pass through a couple of cliques on the prowl and over to the Sado-Masochism aquarium, where a bunch of people are watching the show. The Master is whipping a hot blond with a shaved bush and unbelievable tits. Something deep inside tells me I shouldn't be watching a hot, straight, blond chick getting whipped. Too appealing to my hetero sensibilities. I might be led astray. But oh, how her jugs jiggle! Nevertheless, the voice moves me past the aquarium, past the spinning wheel room, to the only place I should be if I'm going to be away from Lady California: the juice bar, lair of Miss Nowhere.

'Miss Nowhere, how are you?'

'Sam!' She is cleaning the bar. 'It's good to see you. Sit down.'

'Don't mind if I do.'

There's no one in the bar. I was hoping that I might run into Quentin for a little wisdom but like he said, he was a one-shot deal. Unfortunate, more for me than for him.

'What is it going to be tonight, Sam?'

Damn, I left the whiskey with Lady California. 'Give me a cup of joe.'

Without a moment's hesitation she places a black coffee mug on the bar, then fills it with coffee. This evening, Miss Nowhere is wearing brown pants and a black turtleneck. 'You look great,' I say. 'Like Jack Kerouac's girl friend.'

'Oh stop it,' she blushes.

I sip my coffee. There's a silence between us, not awkward, but of anticipation. I put my coffee mug down on the bar and we open our mouths to talk at the same time.

'I'm sorry,' I say. 'Go ahead.'

'No,' she says. 'You talk.'

Time is of the essence. There is only one thing I would like to do better than talk to Miss Nowhere and she's waiting for me downstairs. Nonetheless, there is a reason for me being here. I need to clear something up, to come out the other side so I can go at things with a clear head. The last thing I want to do is fuck Lady California, then go curl up in my bed in Catholic guilt. I need to be of one mind.

I get straight to the point. 'You know I've been with Lady California downstairs tonight?'

Something in me tells me that she already knows. Still, she feigns ignorance. 'Really?' she says excitedly. 'That's great, Sam.'

'Yeah, well, it is, but . . .' Time to lay it on the line for Miss Nowhere. She can handle whatever it is I have to say. She'll trust me more if I give it to her straight, no holds barred. Finally, I see the decided advantage in hanging out with the queer and demented – you can say and be anything you want.

'. . . there's the issue here of gender,' I say. 'While Lady California is more woman than I've ever been with, she is still a man. She has a little penis and balls. I know, I had my hands on them. It was kind of strange, but it wasn't bad. It didn't freak me out or anything, but I guess in some ways it did, because I'm here and not there, right? The main thing is that I don't know what's expected of me. If I didn't care, it wouldn't be an issue. I'd just go down there, tell her to suck my dick, then be done with it. I want to be decent, though.' I take a good drink of coffee and put it back down on the bar. Miss Nowhere is listening affectionately. 'I guess the thing is that I feel like I'm doing the right thing in being with her, but I haven't felt that way in a long time. I don't want to sound like a cliché or a goddamned aftershave commercial, but the bottom line is that she makes me feel like a man.'

Miss Nowhere is smiling. I can't help but feel that she is somehow happy for me. I catch a glimpse of myself in the small mirror below the picture of Divine, and even in the darkness detect a certain glow. 'I'm not quite sure I know what the problem is,' she says in a way that indicates she knows exactly what the problem is, but wants me to figure it out for myself.

'The whole thing is about the approach to caring,' I say. 'If you are going to care, in general, I mean, then how do you go about directing yourself to caring? It's sort of a preparatory question, I guess. I mean, the bottom line is that it's easier not to care, than to care. That much is obvious, right? If you don't care, then you don't have to get involved, but if you do care, then you open yourself up to a whole host of complexities. The real question is, am I up to it? I mean, not only with her, but with the whole thing. The way I see it is, if I open myself up to her, then I'm opening myself up to the whole project. It's like women always wonder why men don't cry. It's because if they did, they would never stop. I want to be real. I want to be there with her when it happens. I know there are lessons to learn, and I want to learn them. If I'm going to open myself up, I need to do it with a pure heart. I'm not stupid. Lady California is significant. I want to make sure I get all there is to get out of it and come out on the positive end. I guess, in the end, it's about change.'

I pick up my coffee mug and drink coffee. Tough. Liberating, but tough.

She looks at me knowingly. She sips her coffee, raises an eyebrow, and asks, 'Have you ever tried speed?'

A weird, but nonetheless interesting question. 'Sure, a couple times.' More than a couple times. A college pal of mine had a solid connection through a security guard. All he had to do was call, and his guy would deliver top of the line crystal meth, anytime, anywhere. One time I stayed up for three days in a row. It was fucking heaven. 'What about it?'

She offers a coy smile. 'What may appear to be the abyss is often the promised land,' she says poetically. 'Now and then we just need that little push to get us there.'

Shit, I've been drinking since nine o'clock this morning, a little speed will do me good. 'I think speed is the push I need, Miss Nowhere. Do tell where I can pick some up?'

She reaches under the bar and produces a large zip lock bag full of bindles.

I murmur, 'You've got to be kidding me.'

She looks at me funny. 'How do you think we pay the rent around here, Sam? Ten bucks a head doesn't cut it, and they won't give a bunch of queers and transsexuals a liquor license.' She adds, 'This is how me make ends meet.'

I drink a toast to Rockets and Missiles resourcefulness. 'How much?'

She pulls out a bindle from the zip lock bag, seals it and places it back under the bar. 'Twenty dollars for a quarter.'

I look around to make sure no one is watching, fish out a twenty from my pocket, and quickly slide it over to her. In the same movement she slides me the bindle. I put it in my pocket.

'Now listen, Sam.'

'Yeah?' I'm excited. I haven't done any good drugs in a long time.

'This is really good speed,' she says soberly. 'Don't go snort the whole thing. A couple lines are good enough.'

Getting up from my stool, 'Okay. Will do.'

'I'm serious, Sam.' A look of tenderness comes over her pretty

Latina face. 'I don't want to see my favorite straight end up in the hospital.'

Standing, 'I wouldn't do that to my favorite tranny, Miss Nowhere.' And smile at her. I move to the door.

I hear her say, in a soft voice, 'Bye, Sam.'

I stop, turn, and face my friend. 'Ecce Homo, Miss Nowhere.'

Her face lights up. 'Ecce Homo, Sam.'

I mouth the words, 'Thank you,' turn my back, and depart.

I make a beeline to the bathroom, stopping for a brief moment to admire the blondy's jugs. Ah yes, how fine they are! I step into the bathroom and shut the door.

I am now in my own mini-disco. The wall is glistening, the strobe spinning, techno in the background, and speed in the pocket. I survey the bathroom for the necessary appliances. Surprisingly, for a place that sells speed, there are few tools. No matter how hard I try, the sink and the toilet stay moist – a death knell for speed. I need a dry surface. The stainless steel toilet paper dispenser is my best bet. It has a flat surface on top, and looks dry as a bone. I wipe it anyway, just to make sure.

I open the bindle: beautiful, yellow, parmesan cheese speed. I carefully place the bindle on the toilet paper dispenser, pull my wallet out of my back pocket, and extract my American Express Card. Don't leave home without it! I knock half the bindle out onto the dispenser, fold the rest up, and put it in my pocket. The speed is chunky. I need to cut it up. I don't have a razor blade, so I'm forced to resort to old trickery. I have a little bottle of Carmex lip balm, great not only for chapped lips, but for crunching up chunky speed. I carefully grind the speed down with the Carmex, making sure to scrape the residue off the lid with the American Express Card. Ground down to snortable form, I put the Carmex back in my pocket and with the American Express Card lay out three beefy lines. Satisfied, I exchange the American Express Card for a one-dollar bill. Roll it up, blow my nose, head down, snort hard . . .

Ahh! Christ almighty I forgot what a tough snort it is! Fucking burns like mad! Goddamn son of a bitch, makes me want to cut my fucking nose off. My nasal passages are on fire, like someone poured acid down them. Shit! It takes every bit of willpower not to sneeze. One blow and it would all be gone. I need to get it in deep, let the chemicals absorb into the blood. I go to the sink, turn the faucet and catch a little cold water in my cupped hand. I hold it up to my nose and snort. Ahhh . . . relief. I can feel the chemicals run down the back of my throat and into my body. My heart quickens, a warmth rises up from my feet. I lick my lips. Time to do it again.

Same process but this time it's easier. I splash a little water on my face to cool off. Things are getting hot, but righteous. I do this thing with my hand that my friends used to call 'the speed gauge'. Beginning with my pinkie finger I touch the middle of my palm. First my pinkie, then the ring, the middle, the index, and the thumb. The faster I go the better the speed is. Two lines and I'm already Eddie Van Halen.

I do half of the last line then give myself a nummie just for kicks. It tastes like shit, but I don't care. Someone knocks at the door.

'Just a second.'

I collect my things, splash my face with cold water again, straighten out my clothes, make a couple of weird facial expressions, then bolt out the door without looking to see who was waiting. Air. Fresh air for the lungs goddammit. Been a long time since I fucking breathed. I need a cigarette.

Down the stairs, bopbopbopbopbopbopbop . . . Everything has a good beat to it. Bopbopbopbopbopbop. 'Yo, hey,' to a good looking raver girl. Bopbopbopwowowow . . . A little reverb action. Distances. *Images*, by Tyrone Green. That old Eddie Murphy shit is hilarious. Kill my landlord, kill my landlord. Really smart. Really witty. What this place needs is an enema! Great line. Can't remember what movie it's in, but a great line. Coke machine. Could use a whiskey. I hate Jack and Cokes. Had a girlfriend who used to drink them, thought they made her look cool. They made her fat is what they did. No never mind. Anybody can be as fat as they want.

Get me that whiskey now, and a cigarette si vous plait. Ya ya ya. You quiero un cigarette, maricone. Ay, lo siento. No maricone es tranvestacion! Gotcha, gotcha gotcha gotcha gotcha gotcha good. To die unsung would really bring you down, although wet eyes would never suit you. Helmet. Good fucking band. I wonder whatever happened to them? New York City, baby. All the way. Always loved New York. Energy, action, the whole shebang. Gotta get me some. Dive into the scene like the days of old. Tripping acid in Times Square. I can feel my heart pounding. Racer X, mother-fucker. Bed Stuy, do or die. We didn't land on Plymouth Rock, Plymouth Rock landed on us. Malcolm X, real cool guy. Always preferred him to MLK. Nice glasses, good looking. Too bad he got shot, he would have made a great sports agent. The lunatic is on the grass . . . Got to try that Pink Floyd, Wizard of Oz shit. On the third roar of the lion they say start it. Perfect for Home Theater Entertainment Center. I need a cigarette. Got to get me my whiskey. Jameson's . . . Irish . . . Blended . . . Right on!

'Hey, baby. What's going on?' My beautiful Lady California still waiting for me on the floor. She hands me the bottle without me having to say a word. I gulp it. The juice of life runs down my chin, I lap it up with my tongue.

'You don't have a cigarette, do you baby?'

She gets up and goes over to her purse. She is a heaven whore, God's bitch. She gets two cigarettes and hands me one, filtered. With a silver zippo she lights me, then her. I take a drag, then take it out of my mouth and break off the filter. She looks at me like I'm strange. 'Need it strong, baby. Big things happening, big things.'

She sits back down on the floor, but I'm more comfortable standing up and walking around the room. 'I saw Miss Nowhere up there, good lady, damn good lady. Reminds me of this girl I used to know in the seventh grade, can't remember her name, though. Maybe it was Tish. Yeah, that's it, Tish. Did I ever tell you about the time we won the City Championship? Oh yeah, I already did. Sorry. It was really cool, though. Really cool. So what's up with you? Anything go down since I been gone? I mean, you know, any kind of action or anything or has it pretty much been the status quo around here?'

She nods her head, smiling.

'You're fucking beautiful, you look like an English Princess, did I ever tell you that? Yeah, what are you anyway, Slavic or something? You have that look. I was in Prague for awhile. It was cool. Lot of action there. People were alive. Velvet Revolution, The Wall came down, Slovakia took off, the whole thing. I mean, hard to explain, one of those things where you really had to be there. You ever been to Europe?'

She shakes her head. I think she might be laughing, but I'm not sure.

'Europe is pretty fucking intense. I mean, you know, when I was over there, it was all hash and partying, those people go on forever. I mean, you know, you don't eat dinner there 'til like ten o'clock, so you have this like full stomach and all this energy into the wee hours. I mean, you know, it's like, you don't even really start partying until like three o'clock in the morning. And I mean, you know, shit, the sex is everywhere and it's pretty fucking good. Weird, you know, I mean, I used to go to this Reggae bar in Prague and smoke hash for like ten hours straight. I met this girl there, though, who uh, kind of looks a lot like you. Yeah, I mean really fucking beautiful, fucking Czech chick. Might as well have been Paulina Porizkova, she was so fucking hot. Just like you, baby, just like you. Except you're better. Yeah, no shit, better, like more interesting and dynamic. That's the word, dynamic. Anyway this chick came over to me, and asked if I wanted to smoke some hash with her and I was like, sure, whatever you want to do. I mean, you know, she was so hot I would have done anything. So I go back over to her table with her – you can smoke right there at the tables – and we had this killer fucking stoner session. She was actually, like, while she was smoking, rubbing her leg against my thigh, so I was good to go and ready. She asked me if I wanted to go to the bathroom. Kind of weird, really. I mean, like, I did sort of need to go, but of course I'm thinking that we're going there to do some fucking, you know, like get it on and fuck. So we go back there – all the bathrooms in the bars in Prague are unisex, which is really kind of cool – and we start kissing and shit. But then she stops, goes over to the toilet, pulls her dress up, and starts taking a fucking dump. Fucking actually taking a dump right there in front of me! I mean stink bombs and everything! So I said, fuck it, when in Rome, whatever . . . I sat across from her, like only ten feet away so we were staring at each other, and let it all fucking go. I mean I was farting, squirting, whatever. I didn't give a shit. So there it is, me and the hottest chick on the planet, staring at each other taking a crap. I mean, you know, it was liberating, but pretty fucking heavy at the same time.' I take a long drag of my smoke then a huge pull. 'Fucking weirded out shit, man. Sometimes life is a fucking trip.' Another drag and slug of whiskey. I can feel small bits of tobacco being washed down my gullet. Right on.

Lady California gets up off the floor, comes over to me, gets down on her knees and starts undoing my pants. I take a huge pull of the Jamesons. 'You ready to get something going, Lady Cal? 'Cause I'm ready. I'm ready to do this like a fucking champ!'

She pulls my pants down to my knees and takes my cock into her mouth without touching it with her hands. She glides my cock deep into her mouth. Back and forth, back and forth. I take a drag of my cigarette. 'Come on, baby. Suck it good. You know I love you, baby. Treat me right, suck it like you love it. Give it all to me. Die for it, praise it. Take it deep. That's right, you're my girl. Lay it on the line. Oh yeah. That's my girl.'

Her mouth is a moving vagina. Socrates, Plato, they knew what they were doing when they diddled each other. Eudamonia. Evkareesto. Antigone. Elektra. What is the good? Get them in the corner and pepper them with questions. The state of Athens will wait for us no longer. Amen, little sister, let's ride . . .

Drag of the cig, slug of whiskey. Drag of the cig, slug of whiskey. Change it up. Drag of whiskey, slug of the cig. Ahh . . .

This is fucking heaven. This is the goddamn way everything should always be.

Going off on the shaft. Mouth of fury, quickening pace. Must hold out, strive, like Captain Kirk. Must ... Hold ... Out ... Can ... Not ... Cum ... Yet ... Be strong, brother Sam. Fight the universal drive to blast home a load in the name of God. Must think of something. Must ... Think ... Of ... Some ... Thing ... To ... Keep ... Me ... From ... Cumming ... Reach deep into the psychological store room. Come up with a doozy. Mom taking a crap! No! Jesus Christ getting nailed up on the cross! Nay! Nein! Nyet! Make up a bunch of German: fassglunten verkshlinkt verboten achtung von streesen nachten. Ya Ya Ya! Ramboosh Ramboosh Ramboosh. Prayer: Hail Mary full of grace the lord is with thee blessed art thou amongst women and blessed is the fruit of thy womb Jesus Holy Mary mother of God pray for us sinners now and the hour of our death Amen. The Virgin Mary sucking on my cock, no! Not a good thought used to jack off to her in the pews back in the Altar Boy days. Something horrible, something really really bad, like a concentration camp. No go! All those naked Jewish ladies with big hairy bushes and boobs. Death, I need death. Mass grave slaughter headless torsos eating sandwiches! Swig of the whiskey. Puff of the smoke, nothing is flying. I can't see anything but the hottest woman on the face of the earth giving me the blow job of the apocalypse. Oh Christ Almighty think of something! Slow it down, slow it down in your head. Come on come on come on come on come on, baby. Think, yeah, that's right. Life is meaningless, a horrible endeavor. No it's not! This is the suckfest extravaganza el capitan de numero uno. I can't hack it. It's too fucking good. Praise to Allah the magnificent, the benevolent, the powerful, the omnipotent, the loving. Praise to all God's firmament. The rats, the cats, the bacteria, the mountains, cars, trucks, mini-vans, Elvis Presley, computers, key rings, life-giving affirmations and new-age sentimentality. I am thankful for being born. Son of a bitch! We are united in the greatest cause of all humanity! Peace and Love! Save the planet! Bring home the bacon. God bless the United States of America. Liberté! Egalité! Fraternité! Eli Eli Lama Sabacthani – No More! Hallelujah. Hallelujah!

'Lady California!' and pull her head away from my cock. 'Time now for the unification of all that's good. Rise up, pull those stockings down, and put your hands against the wall. Daddy's home!'

She does so immediately, spiritually. Her hands against the wall, I waddle over.

Her ass is the ass of all asses. Perfection. Her balls hang like jewels between her thin, muscular legs. I stick my head into her balls, cup them in my mouth and teabag my way into the history books. Sainthood is in the dirt. Life is in the nuts. They taste like Chanel Number Five. The butt juice pours down my forehead, wiping my conscience clean. I step back, cock in hand. Time for the road less traveled.

She reaches back and spreads her tight ass cheeks apart for me. The red eye is the third eye. It calls to my soul. Penetrate and go to the whole, like Allen Iverson on the crossover dribble. Dunk it. Ahh . . . Shalang sholock. Permanent virginity. The 12-year-old pussy of the heavens. The asshole of Lady California!

Her hands on the wall, my hands on her hips, slamming it like a god. Bam bam bam. The Championship Season, the fights, the glory, the nail biters and the hangers hanging on. The superlative effort given for nothing but the game. Fucking beautiful incandescent lights that shine onto the ocean in a benediction. Guide the sailors home. Make it all right for the outcasts. The symphony of the rejects, the purlieus of the twisted architects. The world shines out in its worlding. Bam bam bam. Her moans sing the songs of the ancients. Music is sex. I shall be telling this with a sigh: two roads diverged in a wood and I, I took the one less traveled by, and that has made all the difference. Self-created self-delusional self-fulfilled, writhing flying fearless into the valley of the shadow of death. I'm losing my soul into her. Heaven on earth. Shake the rafters the firmament contorts blissfully in a holy rolling goddamned Christian existential apocalyptic vision. Angels are at the back door. The devil is at the front. Somebody's knocking, should I let 'em in? Lord it's the devil, would you look at him. I don't come no more bringing no more nothing. Life. Kiss it. Chant it out loud brothers and sisters. Chant Life! L I F E L I F E L I F E. International house of pancakes. I H O P I H O P I H O P I H O P. Sacrilege, Monadism, tattooed butt piercings, scarification of anal suffering and miasma. Give me some fruit substance to replace my juices I'm sweating like a pig. My cock has taken off on me, loss of control, mayday mayday we're going down here, we need some help desperately. Das Boot is the greatest movie ever. Jurgen Prochnow Jurgen Prochnow. I want to be a Ramone. Vitamin E. Blood out of the sphincter. Shit projections, legs quivering, the meat conception is upon us in full goddamned force. I can feel it coming! Hoover dam, *Cadillac Desert*. The west was made by Mulholland. Rape the countryside. Build a metropolis. Get the president. There's a crack in the dam. The universe is expanding. Carl Sagan is dead. Bring on the Marines, the Peace Corp, the Caterers. Send lawyers guns and money, the time has come to die! Into the valley of death rode the six hundred.

I pull out my shit covered dick, fall back on my ass, and blow a prayer that lands on my face. Clean. Maybe even holy.

Chapter Eight

CALL IT MAKING peace or a general disenchantment through perverted self-empowerment, but the confines in which I spend my professional life have become less meaningful. The kitten poster? Fuck it, line the walls with action shots of kittens chasing twine. The cheap desk? Give me a TV tray on which to do my work. The laptop? An old Smith Corona will do just fine. It's not that I'm ready to quit this job and follow whatever the new version of the Grateful Dead might be, but recent events have conspired to rid me of certain concerns.

Ironically, I am now at the pinnacle of all that is holy in the world of public relations. I have a laptop with a Pentium Processor that can compute pi to 299 million digits in eight one-trillionths of a second. I have a new $900 desk from *The Office Elite* – a designer office and furniture supply store catering to executives. The desk is ergonomically designed to reduce all physical ailments associated with long-term use of the computer. I have a new trash can, a magnetic paper clip holder, and a top-of-the-line stapler with a simulated wood finish. In addition to the kittens poster, there is now a framed, blown up, satellite photograph of the United States of America with the Liberty Telecomm International logo across the top. They have Bisselled the carpet repeatedly and placed an Ozark water cooler outside my office door. Reception, once sadly comprised of three chairs and four issues of *Field and Stream*, is now a jewel of a lounge, featuring five leather chairs, a courtesy telephone, and the most recent editions of the *Wall Street Journal* and *Asian Business Weekly*. Dina has never been so happy or looked so fine. I'm not sure, but I think Tom has okayed her a petty cash allowance to buy new dresses.

None of these improvements would have been made if it weren't for the long-anticipated orgasm whose time has finally come. Yes, today is the day I interview the President of Liberty Telecomm International.

The man is a flag-waving Christian of the highest order. He has given more than 4 million dollars to various and sundry groups of the Christian Right. He has been on government-funded junkets to Third World in search of war zones and cheap labor. He has farted on the *Communist Manifesto* and wiped his ass with a photo of Lenin. He thinks Oliver North is a saint and Fidel Castro is the antichrist. Watergate, of course, is an overblown sham perpetrated on the American people by the liberal media.

Dick has peered in six times in the last eight minutes. Dina spent three hours last night at a salon getting her hair and nails done. Tom is a wreck. He's wearing a new suit that's at least two sizes too big. He's in the reception area with Dina, disinfecting the telephones.

The hullabaloo of greatness is finally down the hall. He has arrived. I can hear Tom's palms sweating and Dick's nuts shriveling into his stomach. I've made the effort to look sharp. I went to the local suit outlet and scored a brown Armani for three hundred dollars. The inside lining is ripped, but who cares, no one can see it. I am shaved to the best of my ability and smelling of designer cologne. My hands are clean, my eyes are white, my ears Q-tipped. I know all there is to know about this president of ours. I am thoroughly unimpressed. It turns out that he's a man like the rest of us. God forbid.

A small herd of elephants rumbles toward my office. I sit alone, in my chair, facing the door. There are times in life when a sense of importance fills the air like thick, choking incense. For me at least, this isn't one of them. Tom shows up at my door, flush, full of excitement. He mouths, 'He's here!' I continue to sit. A look of sheer panic comes over his face as though my continued sitting is the embodiment of all his fears in regard my behavior in the presence of this great man. To quell him, to rid myself of his face, I stand.

He opens the door and announces, 'Sam, meet the President and founder of Liberty Telecomm International.'

I offer my hand to the man. 'It is a pleasure to meet you sir.'

He ignores my outstretched hand, turns and whispers something to Tom. Tom immediately ushers everyone back to work and closes the door behind him. The president turns to me, offers a perfunctory but stern handshake, then takes a seat in the English leather chair that was delivered to my office this morning for his arrival. I suspect that upon his departure it will find its way into Tom's office.

He doesn't say a word, but surveys the office like a drill sergeant inspecting the barracks.

I take my seat and again try to make contact. 'How was your trip, sir?'

He focuses his attention on me, not so much as an individual, but as part of the decor requiring inspection. I get the feeling that the kittens are okay, but as far I'm concerned, the verdict is still out.

'Productive.' And continues his survey of the barracks.

The impression I got from his photos is of a very clean-looking man. Now that I see him in person, though, the concept that comes to mind is much more severe: antiseptic. There is not a piece of lint on him, nor a whisker in evidence. His hairline is receded, but the hair that he does possess is thick, full, and conservatively arranged. His eyes, nose and mouth are exactly where they are supposed to be. As far as I can tell, he has no pores. Men of wealth have a certain language in their dress. Arch-conservative, except for the one accessory that speaks money. On his wrist, peeking out from his dark blue suit, is a gold, diamond studded Rolex. On his finger is a gold wedding ring.

He reaches into his pocket, takes out a black glasses case and removes a pair of gold, wire-rimmed glasses. He carefully puts them on and returns the case to his coat pocket. He continues to inspect my office. I am uncomfortable with this man, as I would be in the presence of an android.

Finally, after another minute of inspecting, he addresses me, 'Where's your flag?' His voice is higher than I thought it might be.

'I'm sorry?'

'Didn't you get the memo? I had a memo sent out. You didn't receive it?' An accusing tone exists not only in his voice, but in his demeanor. To be in his presence, is to be berated.

'I don't know about any memo, sir.' I try to stay as calm as possible, this isn't getting off on the right foot.

'I sent out a memo stating that small flags be put on desks in the offices. Did you not receive one, or have you ignored it?'

I thought that he would show up here enthusiastically, happy to have a young, rising star immortalize him. I think, maybe, I even had ideas about us hitting it off and starting up an acquaintance. Didn't Tom say that he read the George Johnker's bio and loved it?

'I'm sorry, sir, but I really don't know what you're referring to, and I can guarantee you that, if I had received a memo from your office concerning decor, I would have followed it to the letter.'

He's glaring at me, trying to intimidate. 'I know for certain that a memo was distributed to management concerning flags in the offices. Specifically, it referred to those people in high-profile positions.'

In light of his attempts to intimidate me, I can't help but give him some intentional stupidity. 'Now as far as flags, you're referring to, like, the United States of America flag?'

He looks at me like I'm the stupidest man on the planet. 'Yes, the American flag.'

He continues to try and stare me down. Accordingly, I have never found it so important to maintain eye contact in my life. There is a war going on here. Before we can do one ounce of business, he needs to know that I am cowed. This guy has no comprehension of equality, because everyone he knows works for him. He is surrounded by sycophants. His view of the world is skewed. To him, human relations are comprised of money, order, and maybe a little tennis where everyone lets him win.

I'm not so sure I want to let him win, though. I don't want to jeopardize any sort of integrity that I might have dredged up in the last couple weeks. I've made a small, but nonetheless significant realization, that my thoughts aren't worth a shit unless I act on them.

'I didn't receive the memo, sir,' I say strongly, 'because my position is not considerd a high-profile one within Liberty Telecomm.'

'I'm here, aren't I?' he says abruptly.

'Pardon me?'

'If I am here,' he says, 'then you are obviously thought of as holding a high-profile position within this corporation.'

If anyone else were to say this I might think of it as a compliment. Coming from this guy it's more an indictment of my intelligence.

This little stare of his is starting to get on my nerves. 'Sir,' I say, looking him directly in the eye. 'All I can say is that I didn't receive the memo.'

'And so that's that,' he says in a mocking tone.

'What else would it be?'

The fact that I haven't backed down seems to have invigorated him. I don't get turned on by turning him on, though. I don't want to be the source of any entertainment for this man. I don't want him feeling me out. I don't want him judging me. I don't want him questioning me at all unless it has something to do specifically with the job at hand.

He asks, with a wicked little grin on his antiseptic face, 'Why would an employee of a company that takes a proactive role in the economic development of this nation, and is well-known to anyone associated with it as actively Pro-American, not take the initiative and show pride in his corporation and therefore his country by having a flag in his office?'

'It wouldn't make sense, sir,' I say gently but firmly, 'for me to have a flag in my office.'

'Why is that?' he asks angrily.

'Well,' I say as I lean back in my chair in a display of confidence, 'I don't have a flag hanging in my home, so it wouldn't make sense that I would have one here.' I actually do have a flag in my home, the Jasper Johns. Still, it doesn't seem to count as the kind of flag he's talking about. Interesting, it gives me a kind of insight on it.

A menacing look comes over his face. 'I'm deeply concerned . . .' He's not concerned in the least. I could right now impale myself on a paper clip and it wouldn't phase him. 'I'm wondering why a good American wouldn't have a flag in his home.' He switches to the innocent look thing, as though he simply doesn't get it, when in actuality he's judging the hell out of me. 'How do you perfom your duty on national holidays? You must borrow one or something.'

This guy is a prick royale. Douche bag extravaganza number nine. I'd like to rip into his guts and tear him apart verbally, but it won't do me any good in the short or long term. I can defend myself, but to attack is suicide. The best thing I can do is focus on the biography.

'No sir. I don't have a flag and don't borrow one on national holidays. I live in an apartment, you see, and there's really no place for me to fly it.' I put my hands on the keyboard. 'I know that you are a truly busy man, sir. I don't want to keep you any longer than I have to.' And smile eagerly like an idiot.

'I am indeed a busy man,' he says pompously. 'But I'm not so busy that I don't have time to know the mind of a person who's working for me.'

Hands off the keys. 'From what I understand, sir, you read the piece I did on George Johnkers. What else could there be about me that would be of any interest to you, besides my writing and profiling abilities?'

'There is a quite a bit,' he says in righteous response to my question, 'that is of interest to me. I make it a rule to know who's working for me at all times. No surprises,' he gloats. 'That's why I'm president of this corporation.' He is the sort of man who, when saying good things about himself, is through negation saying bad things about you. 'And now my interests are especially piqued, because you have a flag neither in your office nor in your home.'

I flash on that shithead Joe McCarthy interrogating Hollywood directors:

'Are you now, or have you ever been, a Communist, Mr Sam?'

'No sir, I am not now nor have I ever been a member of the Communist Party.'

'Then tell me, Mr Sam. How do you explain: THE DEMONS!'

The Demons were what me and my pals called ourselves back in the glory days when I landed in the hospital trying to jump my bike in the ditch. One of the things we used to do was get all of our money together (never more than three bucks), then go buy candy and Spaghettios. A fine example of Communism if there ever was one. Back in the McCarthy days, it would have been enough to get me blackballed.

I direct myself to the Joe McCarthy sitting here in front of me. 'I don't have a flag, sir, but that fact has no bearing on the job that I do.'

'Does it not?' he mocks.

'No, it doesn't,' I say sincerely.

'I think it does,' he says arrogantly. 'I am allowing you to write my biography. In so doing I am compelled to elucidate certain intimate facts about myself. You may or may not care, but I am a man who is proud to be an American. I fought for this nation in Vietnam and am fighting for it now on the economic front. I therefore have a real problem divulging my private life to a person whom I can't necessarily trust as being part of the same fold as I.'

I read about this asshole and what he did in Vietnam. His old man, a rich son of a bitch from whom he inherited most of his money, set him up in Saigon in the Army's accounting office. He was there for two years balancing books and never saw a moment of action. He probably never even got a fucking whore.

'Sir, whether or not we are part of the same fold, I can't say. But I can say that not having a flag has no bearing on my performance as a public relations specialist.'

He scoffs at 'public relations specialist.' I shouldn't have said it, but what else do I call it? They're the ones who gave me the title, and I'm sure as hell not a writer. Typical, they give me the title, and once I adopt it they laugh at me. It's all about making me feel small. Once they have you feeling small, they can do what they want with you.

He condescendingly chews his germ-free cud. If I show up at the gates of heaven and anybody gives me a look even remotely resembling the judgmental bullshit on this prick's face, I'll catch the first Japanese bullet train to hell.

He repeats, 'Why don't you have a flag?' I get the feeling that this is somehow cute to him. That his only real joy in life is to see people squirm.

'Sir,' I say cautiously, 'with all due respect, I don't see where that's any of your business.'

This invokes his ire. As far as he's concerned, anything even remotely associated with Liberty Telecomm is not only his business, but his property as well. Back in the Middle Ages, landowners would invoke their right to sleep with the serf's newlywed bride.

'You're in no position,' he says angrily, 'to tell me what my business is or isn't. You see, whatever I choose to make my business, in regard to this corporation, is my business. It's called being the Chief Executive Officer.'

No, what it's called is being an asshole. You are a caricature of a human being. Monkeys relate to each other better than this. Elephants mourn their dead, amoebas bond in a common form.

I have often wondered who perpetrates history's horrible shit. Who were the main torturers in the Khmer Rouge? Who were the Dutch slave traders? What was going on in Josef Mengele's head?

What was up Stalin's ass to make him such a genocidal freak? And concerning the average Joe, what is his major malfunction? What made the average German go from baker to homicidal maniac in the span of a couple years?

I don't put myself above any of it, but in our esteemed and beloved president, I see the sort of man who would have traded in his suit and tie for a can of Zyklon B.

'I understand what it is to be the Chief Executive Officer,' I say. 'I know that it is an incredibly demanding position and that you do a very good job. What surprises me is that a man of your rank would have any interest in whether or not a person in my position has a flag or not.' I hope this piece of flattery derails him.

It doesn't. He is more angry and serious than ever before, 'I don't need you to lionize my position,' he says. 'I know what my position is. Now I've asked you a question.'

Enough. 'And what is it?'

'Why don't you have a flag?'

'To be honest with you, it's a question that I've never really considered,' I say philosophically.

The wicked grin returned to his face. 'Let's consider it then.'

I lean back in my chair and exhale. 'I hadn't considered it,' I say at a leisurely pace, 'because I had never put that much emphasis on the flag. Sure, it's our national symbol and all of that, but if a person wants to honor their country, there are a million ways to do it. This is a free democracy, sir, and as far as I'm concerned the only true way to celebrate it is to be free.'

On the attack: 'So you don't believe in laws?' Dumb question. He is obviously unequipped to handle any sort of intelligent challenge – much like Johnkers.

'I believe in laws, because I believe man is in need of regulation,' I say. 'If man were born good and perfect, we wouldn't require laws. We would be existing in a utopia. However, since man is inherently flawed and prone to all sorts of weird permutations, then yes, we need law to maintain the fundamental order of society.'

I was on a plane once going to Vegas. There was an old man

staring at me like I was the most vile piece of shit on the planet. I didn't take it personally. I thought it was funny. Some old folks are just in over their heads when it comes to dealing with society. It's a matter of pure overload. The modern world is too much. They think everyone's against them, or at least making fun of them in some subtle way that they can't quite pick up on.

The stewardess was walking up the aisle handing out peanuts. I knew what was coming and it took all I had not to burst out laughing in blissful anticipation of the debacle. She got to our row and in the most polite voice asked, 'Would you like a bag of peanuts, sir?' The startled old fart goes, 'What!' She asks again, holding out the basket in front of his face: 'Would you like one or two bags of peanuts, sir?' The old geezer, utterly lost and confused in this world, started yelling, 'Peanuts! Peanuts! Peanuts!'

The President here is on the mentally sharp side of the same sort of paranoia. For him to be challenged is to be attacked.

'What is this about man not being born good and perfect!' He says in panicky indignation – as though I'm saying he's the one who's not good and perfect.

'Well,' I reply, 'I think it's fairly obvious that man comes into this world an unknown commodity. Otherwise, like I said, sir. We wouldn't need the amount of regulation that we do.'

'So you think man is evil.'

'I didn't say that.'

'But you do,' he imputes, 'think that man isn't born good.'

'Yes sir, you can say that.'

A sneaky look comes over his face, 'In the Bible it says that Adam was created in the image of God . . . You do believe in God, don't you?'

The whole process of my existence involves people putting me in corners and forcing me either to shit on the few drops of integrity I have left, or to tell the truth and be vilified.

'To believe in life,' I say like a sage, 'one must believe in God.'

Safe. There is no way in hell this guy's going to ask me if

I believe in life. It's a concept that's beyond him, like buttfucking a transvestite.

'That's good to know. I was concerned for a moment in regard to your religious beliefs. I wouldn't want a godless man prying into my life.' He pauses, only to come up with his next line of attack. 'But if man is created in God's image, then why isn't he inherently good?'

I saw this one coming a mile away. 'We must not forget, sir, that god imbued mankind with free will. It was his greatest gift to us,' I say with a smile.

Got him. There is no being Christian and disputing the whole free will thing. They teach it in Sunday school, it's how the church explains the evil in the world: why do bad things happen? asks little Sunday school boy. The 38-year-old, virgin, Sunday school teacher replies, 'Because God gave us free will and some bad people use it for evil.' Translation: blame everything bad on man, everything good on God.

It figures that the President of Liberty Telecomm would end up being a prick and not a guy I could connect with. I have sex with Lady California, start feeling relatively decent about things, and someone or something has to come along and ruin it. I remember when I got straight A's for the first time in the fourth grade. A fifth grade kid named David Silva beat the shit out of me in front of everyone. In college I wrote a short story that was accepted for publication in the English Department's somewhat prestigious literary review. At the last minute, due to lack of funds, they canceled the review and gave me back my piece. I was so pissed off I threw it in the trash.

The world has a way of keeping people in check. Too many little victories and an alarm goes off in the universe. They send you guys like the president.

'Free will is indeed one of the Lord's most wondrous gifts to mankind,' he says as though he's the one who thought of it. 'That being what it is,' he says haughtily, 'we are put into a position of having to direct mankind to the way of the Lord. Put him back on track, as it were. This nation, the United States of America, is mankind's greatest hope insofar as realizing the godlike potential that's within us.' He pauses, 'We are, after all, God's country.'

Some dipshit in Iran is probably saying the exact same thing right now about his godforsaken nation.

He continues. 'God has a plan for mankind. The plan consists of evolving man toward greater freedom. It is only through greater freedom that man can accept responsibility for himself. And it is only through accepting responsibility for himself that he can come to sit at the right hand of God. God is about responsibility. God is about taking charge of our lives and our own destiny. The United States of America, more than any nation in the history of the world, seeks to imbue its people with the freedom necessary to foster the God in all of us. There are indeed people in our government who would seek to limit our freedoms, who would seek to make us dependent upon them and therefore ungodlike in our weakened state. This is why welfare and lack of patriotism are the greatest evils we face.'

Any asshole who formulates his politics on the existence of God needs to be shot. Any asshole who justifies eliminating welfare on the basis of America being God's country needs to be handed over to the Yakuza with a letter of introduction that reads, 'FUCK YOU MR MOTO.'

I've been in this conversation before. There's no winning it. Every college monkey goes through a Communist phase, and I was no different. I used to pounce on my business professors and argue the Marxist critique of a Capitalist society 'til the cows came home. They of course countered with Smith and historical evidence showing Communism to have failed miserably. With an intelligent partner, it's a great argument and a fine way to spend an afternoon. With the president of the company I work for, though, it's probably not the best way to go about things.

When there's no escaping or winning an argument, cleverness must come to the fore. There's no such thing as losing an argument if your intention isn't to win it. Undetected sarcasm is like fucking

a date after she's passed out. It might be immoral, or even lame –
but it's still fucking.

'Sir,' I say as though H.R. Haldeman to my own personal
Nixon, 'are you implying that welfare in it's current form is an
immoral state of affairs meant to curtail the advancement of the
American race as enabled by the more enlightened policies of our
government?'

'Yes I am,' he says, registering a slight bit of surprise. 'Welfare
can only hold us back.'

'So am I also correct in assuming, sir,' I say with the utmost
earnestness, 'that you consider all other social programs that
profess to aid the so-called disenfranchised of this nation as
little more than conspiratorial efforts to hinder the evolution
of the American people – the only race of mankind uniquely
and magnanimously empowered by its government to lead the
evolution of human kind?'

The android is getting excited, 'Yes, that is exactly what
I'm saying.'

'Then sir,' I say passionately, 'may I be so bold as to expound
upon your most advanced theories and say that the liberal factions
of our government are not – as they proclaim to be – upholders
of our freedom and the voice of the American people? In actuality,
they are a repressive force whose only intention is to weaken
us through their policies by making us descend to the level of
the lowest common denominator. And not, as they ought to be,
forcing those lowest common denominators to ascend to their God-
given potentials as embodied in our more enlightened, conservative
representatives, and if I may be so bold, in men like yourself.'

His gold-framed eyes are saucers. He gleams like a misunder-
stood genius finally recognized. 'I would say, unabashedly, that
you have captured the essence of my argument.'

'Sir,' I say most determinedly, 'then we are co-revolutionaries,
luminaries if you will . . .'

He has the strange look of a man who is at once surprised,
saddened, happy, fulfilled, and empty.

'I had no idea that you thought these things,' he says.

'Sir,' I say with overkill respect, which of course he views as sincere, 'there is no thinking involved here. This is merely statement of fact. The current state of America is a dire one. It is a battleground between the righteous and the godless, between the perverts and the holy, between those who would spit on our way of life and those who would die to maintain it.' I pause and lean forward on my desk. 'You are a patriot are you not sir?'

He nods his head vigorously. I'm enjoying this more than I should.

'What, sir – if I may be so bold as to inquire – is it to be a patriot in what our liberal rivals would refer to as "contemporary America"?'

He rolls his head back and scoffs aloud in disgust. 'You ask me what it is to be a patriot?'

'I do indeed, sir.'

'I'll tell you one thing for certain, Sam. It certainly has nothing to do with being contemporary or post-modern!' he exclaims, punching his hand with his fist.

'Pardon my language, sir,' I seethe, 'but you're damned right.'

He holds his hands out to signify that he is about to begin his soliloquy on patriotism. If I had a video camera, I'd tape him and play it on one of the TVs at Rockets and Missiles. I'd be the hit of the queers.

'This is a question that I've been asked before, Sam,' he says officiously. 'And I must say that I enjoy answering it. For to be a patriot, one must publicly love his nation. It must seem to you as though I am stating the obvious, but I am not. This is a time when men are fickle in their affections. One moment they claim to be Americans, and the next moment they desecrate the flag. Their love of the United States of America is dependent upon their current state. If they are doing well, if they can buy their wife a new dress or their child a new toy, then the United States is the greatest nation on the face of the earth. On the other side of the coin, if they are unemployed or if their wife has left them, then without a second thought they turn their backs and decry this great nation. A patriot is a man who loves his country through thick and thin, Sam. He is a man who stands by his nation as did Job with his Hebrew god. A patriot upholds what it is to be an American!' He again slams his fist into his hand. 'America does not change, but a capriciousness has infected the hearts and minds of its people. The qualifications for patriotism are the same as they were in 1780. The uniform unchangeability to which I'm referring is the work ethic and the corresponding morality that has made this country great.

'You see, Sam, Americans are a simple people. We go to work, we go to church, we play with our children, and we save for our future. We need nothing more! When we try to make our lives complex, we suffer, and our nation suffers.' A look of sadness comes over him, but he quickly rights himself. 'To be a patriot is to connect to the traditional American values as adduced by our forefathers and then, most importantly, to live by them every day! Each of us has our place in society. A ditch digger can't do my job any more than I can do a ditch digger's job. It's a man's duty to strive, but he must strive within his place. God created the laws of nature, and those immutable laws say that some men are leaders and some are followers.' He clenches his jaw decisively so as to leave no doubt as to which group he is a member. 'When our forefathers constructed the framework for this great nation, they set forth to create a society where great men would rise up to lead the weaker. I believe that to be a patriot is to the love the natural order that is America. For we are the most natural nation in the history of mankind – and God has willed it so.'

He leans forward and speaks in a more hushed, but nonetheless authoritative tone. 'I probably shouldn't use this as an example, Sam. But I was watching television the other night when I came across a documentary on the Mafia. Now, of course, I am totally against everything the Mafia stands for, but I could not help but appreciate one aspect of their organization . . . The reason they were able to remain so successful for so long was that their chain of command was never questioned. Mafia ways have been passed down from generation to generation, and to question those ways, or anyone above you in the chain of command, means certain death. America has only gotten in trouble, Sam, when it has questioned those in authority who protect our traditional American values. Richard Nixon was a great president who represented all that is good and God-fearing in America. A small group of infidels questioned his judgment – and where did it get us? Ultimately to Jimmy Carter, a man responsible for our humiliation at the feet of the maniacal Arabs, not to mention an inflation rate of 19 percent and the near economic collapse of this nation. That's what happens when we question, Sam. That's what happens when we lose sight of American morality, belief in God, social structure, and the work ethic.' Finished, he leans back again in his big chair.

I wish I had the courage to stand before him and bust a nut. To critique, theorize, pontificate, and expound. All I want is five minutes of sheer, unadulterated bravery.

'So you're saying, then,' I say fervidly, 'that to be a patriot is to accept authority and thereby maintain the more than 200-year-old traditions of this nation?'

Proudly, as though vindicated. 'Exactly right, Sam.'

A most worthwhile piece of scholarship would be to research the history of Europe and America and uncover the magnificent, but nonetheless anonymous figures, who threw themselves onto the gears of the machine. The tome would serve as a modern-day book of saints. Chances are slim, but it might have even motivated a man such as me to stand up to an asshole such as this.

I thought I had this so under control, that I could play games with him and win out with sarcasm and cleverness. Such a strategy can work only for a man resolute in his beliefs, who is comfortable with his own being. One cannot shake hands with the Devil and escape untarnished. Crossing the fingers means nothing for a man who lives with his fingers crossed.

In the name of my job and therefore my piss ass way of life, I am reduced to a sarcastic little kiss ass.

'Sir, your ideas are absolutely phenomenal insofar as they are espoused by a man with phenomenal ideas.'

He is, of course, touched. 'Thank you, Sam.'

'No sir,' I smile. 'Thank you for the thanks.'

He holds one finger in the air and says, 'There is still one thing that bothers me here, Sam.'

'What is it, sir?' I ask with the utmost concern.

'Your lack of an American flag,' he says. 'It seems to me that a man of your beliefs would have a flag. I know we've been over it, but it does seem odd . . .' and he waits for me to offer a satisfactory explanation.

In a society dominated by selfishness, integrity is an obstacle that needs to be overcome. Nix that. A new breed of integrity needs to be cultivated – nothing more than the drive to succeed. The feeling that success gives to a person outweighs any sense of lost integrity. What the hell is integrity anyway but a feeling of doing what's right? And what's considered right, but what society says is right? And what does American society say is right? Success.

'Sir, I can only say that I sit before you guilty as charged. I should have the Stars and Stripes in my office, not because you sent out a memo, but because, as an American, it is my duty.'

Smug with victory, he says, 'It makes me happy to hear you admit to your mistakes, Sam.'

'Yes sir,' I continue, 'we are in a cultural war here, and it's high time I started showing my true colors.'

(If I only had the courage . . .)

'Indeed it is, Sam,' and he folds his arms behind his head. 'And I have some good news for you,' he says with an air of superiority.

'What is it, sir?' I say excitedly.

'I'm going to allow you to do my biography.'

'Really?'

'Yes, really. You've passed the test.' He pauses, smiles and nods his head at me. 'You're a good American, Sam. A good American.'

Chapter Nine

IT'S BEEN A long time since I picked up any books. Shit, I can't remember the last time I went to a bookstore. In college it was a common occurrence. When I was in Europe, I used to go all the time. The best thing in the world was to get baked on hash, go to the bookstore, and hang out. Prague was the best place for it, they encourage that kind of thing.

With all the interesting shit there is to do and explore in the world, it's surprising and sad that a man would waste most of his life in an office playing public relations specialist.

That was pure shit with the president. Had to suck it up and take the hit, though. Where would I be right now if I had walked out and quit? Scrambling, nervously pouring over the want ads, wondering how the fuck I was going to make rent. It's not like any other public relations job is going to be any better. So now, instead of shitting my pants looking for work, I'm fully employed and on the fast track.

The whole thing balances itself out in the end. I spend a dehumanizing time with the president of the company, but since I stuck it out, I have the money to spend a reinvigorating night at the bookstore. The system has its rewards, but why does a system need rewards? It's like they have to bribe people to stay in it. You give us this, we'll give you that. Deal with an asshole, here's money to go buy some books. Nothing but a prolonged bribery.

Nonetheless, a great night at the bookstore. So warm, almost healing, bookstores make it seem like anything's possible. Such a change from the corporate environment where the world seems wired for persecution. I like the travel section. To work for Fodor's or Lonely Planet, to travel all over the world and write about it.

I think I'd want to do something on Antarctica. Make up a bunch of lies about how balmy it is in June. Tell people not to burden themselves with anything more than their bathing suits. Inform the public that the continent is littered with bed and breakfasts run by friendly locals. Be responsible for the ignominious deaths of hundreds of tourists from Arizona and Japan. To some, I would be a monster. To others, a hero.

I'm a goof when it comes to buying books. There are the books that I understand, and there are the books that I buy. The habit stems from this asshole teacher I had in the fourth grade. He saw me pick out a copy of Freud's *Interpretation of Dreams* from the library, and he said, 'I don't know who you think you're trying to impress!'

It was all over after that. He was my homeroom teacher, and as part of his duties, he had to take us to the city library twice a month. I had the fat fuck for two years. I would get the most outrageous books just to spite him: *The Critique of Pure Reason* by Immanuel Kant, *The Decline of the West* by Oswald Spengler. He must have wanted to be a doctor or a nurse because it particularly killed him when I'd get a book from the practical sciences section. I couldn't understand a word, but would memorize the names of the authors and a term or two to really rub it in: *Psychiatric Nursing in the Hospital and the Community* by Ann Wolbert Burgess, *Principles and Practices of Intravenous Therapy* by Ada Lawrence Plumer. His name was Mr Foosger. 'Isn't it amazing, Mr Foosger, how Ada Lawrence Plumer does such a good job of explaining basic venipuncture?' Or, 'Do you think, Mr Foosger, that Ann Wolbert Burgess is right in her psychodynamic theory of involutional depression?' The librarian thought I was a prodigy. She wanted to bring me in for genius testing. She even went so far as to contact the school. She refused to believe it when the principal informed her that my IQ was a measly 125.

I guess Mr Foosger got his revenge, though, because I can't buy a book unless it's totally beyond my comprehension. I'm not an idiot, but there are books out there that are impossible to read. Outside of a select group of asshole professors, who has actually read *Finnegan's Wake?* In college, when you have a teacher there to guide you through it, fine. But after a day of kissing ass and mind-numbing paper pushing, no one wants to come home and be made to feel like a moron by a one-eyed lunger.

Today, I picked out the *Collected Philosophical Writings of the Marquis De Sade* for the obvious reason that he is one of the most twisted, incomprehensible wackos of all time. In the store, I came across a fascinating letter. Since I've been home I've read it three times, understanding more with each read. I can't get rid of it. I want to think these thoughts and live by them, though they are safely beyond the depth of my character. He wrote it to his wife while he was locked in the Bastille.

Hit of the whiskey. There's something about reading that gives the apartment a vibrant, glowing hue. The living room feels warm. I take another sip of whiskey, put the glass down on the table, pick up my new book, and reread the letter. Every time I start it I feel like I'm embarking on an adventure of bravery. A needed fantasy.

'*My manner of thinking, so you say, cannot be approved. Do you suppose I care? A poor fool indeed is he who adopts a manner of thinking for others! My manner of thinking stems straight from my considered reflections; it holds with my existence and the way I am made. It is not in my power to alter it; and were it, I'd not do so. This manner of thinking you find fault with is my sole consolation in life; it alleviates all my sufferings in prison, it composes all my pleasures in the world outside, it is dearer to me than life itself. Not my manner of thinking but the manner of thinking in others has been the source of my unhappiness. The reasoning man who scorns the prejudices of simpletons necessarily becomes the enemy of simpletons; he must expect as much, and laugh at the inevitable. A traveler journeys along a fine road. It has been strewn with traps. He falls into one. Do you say it's the traveler's fault, or that of the scoundrel who lays the traps? If then, as you tell me, they are willing to restore my liberty if I am willing to pay for it with the sacrifice of my principles or my tastes, we may bid one another an eternal adieu, for rather than part with those, I would sacrifice a thousand lives and a thousand liberties, if I had them. These principles and these tastes, I am their fanatic adherent; and fanaticism in me is the product of persecutions I have endured from my tyrants. The longer they continue their vexations the deeper they root my principles in my heart, and I openly declare no one ever need talk to me of liberty if it is offered to me only in return for their destruction.'*

This guy's standing tall against the entire moral edifice of Western Civilization, facing life in the Bastille and possible execution. All that could happen to me if I were to express my true sentiments, is that I would lose my job. That's why he's him and I'm me. Two hundred years from now nobody's going to be reading the letters of Sam.

I wish Lady California were here. No so much so that we could fuck, but so we could hang out, maybe read together. It's a sign of a good person, that when you do cool things like going to the book store, you wish they were there. Next time I see her I'm going to try and get her number, or at least that's what I tell myself now. Fact is, when it comes down to the reality of hanging out with a transvestite in public, I'm not up to it. Everything controversial about me begins and ends in my head, or behind closed doors. A quiet life of desperation.

In the hypnotic light of possibility that was the bookstore, I bought another book that now seems ridiculous. The latest edition of *Writer's Market*. Oh yes, for a glorious 20 to 25 minutes there I was going to reinvent myself as a writer, to give birth to the brilliant man of letters lurking inside me and every other goddamned educated American. I am, of course, a great artist, but I am also pragmatic and realize that I must first take care of the material side of life before I embark on the inevitable creative journey that will result in mass recognition.

If, by some outrageous alignment of the stars, my drive to write endured beyond the ride home from the bookstore, it would have been killed upon opening this book. One of the first pages in the *'Writer's Market'* is a photo of the archetypal yuppie with a shit-eating grin. His name is Everett Weinberger, and the headline above him reads: *Investment Paying off for New Writer!*

'The difference between a "wannabe" and "gonnabe" often boils down to an investment of time, energy, and sometimes money. As an investment banker, Everett Weinberger recognizes the potential rewards of taking risks. And he's willing to go out on a limb, whether he's trying to break into Hollywood or developing his own supplementary marketing program to spread the word about his first published book.

'Weinberger left his Wall Street investment banking position to return to school, hoping a Stanford MBA would be helpful in pursuing his dream job of movie producer.'

The Marquis de Sade is rolling over in his grave, but so fucking what? Literature has been dead for years and nobody misses it. Everyone, obviously, has found the meaning of life and is entirely happy with the way things have turned out. I, for one, think we're doing a great job, and to criticize it through something as meaningless as a book . . . well, if some bitter, no-account writer wants to sit around in a garage and waste his time spewing idiotic thoughts out at the world, then let him rot.

I did, embarrassingly enough, go through a period in college during which I dedicated myself to becoming a writer. I produced one piece – the short story that was canceled when the English Department's literary review lost its funding. Now and then I have tried to blame that inauspicious loss of funds for my general failure as a human being, but I am too aware of my own failings to allow myself to get off the hook so easily. As usual, stuck in the middle.

It began as a story about the championship football season but quickly took on a mind of it's own, so I scrapped the football idea altogether. From what I gather, things like that happen in writing. You may start with one theme, but you always end up writing about what's really on your mind. It's a story about a man facing a terrible decision.

The end of World War II, he and his regiment are in Germany.

He's an intelligent young man. He has maintained his humanity in spite of enduring some of the greatest horrors of the war. He has served his country well and wants nothing more than to return home. He doesn't dream of easy street, but of an interesting life full of challenges. He's done with the idiocy of war. There is more to him than carrying out the orders of army bureaucrats.

Germany is on the verge of accepting its defeat, the boys are celebrating their imminent return to the States. He is drunk, happy. The whole world lies before him. He has proven himself to himself.

The colonel orders him to lead a squad to Dachau to complete its liberation. The mission is a peaceful one, as there are no Germans left in the area. He is to visit the camp, return, and make a report to that effect. The colonel tells him that when he returns he will arrange for a plane to take them back home early to the States. Otherwise, it will be more than two months before official evacuation begins.

He returns to his squad and jubilantly informs them of the mission and it's reward. They leave for Dachau at five the next morning.

They arrive at daybreak, having no conception of the nightmare that has transpired. There are twisted mountains of emaciated bodies, dried up oceans of human wreckage, whole continents of teeth and hair. The sky above is blackened from the incinerators. The air is noxious with human remains. To breath is to inhale death.

He has lived death for two years. Still, he is cast into a pit of anguish at the sight of the endless and immense suffering. He walks amongst the bodies, crying. In the dead face of a young girl he sees his sister. In an old man, his grandfather. He loses himself in the nightmare, becoming separated from the rest of the men. Overwhelmed, he sits in the door way of a building and puts his head in his hands. It has begun to snow.

With every fiber he regrets having taken this mission. Two more years of war would have been preferable. He knows that he will never rid his mind of these images. That he has become part of the horror.

His only consolation, the only thing that keeps him from losing his mind, is that a plane is waiting for him and that in 15 hours he'll be home, thousands of miles from this nightmare. There are no Germans remaining, but they have left this as a final means of psychological assault. With this in mind, he determines not to let this evil injure him or his men any further. He summons all of his courage, wipes the tears from his face, stands and readies himself to unite the squad and evacuate immediately.

A sound comes from within the building . . .

He stops, hoping that he'd imagined it. Again, a low, barely audible moan, like soft wind over the top of a glass bottle. He is scared, but brave. He's done all that has been asked of him and done it well. Rifle ready, he moves into the doorway of the building and nudges the door open with his foot. No sign of life, he enters.

A medical lab, sterile. The only light comes through a crack in the blinds at the far end. There are file cabinets, all emptied. Six beds, all unoccupied, except for the last one by the window. There, with streaks of light running across her withered and naked body, lies an old woman.

He moves over to her. She is more dead than alive. He covers her with a blanket from off the floor. He stands over her for more than a minute before she opens her eyes. An almost imperceptible look of tenderness comes over her dying face.

He strokes her white hair. To move her would be to kill her, yet it could be hours before she dies. He must either round up the men and stay with her until she passes – thereby missing his trip home and having to stay in the hell for another two months – or leave her alone, in the nightmare, until she dies. He is her last hope. Not at life, but at dignity.

He nervously checks his watch and caresses her hair. With every second he stands over her it becomes harder for him to consider leaving. He has to make a decision soon.

She shows no signs of improvement nor of worsening. He can sense, however, that his presence is making her death easier. He again checks his watch. The men must be concerned about where he is.

He takes his gun, points it at her face so she can see, hoping that she'll understand and somehow ask him to shoot her. She doesn't register. She continues only to exist somewhere in the land between life and death.

Tears streaming down his face, his mind spinning out of control, he kisses the woman on the cheek and leaves. As he steps out the door, he hears her moan . . . .

The story ends with a cool, but nightmarish little twist. The colonel had lied. He never had any intention of evacuating them early and took off in his own private plane that morning after a hearty breakfast of steak and eggs.

It's too bad I tore up the story. Maybe Everett Weinberger, the investment banker, could have helped me get it published.

Enough of books and writing. The Marquis De Sade will, I'm sure, find his way into a dusty and forgotten corner of this apartment. The *Writer's Market* will be disposed of forthwith. Now where's the goddamned remote . . .

'Don't dismiss me, Joanne!'

'I'm not dismissing you, Vance. I just can't deal with this tonight!'

Amen, sister. Neither can I.

Hushed tones, mumbled voices. Hopefully, it will stay that way.

No remote. Damn. I don't want to read. I'm tired of the Marquis de Sade throwing his bravery around in my face, and I sure as hell don't want to read about how Everett Weinberger's marketing strategy is going to make him the next Steinbeck.

I'm not hungry. I don't need to go to the bathroom. I don't want to go anywhere. I don't want to talk to anybody on the phone. I don't feel like jacking off. What the fuck to do then? It's a serious question. I guess my only recourse is to sit here, drink and attempt to think. The drinking part is easy enough. I take a big drink just to prove it. What can I think about, though, that's not going to make me feel like shit? Work, my twisted sex life, the neighbors next door, how great Jerry Seinfeld's life is compared to mine, Catholicism, America, loneliness, depression, Dina's rejection, taxes, loss of God, my crappy car, violence, genocide, pseudo-happiness, loss of my dreams, my general failure to become anything I might have wanted to be, cowardice, aging, physiological disintegration, loss of identity, political corruption, the Pittsburgh Steelers sucking this year, cancer and death, television making me stupid, low self-esteem, selfishness, schizophrenia, manicness, boredom, hatred of self, universal annihilation and cosmological concepts that I can't understand, hot weather, Iran, Islam, prophets, fame, the middle class, computers, confusion, boredom, starvation, disease, tragedy, harmlessness . . . An innocuous, mother fucker.

'You don't put your work above your husband! I won't tolerate you bringing it into this house!'

Go fuck yourself you insecure fuck. Another whiskey, pour a nice full glass out of the bottle and slug away.

'I have to do this, Vance! The presentation is tomorrow and they're depending on me!'

That's the key right there: to convince yourself that what you do actually matters, that there are people depending on you, that if you don't come through and produce the quality work that the world has come to expect of you, then buildings will fall, guillotines will be wheeled out and innocents beheaded.

The president was right, Americans are simple. It doesn't take much for an American to live a meaningful life. It's Wonder Bread instead of wheat. Fritos instead of Cheetos. It's giving a good presentation to a bunch of guys who are staring at your tits. The stupid don't know they're stupid, and the intelligent have taken themselves out of the game. To think is to be full of sorrows, and yes, leaden-eyed despairs . . . Funny how poetry always finds its way into the mundane belly of the average beast.

'Please, Vance!' She pleads and whines. 'I have to get this done tonight!'

'You don't have to do shit except listen to what I have to say!'

It seems like I started off life with 29 pages of things that were meaningful to me, but every year I peeled off a page and threw it into the trash. What the fuck happened? I feel like I've been broadsided. I can't convince myself that anything I do is worth a shit. There is not an activity in my life that gives me a sense of well-being or meaning great enough to overcome the crap. There is only one thing that has even come close to it, and that was making love to Lady California. The fact that the most twisted act of my entire life is also the most meaningful in recent memory casts aspersions on everything that I am.

The world is a trap. You can deny it, you can rebel against it, you can give into it, it doesn't matter. I am what society says I am. The smart thing is to give in and accept it. A man can only fight the stream so long before he drowns.

'Get in here now!' he yells from the kitchen.

'Please, Vance. Just let me finish this!'

Stomping around, some wrangling, muted noises.

Like the president said, the table is set. Pull up a chair, anything I don't like I'll get used to. Who would be such an idiot as to skip out on the greatest, most decorated feast in the world?

If it's all so good, though, why do I feel at odds with it? Shouldn't I be jumping with excitement over the life which has been given to me? Or am I just a fucking spoiled brat who needs to complain to feel like he's worth a damn? What is it that's keeping me so fucked up and miserable?

'What is it Vance?' she screams angrily in the kitchen. 'I'm here now, you've taken me from my work. What is it that you want?'

'Don't come in here acting like you're doing me a favor, Joanne! I won't stand for it.'

Emotional mumblings, some stamping on the kitchen floor.

Maybe I am a spoiled brat. Maybe I've had it too good in life. If a 29-year-old guy from Bangladesh could be here in my place, he'd think he died and gone to heaven. Okay, fine. I'm glad I have my whiskey and a Home Theater Entertainment Center . . . There, I feel so much better.

There is a dialogue in my core that has nothing to do with the material world. I see myself in darkness, small and weak, trying to convince a faceless jury of my worth. Yet, when it comes time to make my argument, I'm at a loss, an idiot. For my punishment, they leave me alone in the darkness. They know the worst thing in the world: force a meaningless man to deal with himself.

'I told you not to bring your goddamned work into our home! It's a direct slap in my face!'

The beginnings of hysteria, 'Why is it a slap in your face for me to bring my work home, Vance? You bring your work home all the time and all I do is support you!'

'Because I don't fuck the people at my work, Joanne!'

I can hear her crying.

I've already started the president's biography. It's flowing perfectly – a sad commentary on how far I've come. When I'm finished, I'll get a raise. With the money I'll be making, I'll be able to move out of here and these people will be nothing but a bad memory. In a few years, I'll be able to live in a gated community in the hills. The job will take up 80 percent of my time. With the other 20 percent, I'll take trips, make new purchases, get married. The main thing is to insulate – from myself as much as from the world.

'I can't take this anymore!' she cries.

She has taken it, is taking it, and will take it for the rest of her life. Life is nothing without tragedy, not because it allows us the chance to redeem ourselves, but because it chews up large junks of time.

'Not only,' he screams seething hatred, 'do you make a fool out of me by fucking those pricks you work with behind my back! But you insist on bringing your work home to remind me of it! You have destroyed the sanctity of our home!'

'I have not, Vance!' she cries. 'I have not!'

The fact that he would use the word sanctity in reference to their home is laughable. There is nothing sanct on this planet, let alone the home of an abusive lawyer! Still, in his mind there is no life more holy and important than his. Truth is whatever a person believes.

'You have, Joanne! You have brought your filth into this home!'

Catholicism taught its own weird version of truth. The crucifix above the head, Christ staring down at me, bleeding to death like it's all my fault. They had a way of making you feel like shit for not being the next messiah. I realized pretty quickly, though, that absolute truth was a joke. That it had nothing to do with the individual and everything to do with what they thought an individual should be.

'Leave me alone, Vance!'

'You're a fucking whore!'

So I looked inside myself. I found nothing . . .

'I can't stand this!'

Is it possible that in my lame wanderings I might have skipped over a couple rocks that I should have investigated? That what has left me an innocuous motherfucker is an unwillingness to give myself a chance. That whenever I might have had an inclination to do the right thing in the name of something better, I crushed it out of a half-ass belief in nothing. That I came to the crossroads, and instead of picking a road, picked neither – and have since just sat there.

What if I made a choice? What if, instead of teetering on the brink of the abyss I dove in head first and accepted the consequences. Wouldn't I be better off than I am now?

There is nothing inside of me strong enough to push me over. I am suspended by a lame will. Another drink of whiskey.

'Why! Because it's the truth!' Then a thud. I think it's the thud where she gets pushed down on the floor and not the thud where's he smacking her. I hear hushed mumbling. A good sign, usually.

My lack of inertia is common. Men don't freely jump into the abyss. People have to be railroaded, by God if necessary, to do something meaningful. God dogged Saint Francis for days before he accepted the righteous path and put his neck on the line. If God were to come down to me in the form of a burning bush and tell me to quit my job and walk the earth, shit, I'd do it in a second. All I've ever wanted was the word – like a sentinel waiting for the dawn.

'Get up! I told you to get up!'

Fucking asshole, I wish he'd shut the fuck up.

'You pushed me!' She cries aloud. 'You promised you wouldn't push me!'

That yearning has to stand for at least something, right? That in spite of all the bullshit and ugliness, there's something in me worthwhile. I would tear my insides open to find it. I would flay myself to reveal beauty. Yet, I am coward. I have to know that truth exists. I must be sure that leaping into the abyss would pay off.

There are no guarantees. The abyss is mystery. I could dive into nothingness, or worse, be faced with mediocre distortion. How could I live with myself if after daring the question, I awaken from a 29-year illusion to find that I have no soul. That my inner core is comprised of everything that disgusts me and that there is no way out but acceptance.

'You are nothing but a fucking whore!' he screams again.

'Please don't say that!' she yells in pain.

'And what makes it even worse,' he screams, 'is that you're turning our daughter into a whore!'

Anything but the daughter . . . I can sit here, listen to him beat the shit out of her all night, and jerk myself off with meaningless questions. But I cannot be reminded of the daughter. I was hoping she was gone tonight, but I know she's in her room. I imagine her curled up on her little bed, desperately clinging to her favorite stuffed animal, praying for her parents to stop fighting and for daddy not to hurt mommy. She is helpless. The baby seal left alone in the dark ocean, crying for its mother. The sharks are circling, they rip at her with their teeth and pull her under until she's almost drowned, then let her up again so that the next shark can have it's fun. The water around her reddens with her own blood. She wails out for her mother, more sharks arrive. The seal will die, but the girl will live on – a mutilated, bloodied, disfigured soul.

'I'm not a whore!' she cries. 'I'm a good mother!'

I can hear him laughing, mocking her.

I drink my whiskey and think of the darkness . . . There are no questions that can be asked when a little girl is dying in the room next to me. Every thought is nothing more than an indictment, a proof, of my own weakness. Where is the boy that made that tackle . . .

'All you are is a whore!' he yells in a mocking lilt. 'You think you're a successful, powerful woman, but all you are is a company slut! You make fools of all of us the minute you step out the door! You're a joke! A piece of shit! You're not worth my spit!' Another thud and scream.

Where is it? Where is who I am? All I have is questions but no answers. Why can't something rise up in me and make me feel again. Where is my heart? Reach inside! There must be something about me that makes me worthwhile! I am not the vile piece of shit that I have billed myself to be!

'Stop it, Vance!'

'SHUT THE FUCK UP!'

I can hear it now. He's beating her.

'YOU'RE A WHORE' THUD THUD THUD. 'YOU'RE A FUCKING WHORE!' THUD THUD THUD! 'YOU'VE MADE A FOOL OUT OF ME!' THUD THUD! YOU'VE DESTROYED THIS FAMILY!' THUD THUD THUD!'

I drink my whiskey. I hadn't noticed but I'm shaking. I start searching frantically for the remote, flipping over couch cushions, kicking the books out of the way, knocking over my whiskey. The Jasper Johns flag on the wall stares back at me like a mirror. It looks ugly, like a filthy rag.

'I'M SORRY!' I can hear her running. 'PLEASE STOP HIT-TING ME! I'M SORRY!'

'GET THE FUCK BACK HERE YOU FUCKING WHORE! I'VE HAD ENOUGH!' I hear him chasing her.

There's a loud crash and I know he's tackled her. She shrieks. THUD THUD THUD. 'YOU'RE NOT GOING TO EVER FUCKING LEAVE ME!' And I can hear him dragging her back into the kitchen. She is screaming, begging hysterically for him to stop.

'PLEASE VANCE DON'T HURT ME! I'LL QUIT MY JOB I'LL DO WHATEVER YOU WANT! JUST PLEASE VANCE DON'T HURT ME!'

I fall back on the couch with my face in my hands. I could call the cops, but that won't change anything. She'll never leave him. I should just leave. That's what I'll do. I'll go see a movie. By the time I get back, it'll all be over and they'll be in love again . . .

'Mommy are you okay . . .'

No, please, not her.

'GET BACK INTO YOUR ROOM, KELLY!' the monster yells.

'But daddy,' she sobs, 'mommy's bleeding.'

'I TOLD YOU TO GET BACK IN YOUR ROOM! NOW GO!'

The little girl's voice awakens me, as though I were in a trance. I hear her run back into her room and close the door.

There is a crystal clarity about the room, now. I feel alert, yet strangely calm. There are screams and thuds in the background. He's beating her:

'YOU'LL NEVER LEAVE ME YOU FUCKING BITCH!' THUD THUD THUD. 'I'LL FUCKING KILL YOU FIRST!' THUD THUD THUD.

I am awash in emptiness. It is an eternal sea of which I am an infinitesimally small part. There is no truth inside of me. No glimmer, no silver lining, no hope. I am a question mark waiting to die.

Yet, what is it to be this question mark? Am I not still unresolved? Is there not a world out that awaits my actions? Am I not free? The history of the world may be filled with ugliness, but it also consists of those who have chosen light over darkness. Within them was the same doubt, evil, confusion, and sense of helplessness that exists within me. A man must overcome himself before he can overcome the world.

'YOU NEVER LOVED ME! YOU NEVER LOVED ME AND NOW YOU'RE GOING TO LEAVE ME!'

When faced with challenge I have always found something defective within myself or the world to justify my withdrawal. I have convinced myself of a lack of integrity so that I would never have to act virtuously. I have convinced myself that I am a coward, so I would never have to be brave. I have done this because to stand up to the evil in the world is to take responsibility for it.

'WHAT THE FUCK DID YOU SAY?'

'NOTHING, VANCE! OH GOD, PLEASE! I DIDN'T SAY ANYTHING!'

'YOU WILL NEVER INSULT MY MANHOOD, YOU FUCKING WHORE! YOU'RE GOING TO FUCKING GET IT LIKE THE MOTHERFUCKING WHORE THAT YOU ARE!'

'OH GOD NO! NO VANCE! PLEASE NO!'

A man is defined by what he is willing and not willing to accept.

'I'M GOING TO TEACH YOU A FUCKING LESSON YOU STUPID BITCH!'

When the boundaries have been pushed and pushed, when there is no more room for a person to live, he is forced into making a decision: either give up the boundaries or take a stand.

'OH GOD PLEASE STOP IT VANCE. YOU'RE GOING TO KILL ME!'

'SHUT THE FUCK UP, YOU STUPID WHORE!'

On the edge of the abyss, looking down. I think of Lady California, of the football team, of my old friends. I see that goodness and freedom live hand in hand, that we enslave ourselves, and the prison is far too full.

A horrific scream. 'OH GOD NO!'

'I'M GOING TO KILL YOU!'

No one is born with integrity. A man is a man because he chooses to be one.

'DADDY WHAT ARE YOU DOING TO MOMMY! STOP IT! PLEASE STOP IT! YOU'RE GOING TO KILL HER FOREVER!'

I run to my door, tear it open and suddenly find myself standing in the hall outside their door, alone.

'YOU FUCKING WHORE I'M GOING TO KILL YOUR FUCKING WHORE ASS YOU FUCKING BITCH! YOU'VE FUCKED BEHIND MY BACK AND DESTROYED MY LIFE!

WHO THE FUCK DO YOU THINK YOU ARE TO FUCK WITH ME? I'M GOING TO FUCKING KILL YOU! I LOVE YOU AND THIS IS WHAT YOU DO TO ME? HOW COULD YOU DO THIS TO ME AFTER ALL I'VE DONE FOR YOU YOU FUCKING BITCH I LOVE YOU?'

With the bottom of my fist I slam into the door and scream, 'What's going on in there?'

'I'VE GIVEN YOU EVERYTHING AND THIS IS WHAT YOU DO TO ME! YOU TURNED ME INTO A JOKE YOU FUCKING BITCH! HOW COULD YOU DO THIS TO ME? I LOVE YOU HOW COULD YOU DO THIS TO ME? I'M YOUR FUCKING HUSBAND, AND NOW I'M GOING TO KILL YOU LIKE A MOTHERFUCKING WHORE!'

'DADDY PLEASE STOP IT YOU'RE KILLING MOMMY!'

I reach for the knob and twist, but it's locked. With all the strength in both my hands I try and twist it open. A sharp edge digs into my hand and blood spurts down my wrist. It's no use. I bang on the door and yell: 'WHAT ARE YOU DOING IN THERE! YOU BETTER NOT GODDAMNED TOUCH THAT GIRL YOU MOTHERFUCKER!'

'I'VE LOVED YOU FOR FIFTEEN YEARS AND THIS IS WHAT YOU DO TO ME! I'VE GIVEN YOU MY LIFE AND YOU CRUSH ME! YOU'RE A WHORE, YOU FUCKING WHORE CUNT, AND YOU'RE GOING TO DIE IN HATRED! YOU ROTTEN WHORE I LOVE YOU GODDAMNIT I LOVE YOU!'

'OH GOD DADDY PLEASE STOP! PLEASE STOP YOU'RE KILLING MOMMY! MOMMY ARE YOU OKAY? MOMMY? MOMMY? DADDY SOMETHING'S WRONG WITH MOMMY! PLEASE STOP! SOMETHING'S WRONG WITH MOMMY!'

'GET THE FUCK OFF ME YOU LITTLE BITCH! YOU'RE GOING TO GET IT NEXT YOU LITTLE FUCKING WHORE!'

'OH NO PLEASE NO I'M SO SORRY DADDY! OH MY GOD PLEASE DADDY NO DON'T HURT HER!'

'SHUT THE FUCK UP YOU LITTLE WHORE!'
'NO DADDY NO!'

A man looks out over the world and there's only one decision that confronts him – whether or not he's going to be part of it. There's no sunset, no beaches, no children playing in the park . . . Only an empty landscape that offers no guarantees. What is a man? Man is a choice. What does he bring to the landscape? Life.

The emptiness floods out of me, and in the rushing darkness, I am made whole. I am in the ditch again, pedaling toward the hill. I can hear my friends cheering, the landscape screaming past me in the periphery. Pedal, pedal faster with all your might! The abyss is the other side. All it is is jumping a hill on a bike. That's all it's ever been.

I take a few steps back from the door, lower my shoulder and slam into the door.

'PLEASE HELP ME!' cries the child.

The door hangs by the top hinge. I step back, lock my hands together and come down on the door like a hammer. BOOM! The top hinge blows off. I fall with the door to floor. Blood on my hands and arms, I raise my head . . .

There is only one true horror: when the soul of a man has died, and out of revenge he has brought his emptiness into the world.

'WHO THE FUCK ARE YOU? WHAT THE FUCK ARE YOU DOING HERE!'

The woman lies on the floor. Half of her face is torn off. It falls over the other part of her face that is still attached. Her white cheekbone reflects the light that seems to die off in the area around her eyes. There, in the darkness, two, dead, blue eyes stare up at the ceiling as though in prayer. Blood drips from the counter onto the linoleum floor, like holy water in a baptism. Her arm is bent behind her, contorted and broken. Her collar bone and chest are dented in. A rib pokes through her skin, as though it were trying somehow to escape. She drains blood like a can of red paint that's been knocked over. One of her fingers has been torn off.

'HELP! PLEASE HELP ME!' screams the child.

'GET THE FUCK OUT OF HERE YOU FUCKING COCKSUCKER! GET THE FUCK OUT NOW OR I'LL FUCKING GUT HER!'

He holds the little girl by the neck with one hand. The other hand, white knuckles clenching, holds a 12-inch butcher knife. His white, button down shirt is covered with blood, as are his teeth. He looks like a hyena after a feeding. The little girl fights his every jerk and pull. She is terrified, and desperately wants to live. Her brown hair is matted with blood. He has cut her once already, a gash in her arm bleeds down onto her wrist and hand.

'PLEASE HELP ME SIR HE'S GOING TO KILL ME!'

Waving the knife in the air, 'I'M GOING TO FUCKING KILL HER UNLESS YOU GET THE FUCK OUT OF HERE RIGHT NOW YOU SON OF A BITCH! GET THE FUCK OUT OF MY HOME YOU PIECE OF SHIT! I'M GOING TO FUCKING KILL . . .'

I'm on him . . . Tearing into him with my hands, gnashing at his face with my teeth. I can feel his bones crushing under me, his ribs cracking, his writhing twisting body smashing into the wall . . .

The world is a dream. Silence, pieces of time, the washing away of sorrow. Screams from the inside! Go you son of a bitch go! Tell' em! Tell 'em!

I become aware of being on top of him. He has stopped moving. My fists sink into his broken face. With every punch blood sprays up and colors my vision red. It's beautiful, I can taste him in my mouth. His eye is crushed inside the socket. His bottom lip hangs out over his jaw. I stop, reach back, and with all my strength bring my fist into where his nose used to be. I blow past bone and am blinded by a spray of blood. I feel the last vestiges of life fall from him. Wiping the blood from my eyes I roll off him onto the floor. Exhausted, I lie on my side, between the two corpses.

It sounds like my own breathing, but then I realize it's outside of me. Sobbing. Weak, lonely sobbing . . . I remember the little girl. I can see her out of the corner of my eye. She is holding herself, staring out in lost horror, rocking back and forth. I should go to her. I try to sit up. Every movement takes all of my strength. I'm glued to the floor.

I make it up and drag myself over to her. I don't feel right. Nauseous, like I'm heavier than I've ever been, but light at the same time.

I say, 'Come here, honey.'

I lift my arm up and put it a round her. I lean back against the wall and a sharp pain rips through my body. I slowly reach down to my lower back . . .

The butcher knife is stuck there. There's so much blood, it feels like someone has dumped a bucket of water on me . . .

The girl is holding on to me with both arms, weeping, digging her head into my chest.

I try to speak, but can barely whisper. 'It's not like this, honey. It's better than this.'

I think maybe somebody's turned down the lights. It's time to go home, grab a whiskey, and catch the last part of the game. That tackle, I did a good job on that. A good job. I can't feel anything. The communion wafers all over the street. That was fun. It's going to be all right, honey. We won, didn't we? Yeah, we won. It's going to be all right. You got to make it out of this for me, because I'm not going to be here anymore . . . You got to make it, because there are things to do, baby. You have to be strong. There are things to do.